HIS TO OWN

50 LOVING STATES, ARKANSAS

THEODORA TAYLOR

To my fascinating neighbors,
Thanks for the story!

1

MASON

*F*uck if he isn't going to have to end this deal with a body count. Mason silently tallies the number of Hijos de la Muertes standing in front of him, while pretending to listen to their leader's ridiculous "request." How they'd like fifteen more glocks added to their order. On the house, of course. Blah, blah, no fucking way, blah.

Mason's got plenty of time to run diagnostics on the situation. The head guy likes to talk. A real pompous ass. He ain't wearing a shirt—maybe because it's summer. But more likely because the front of his torso is entirely covered in what has to be thousands of dollars' worth of quality ink. Beneath two beautifully rendered tattoos of ornate Mexican cartel revolvers, the boss man's pecs stay puffed up like he's part rooster.

Mason knows the soon-to-be-dead fuck's name is Razo. Not because he introduces himself proper or anything like that, but because the asshole's name is inked clear across his stomach in large, ornate script: RAZO. And Mason has to admit it looks pretty slick beneath the huge HIJOS DE LA MUERTES etched along the guy's collar bone. Every single bit of his front torso, including his arms, have been turned into a living canvas.

Mason spots a few less skillful tattoos buried under the quality stuff, but he can see that somewhere down the line, Razo got real smart about his body art. Hooked himself up with a talented visionary. A *real* artist...nothing like the washed out old man Mason knows back at the SFK clubhouse, the one who inks new members with the official SFK seal.

Given that Razo is a full foot shorter than Mason, he's sure the little bitch shows up shirtless to every deal. After all, the tats make him look more bad ass in every way. Tougher, bigger, more powerful. Like the overlord of a serious Mexican drug cartel rather than the leader of a small-time Latino street gang. The intimidating ink combined with the handle of the GAT sticking prominently out of Razo's pants have most definitely convinced other sellers to give him what he wanted.

But not tonight. Because now this beaner prick is dealing with Mason Fairgood.

"Sorry, hombre. Southern Freedom Knights don't do nothing on the house," Mason answers when Razo's finally done flapping his lips. And he doesn't bother to sugarcoat his words with a friendly tone, like his cousin D might have done. No, Mason's voice is flatter than all those miles of highway he traveled to get here from Tennessee.

The Hijos de la Muertes have holed up in what the SFK often refer to as a roach town. The brown roaches move in, and the whites move out. Ceding their pretty properties to beaner scum in favor of new and improved—and as yet un-infested—suburbs. What was once a nice neighborhood is now completely occupied by Razo's crew. Their distinctive graffiti tags cover every street sign, dividing wall, fire hydrant, and sidewalk. Damn shame.

But there are only three guys standing behind Razo. Likely his most trusted and strongest gang members. Not that it really matters. Nobody beats Mason in a fight. Not even hardened street cholos like these. No, the odds aren't fair for Razo and his men. They might look tough but Mason knows these inner city gangs don't weapon train for shit. No mandatory time spent in target practice. No game hunting in the woods. Just time spent shooting at each other in brief street skirmishes, like something out of a lame-ass video game, using illegal weapons provided by the SFK and other distributors.

The thought of these pussies referring to themselves as "soldiers" turns Mason's stomach. But whatever, at least it gives him the advantage in close situations like these. He supposes he ought to be grateful that these low-rent assholes lack basic shooting and hunting skills, even as more and more of them sprout up across the country. More gangs equal more business opportunities. And more target practice for Mason.

The only Hijos he really has to worry about are the five or six guys milling around on the front porch of the house Razo exited to do this deal with Mason. There could also be a few men hidden in the surrounding cul-de-sac.

And if any them actually have something with a sight on it, well...hello bullet straight to the head. Even a kid could hit a moving target with that kind of set up.

"You Knights don't do nothing on the house?" Razo asks. "That ain't what I heard, man. I heard your cuz gave the Lightning Bolts in Little Rock a couple of AKs. Like as a bonus and shit."

Mason shrugs. "My cousin and I handle things different."

Unspoken: *Also, I'm white and you ain't. Which means no extras as far as any business deals go.* The truth is, the SFK board doesn't exactly like to advertise that they do business with buyers who don't—how to put it—match their preferred client profile.

But the SFK likes money, and thanks to the growing heroin problem across the Midwest and Deep South, these fucking beaner gangs are flush with cash. Too much to just leave on the table.

So the SFK board decided to strategically split off the gun sales. They sent Dixon, Mason's pretty boy cousin—who also happens to be the gang's prez—to make deals with preferred customers (read: white gangs). And they sent Mason, the enforcer, to run all the beaner deals. Well, at least that was the original plan. Until D up and disappeared a few months back. Ever since, Mason's had to handle both sides of the coin for the SFKs.

But that's a whole 'nother shit show. So to Razo, all Mason says is, "You're dealing with me now. Not my cousin."

He doesn't notice the hand-rolled cigarette Razo's smoking until the shorter man puts it to his lips. He takes a long, thoughtful drag before pointing out, "This is a big order, *bolillo*." Razo nods towards the suitcase of money one of his men handed Mason a few minutes ago. "Fifteen more glocks. It's the least you can do, in my opinion."

Bolillo. White bread. Mason works hard not to let the slur throw him off his game. After all, he knows a thing or two about slurs.

"Well, you know what they say about opinions," he responds. Like any creature raised to kill and maim, Mason lacks a certain finesse.

"You sure about that, man?" Razo asks, his voice pleasant as the cheerful picket fences surrounding the perimeter of each house in the cul-de-sac. He casually rests his cigarette hand on the butt of the piece sticking out of his waistband. The gun is even more ostentatious than his tattoos: gold plated with a pearl grip, featuring a huge honking silver cross. Pretty as a girl, but lethal beneath the sexy exterior. A clear message to Mason that Razo doesn't give a flying fuck what anyone says about opinions, and if Mason knew what was good for him, he'll give Razo what he wants.

Mason suppresses a smile. He almost has to give the guy some respect. Razo's balls are a thousand times bigger than most of the two-bit dipshits Mason usually deals with. And he clearly knows how to read a situation.

See, Mason always does these secret side deals alone. To protect the fragile egos of the Kool-Aid drinkers among the ranks of the SFK who might take issue with the fact that some of the funds in their "race war" hope chest come from selling guns to non-white clientele.

Razo, like Mason, had clearly run his own diagnostic: Mason was one guy to Razo's four (and that didn't include his men on the porch, or any other gang bangers he might have hidden throughout the cul-de-sac). So as far as he was concerned, Mason would either give him what he wanted to get out alive, or Razo and his boys would take out a major player in one of the nation's top white supremacist organizations. Either way, it would give the little cholo something to brag about over tacos at the next gang banger potluck.

It would actually be a pretty solid plan *if* Razo was dealing with anyone other than Mason Fairgood. So even as Mason grudgingly gives the gang leader his due, he's working out exactly how to eliminate this motherfucker in the best way possible. Point blank? Too fast. Maybe snatch that pretty gun Razo was so casually threatening him with and use it to shoot the three beaners lined up behind him. Then use Razo as a human shield to stave off any fire that came from the houses. Yeah, that sounds like a plan—

KABLOOM!!!

The echo of a projectile hitting the conversion van he drove here in reverberates across the cul-de-sac. No, not a projectile...a soccer ball, he realizes, when a raggedy orb rolls past him as he runs toward his van.

What the hell!? What they do, shoot the damn thing out of a cannon? His van's still rocking from the impact.

And when he yanks open the back doors, his heart freezes at what he sees.

His baby. The sweet baby he'd brought along for the trip, lying on her side.

Imploding deal all but forgotten, he pulls his poor motorcycle out of the van and sets it carefully on the sidewalk. "You okay, baby?" he asks the lovingly restored chopper as he checks it everywhere for damage.

Only after he's sure she's okay, does he turn his attention back to the street. Was it a distraction? Maybe this is all a set-up, designed to confuse him. Bracing himself to get jumped he pulls out one of his Colt M1911s. Not nearly as fancy as Razo's piece, but it'll do the trick, he decides, scanning the darkened cul-de-sac for the motherfucker who'd dared kick a ball into his van.

"Oh, man, is that your bike?!?!'"

Mason stops, his eyes narrowing when he spots a kid standing there, the same worn soccer ball that hit his van tucked under his thin arm. The boy is small and scrawny as fuck. Nine, maybe ten at the most. Darker than Razo, possibly mixed with something other than Mexican. Black maybe. Some kind of kin to Razo? Maybe a son? Nephew? Whoever he is, the kid is goggling Mason's bike so wide-eyed, he's completely failed to notice the gun Mason's aiming at him.

"What the fuck do you think you're doing out here, kid?" Mason demands.

The boy finally looks up from the bike, finally sees the gun in Mason's hand.

"I was just...I was just..." he says, taking a big, nervous step back.

"You were just what?" Mason asks, cutting off the kid's sudden case of the stutters. "Looking to get killed?"

The sound of running footsteps startles him, and Mason realizes maybe this is all a set-up, designed to distract him so the beaners could get the jump on him from behind.

Mason aims, preparing to shoot first and ask questions later. But then his vision is completely filled with the figure of a girl.

But not a little girl. Not with those curves. This is a young woman, he realizes, his finger freezing on the trigger.

She's darker than the boy, with a wider nose—a black woman. Which is strange, because he usually don't see blacks, like at all, on these runs. But aside from the color of her skin, she looks exactly as you'd expect a girl living in a cholo neighborhood to look: tight white tank top that barely contains her large breasts, and a pair of fringed denim shorts that cover her thick hips, but leave the bottom of her ass exposed. She's even wearing an L.A. Dodgers cap over her long straight black hair. All she's missing is the chola teardrop tattoo next to her eye...

Definitely beaner girlfriend material. Maybe even Razo's woman. She looks like someone he'd want. Arresting and different.

She's parked herself in front of Mason's gun, and doesn't seem to be thinking about moving, even though her eyes are wide and terrified beneath the wide blue brim of her Dodgers cap.

And she stays put as the kid behind her says, "Sir, sir...please put away the gun. She didn't do nothing to you."

Mason Fairgood doesn't take orders from anybody, especially colored kids.

But he re-holsters his gun, even as he spits out, "That ghetto monkey of yours just kicked his fucking soccer ball into my bike."

His eyes flicker over to his baby, and then back to the girl. She visibly swallows, but still says nothing.

"You hear what I'm saying?" he asks.

No answer. Just more standing there like she don't exactly trust him to keep his gun out of sight.

"You retarded?" he finally asks.

"No, sir, she ain't retarded. She just don't talk much," the boy answers from behind her. His young voice is perfectly friendly as he asks, "Did I hurt your bike? Because if I did, I apologize. But if I didn't..."

Mason squints at the kid. "You still need to apologize. Do you know how much work went into that bike? Me and my cousin built it from the ground up. That's a 50K custom job right there. Bike's worth three of you—"

The woman startles the shit out of him with a sudden movement. She turns her head, and shakes it at the boy over her shoulder.

"She don't agree with you about that bike being worth more than my life," the kid translates, before asking, "Did you really build it yourself? How long did it take?"

What the hell is this kid's damage? Still no apology, and now he has the nerve to ask questions. But despite himself, Mason answers, "Few months. Hammered out all the body panels, mixed the paint. Even skinned and tanned one of our old cows to make the seat."

"Whoa!" the boy says, stepping around the woman, and moving toward the bike as if drawn by a magnet.

More sudden movement from the girl. This time, she grabs the kid by the back of his shirt, drawing him to his original position behind her.

"It's okay, June. I just want to look—"

"Why you two out here?" Razo's voice cuts him off.

The woman goes completely still, like prey scenting a

predator in the wild. And the night seems to tick with a new tension as she urgently motions the boy back towards a house that's parallel with the passenger side of his van.

But the kid just laughs, like he's run into an old friend on the street. "Hey, Razo!" he calls out. "I didn't know there was anybody out here. I was just kickin' a few balls before June left out..."

Mason's now wondering if the kid, not the girl, is the retarded one.

The girl—June—is obviously terrified. He can see the whites of her eyes, reminding him of a deer he shot last season, just before he pulled the trigger. The woman starts pushing the kid towards the house. When he doesn't budge, she squats down to his eye level and they have some kind of argument, made up mostly of head shakes and pointing. One she apparently wins.

Under the orange light of the street lamps, Mason can see the shadow that falls over the boy's face. One so familiar, it feels like he's staring into a dark mirror. The kid gives up, and without another word, skulks away. Back to the house the girl was pointing at.

At least that's where Mason figures he's headed. The boy disappears from his view, but Mason's eyes stay on the woman.

That's when he realizes he actually can't stop staring at her. Because even when the boy moves away, Mason's eyes remain where they've been since she stepped in front of his gun. Stuck on her, and only her. *What. The. Fucking. Hell?*

There's no reason for him to react like this to her. No reason he should stand in the street, not caring that he's surrounded by gang bangers who could turn on him at any second.

She's...not beautiful. A black girl can't be beautiful. He wasn't raised to think like that.

But she *is* mesmerizing. So mesmerizing, it feels like it's just him and her standing out here in this roach-infested cul-de-sac.

And for some reason, his dick—which is supposed to be deaf, dumb, and blind to her kind—is thrumming like an engine revving inside his pants.

Mason doesn't understand. Cannot reconcile it. This girl ain't white. She ain't even one of them darkie spics who won't let you call them black, far as he can tell.

So why can't he stop looking at her—?

He's released from her spell abruptly. Because suddenly Razo's standing between them, grabbing her by the throat. "What I tell you about him and that fucking soccer ball, huh, *puta*? What I say you about staying out the way when I'm working?"

It's not exactly fair. Mason prefers to keep his business meetings on par with the most fucked up of cable guys. He provides a vague window of days during which he might stop in with the goods, and usually shows up around dinner time on the first day when he knows they'll least expect him. Ain't no way this woman or that boy had any way of knowing who he was, or why he was here, when they left the house.

But the girl doesn't try to argue with Razo or make excuses. Her body just stiffens, her eyes rolling to the side of her face that's the farthest from Razo, in a way Mason recognizes more than he cares to admit. June knows she's about to get hit but doesn't want to see it coming.

And she's right.

Razo gives her a short, vicious punch. He's obviously had a lot of practice. It's just enough to deliver a painful blow without damaging her face. The woman's head lulls, but she doesn't throw up her hands, doesn't try to protect herself. It's as if she's flipped on a zombie switch. Figured out a way to disappear while her boyfriend's doing this to her. At least Mason assumes Razo's her boyfriend.

June's lack of fight seems to diffuse the tension and stop

Razo from hitting her again. Instead, he shoves her, sending her stumbling backwards onto her butt. "Get back to the house, bitch," he spits at her. "I'll deal with you later."

Get back to the house. Familiar language you'd only use with someone you were intimate with. *Definitely Razo's girlfriend*, Mason thinks. His to command. His to hit. His to do with as he pleases.

But for some reason, Razo's command to go back to the house brings the girl out of zombie mode. She starts pointing toward something at the end of the cul-de-sac.

"You think I'm gonna let you take the bus to go see that fag now?" Razo answers, voice nearly screeching with anger. "After this!? You out your mind, *puta!*"

He grabs her by the arm, yanking her to feet—but not out of any sense of chivalry. No, this assist is only given so he can really get up in her face. Bare his teeth at her as he....

Mason doesn't see it coming. If he had, he would have turned away. But the next thing he knows, he's watching Razo push the orange end of his cigarette into the woman's chest, pressing so hard, it collapses like a small, white accordion against her dark skin.

Again she doesn't make a sound. There's only a grimace, quick as a flash, like her face has become a valve for releasing pain in silence.

But for Mason, it's too late. His heart stops, seizing up as his brain's engine reverses hard into memory.

It's an old, old male Fairgood tradition, dating back almost to when Winstons first hit the shelves back in the fifties. Fairgood men put their cigarettes out on their boys. It wasn't considered cruel. It was training. Training the boys up to be men who knew how to endure, so they wouldn't become too soft, so they could handle pain...

"Now get in the house like I told you!" Razo calls out in the distance.

But in Mason's mind, his father, Fred Fairgood, is telling him to get back to his room, while he "deals" with Mason's mother.

She said something wrong again.

Did something wrong.

Maybe asked the wrong question.

Or looked at Fred the wrong way.

Got too fucked up on the drugs Fred plied her with.

There are a million things that could set his parents off. So many, it's almost not a surprise when a hot cigarette burns against the back of Mason's neck and he's told to go, *now*.

And Mason does, just like that half-darkie boy. Wanting to stay, but knowing from experience he'd only make it worse. That any action or word he could possibly think of would prolong his mother's suffering rather than end it.

He goes, but the fighting follows him down the hallway. The sound of his father's low menacing voice growling at his mother. And, depending on how high she is, his mother shrieking right on back at him, telling him he's washed up, that both him and his brother are disappointments to the SFK board. That he's lucky to have her. How she knows he's sleeping with [insert name of latest SFK groupie here]. How if it wasn't for Mason, she'd have left his ass the first time he laid hands on her. How he'd better not ever sleep too deep, because one night she'd cut his dick off—

And so it goes, a verbal release before the beating. The more creative his mother gets, the longer she staves off the inevitable. His father almost seems to enjoy listening to her. To Mason, her shrill voice sounds like the equivalent of squeezing hard on the throttle. Of someone getting a motorcycle nice and angry, so it'd make the biggest amount of noise as it speeds down the road.

By the time Mason reached the soccer ball kid's age, he'd

learned to climb out his bedroom window during this part. To be anywhere but there while his mother was still shrieking.

But when he was little...

When he was little, all he could do was cower behind the bedroom door. Listen to the shrill screams and the low-pitched yells until the noise of the beating ended all the talk.

Then it was just the hard, dull slaps of fists raining down on skin. The kind of sound that doesn't remotely resemble what you hear on TV or in movies. This would go on for a surprisingly short time. Five...ten minutes, tops. Then the aftermath. The weird quiet after the beating. Also not what you see on TV. In real life, there ain't no sobbing after your father's done beating on your mother. Not if he's done it right. Not if he's a Fairgood. After a Fairgood beatdown, the only sound anybody's going to hear is *him*...his breath, panting from the exertion of putting his old lady in her place. The soundtrack of him standing over her, waiting to see if she dares get up. Or say so much as another word.

And then he stops breathing hard. And there's nothing left but the quiet. And if you're a Fairgood boy who hasn't learned to climb out the window yet, you just have to wait and see what happens next. Because maybe your father will leave out, go have a few more drinks at the clubhouse. Maybe he'll head to his room and pass out from drink the way your mom has passed out from her beating. Or maybe he'll come after you. Finish releasing the rest of his anger, finish what the cigarette burn started—

When Mason returns to reality, everything has changed. The woman is gone. And Razo and his original three-guy crew are in front of him. Exchanging unsettled looks with each other in a silent conversation Mason can easily translate as, *What the fuck is up with this loco gringo*?

Bad things happen when he's triggered. Most often people

get hurt. Sometimes they get dead. Are they looking at him that way because he snapped?

But no...he looks around the cul-de-sac. No blood, no dead bodies, and the porches are empty now—but in a smart, disappearing act way, not in an aftermath sort of way. He knows aftermath. Really well. And this ain't it.

Mason lets himself breathe again, somehow knowing she's inside one of those graffiti-covered houses. Maybe the same one as the boy. Safe. At least for now.

"Hey, you alright, man?"

His eyes flicker back to the cholos.

"You was just standing there," Razo tells him. "Breathing real weird. Like you fixing to explode or something."

The other three snicker at their boss's observation.

Only to stop short when Mason hits them with a look. The one he usually saves for right before he pulls out the bowie knife his uncle, D's dad, gave him for his twelfth birthday. *"You can use it on any animal gives you trouble. Don't matter if it's on four legs or two."*

At Mason's look, Razo actually shrinks back, but then manages to regain his poise and find some courage inside his small chest. "We doing this or what?" he asks, lowering his voice a few octaves and tapping both hands against his HIJOS DE LA MUERTES tattoo.

Mason blinks, a deliberate motion that serves to reset his face into business mode.

Yeah, crazy shit happens when he's triggered. Take, for example, right now when he opens his mouth and unleashes words. Three of them, directed at Razo. "That your girl?"

Razo's brow furrows, his confusion at Mason's unexpected question written clearly across his face. "Yeah, and don't worry, homes. I'm going to make her pay for what happened with your bike. As soon as we get our fifteen extra, you know."

It's both a promise and a threat. The original request for fifteen extra guns hangs over the conversation like a storm cloud, warning of shit to come.

But Mason ignores the cloud and asks, "You sick of fucking her yet?"

A thoughtful beat. Then as if just now realizing it himself, Razo answers, "Gettin' there. I mean she fine, but that kid and—"

Razo cuts off, the obvious question suddenly occurring to him, "Hey, why you askin' about her?"

Crazy, crazy, shit, Mason thinks. But he asks the next question anyway.

"How much you want for her?"

2

MASON

Twenty glocks. His custom bike. And five thousand dollars.

That's what Mason pays for Razo's girl. A fucking *black* girl. And one who comes as a package deal, no less.

"You take her kid, too," Razo demanded during the negotiations. "No way he staying here with us. Ain't good for shit. Can't even trust him on runs cuz he talk too much."

Well, fuck...

So that's how Mason ends up jammed in the front of his van with a silent black woman and her kid...one she maybe had with Razo. She sits as far from him as possible, slumped against the passenger side door so heavily, he's half afraid she's going to accidentally depress the handle and roll out into the oncoming traffic of the 303-N.

Sure, it would solve the current situation. But it'd be messy. And create a whole bunch of other problems he *really* doesn't need right now.

Fuck, fuck, fuck...

Mason drives, trying to ignore the kid seated between him and the woman. The boy clutches that goddamn soccer ball in his lap like it's a beloved pet. And he's been yammering since they peeled out of the cul-de-sac. Forty-five long-as-hell minutes and barely a pause to breathe.

Turns out, the kid only needs someone with a pulse to keep a conversation going. And apparently, he was born completely without the ability to read a fucking room. Because despite Mason's aggressive lack of response and his mom's leaden silence, the boy jabbers all the way to Beaver Lake. About Arkansas's lack of a major league soccer team. About the last World Cup. About that one time he kicked his soccer ball all the way over the house. About that other time he kicked his soccer ball down an open manhole and a worker from the city's water and power department had to get it for him.

The kid's one-sided conversation definitely has a running theme, and it doesn't occur to him to ask a single non-soccer related question until Mason pulls up in front of a lodge with a burnt out neon "Vacancy" sign.

Even then, the boy's voice sounds more curious than afraid when he asks, "Where we at?" He doesn't even seem the slightest bit worried that Mason has driven him and his mom to a very remote area of Beaver Lake. With backwoods so dense, you can barely make out the sky above.

"Motel," Mason grunts back, even though that's not exactly true. More like a bunch of run-down cabins and a few camp-sites. Not the ritziest place on the lake, but one that—for obvious reasons—always has vacancies. Also its owner accepts cold hard cash and doesn't require signatures or paperwork.

"You looking for a room, son?"

Speaking of the owner...

An old man, about the same age as Methuselah, charges out of the lodge towards them. His question might have come off as hospitable if not for the Model 60 Marlin Rimfire in his hands, barrel pointed directly at the van.

"Relax, Burt. It's me." Mason says, rolling down the driver's side window.

"Oh...hey, Fairgood!" Burt lowers his gun with a cackle, recognizing Mason as that guy who's been coming here once or twice a year for the last five. "Haven't seen you in a while! Didn't recognize you in that vehicle." The old man narrows his eyes, peering further into the dark recesses of the cab. "I see you brought some friends..."

Burt knows who Mason is. What Mason is. He's seen the patches on Mason's vest, and once, Burt even came by to warn him he had some colored folks staying in one of his cabins. "I ain't lookin for no race war on my property, so if it's going to be a problem..."

It hadn't been a problem. Mason knew how to keep to himself, and ignore the fact that the rest of the world isn't as lily white as the one at the SFK compound.

But tonight, with the barely functioning neon motel sign flickering in the background, there's just enough light to illuminate the interior of the van. Burt squints and strains to get a better look. Obviously trying to figure out if he's seeing what he thinks he's seeing. "You...ah...looking for more than one campsite today?"

Mason pushes a wad of cash at the old man through the van window. "I'll take one of the king kitchenette cabins. Going to be here for...a few weeks."

Burt's watery eyes light up at the bills. There's way more in that bundle than what the cabin's worth, even at the weekly rate.

The old guy reaches over and takes the money. "3C, last on the left. It's all yours," he says without looking up from counting his cash.

Mason leaves him to it.

"How old was that guy?" the kid asks as they drive away. "A hundred?"

Mason glances over at the silent woman, still pressed up against the passenger door. Her hands are folded primly in her lap, making her look like a Catholic school girl in chola clothes.

She still hasn't said a word. Hasn't so much as looked in his direction since Razo's guys shoved her at him after the exchange of glocks, money, and Mason's bike.

The kid and her had climbed into his van with nothing but a backpack between them. And now she's shrunk up against the passenger door in a way that makes Mason wonder if she's permanently flipped on her zombie switch.

"Stay here," he growls at her and the kid. The van is a stick, which he knows most women can't drive. But just in case, Mason yanks the key out of the ignition. Sure, she can still escape on foot, but at least now he can give chase if she tries.

Hold up. Why the fuck is he planning how to catch her if she runs? Why in the hell is he figuring out how he'll track down the woman he had no business buying in the first place? If he had any goddamn sense, Mason would be praying for her to haul ass. And take the kid with her, save him the trouble.

But he sends up no prayers, and not just because he's been a secret non-believer since his mother died the way she did. No, it's mostly because of the woman. Because despite her not wanting to be anywhere near him, he gets hard at the thought of her.

And though he knows he can't keep her for long, his head is filled with thoughts that someone like him should definitely not be having about someone like her. Mason wonders about the body under her tacky clothes. Wonders if it feels as soft as it looks. Imagines her thick thighs wrapped around his waist as he—

Fuck, fuck, fuck!

He shakes his head and tries to clear it of those unwelcome thoughts, all while striding towards 3C. If it wasn't already clear that his cousin's disappearance is fucking with his head, it's sure as shit clear now.

The cabin door turns out to be sticky, so Mason kicks the damn thing open with a heavy motorcycle boot. But this relatively small release of anger does nothing to reduce his pent up frustration. As he turns on every single light in the cabin, and opens every single window not already welded shut, he reflexively and repeatedly pulls on an invisible gun trigger. He wishes he'd killed every one of those cholo motherfuckers. Wishes he'd never met this woman...even as he swears if she so much as thinks about leaving, he'll hunt her down like a dog.

Mason shakes his head again. He's all messed up. His mind is a jumble of thoughts about hunting, and gun running. About fucking the black girl waiting for him in the van.

He won't stay at the cabin tonight. But for June's sake, he performs a final sweep of the room. Opens the stove, the fridge, and kicks the bed to scare out anything lurking beneath.

Truth is, Burt isn't exactly known for his high quality housekeeping standards. Last time he stopped in, Mason witnessed a whole family of raccoons crawl out through a partially open cabin window.

But this time, there are no signs of animal life inside. Mason's about to fetch his two passengers, when the kid appears behind him in the doorway.

"Whoa!" he says, looking around the cabin.

"I thought I told you to stay in the van!" Mason barks, irritation pounding in his head worse than a headache.

But the boy only walks further in, not remotely intimidated, his eyes wide as saucers. "Double beds? A fridge?! Ah, man, we even got a stove!" Looking like he's just been shown into a room at a luxury hotel, the boy rushes to the old gas stove. "June! Come see!"

June...

She stands in the doorway.

And Mason's stomach revs up at the sight of her, on cue. He realizes he's staring. Unable to look away.

June stares right back. But he can tell she's definitely not checking him out. More like taking him in, getting the measure of him.

Mason lets her, even though he's sure she ain't going to like what she sees. He knows he's scary as hell. Partly thanks to genetics, partly because of him going the extra mile to cultivate a look that says, "*the last thing you'll do on this earth is fuck with me.*"

Yet for one crazy second, he wishes he looked more... normal. Less threatening. That the black girl named June in the cabin doorway could see someone else when she looked at him. But those fragile wishes burn to ash when her eyes wander down from his face to the patches on his leather vest...

Oh fuck. Mason suddenly becomes aware that she might not have gotten a good look at his vest under the orange streetlights in Razo's hood. What with all the drama, she might not have taken in every single bit of him the way he'd taken in every single bit of her.

Her brow furrows as she studies the patches. Puts two and two together.

Then a look comes over her face...

One that stabs Mason in his chest, with a rough, sawing pain far uglier than any inflicted by the serrated blade of his ever-present bowie knife.

"Are you seeing this, June?" the kid asks excitedly from the kitchenette, still clueless about the newly arrived tension in the room. "You can start cooking again like you been wanting to!"

The girl's excruciating gaze finally swings away from Mason and towards the kid.

And she smiles. For the boy's sake, Mason senses.

But then her forced smile wobbles, and she doesn't so much sit as collapse on the bed nearest the door.

"June!"

The kid rushes to her, face drawn into a frown of concern rather than the usual "happy-all-the-time-for-no-fucking-reason" look he's had on since Mason met him.

The woman's about to pass out. Mason can tell. But she squeezes the kid's hand and gives him a reassuring smile. Her face is on par with an angel's, even as her lids flutter and she keels over on the bed.

"June? June?!" the boy calls out, his voice cracking with worry.

Mason pushes the kid aside and crouches down over his mom to run diagnostics. This is definitely not how he pictured their first touch, but he shoves that thought to the back of his head and does what he has to: checks her eyes, her pulse, and all that other shit.

The good news is she doesn't seem to have a concussion. She's hasn't really even passed out. She wakes easily when he pries one of her eyes open. And when he shines his pocket flashlight into it, she doesn't flinch. Only closes her eyes as soon as he's had his look.

"She on anything?" Mason asks the boy.

The kid shakes his head. "No, she don't do any of that. That's how her mom died. She don't even drink."

No drugs. No alcohol. But the kid's not quite looking him in the eye. Mason squints at him, trying to figure out what the fuck is going on.

"You hungry?" the kid asks all of a sudden, like his mom's not near passed out. "Maybe...maybe we should get something to eat."

"Kid, what in the hell does food have to do with—" Mason

starts to asks...but then his instincts switch on. "Hold on...when was the last time she ate?"

A long, sober beat passes...then the kid's answer comes back in a tone way more quiet than any he's used so far. "Uh, well, Razo brings us food and tells us when we can eat. But sometimes he forgets. And if you remind him..."

The kid trails off in a way that tells Mason everything he needs to know about what happens if anyone asks that little beaner shit for food. It all makes sense now. June's complete lack of reaction to all that's happened to her thus far, her slumped position in the car, her sudden need to take a nap. Like, right fucking now.

Mason stands, shaking his head. He *really* should have killed that cholo prick when he had the chance.

"She was supposed to get something tonight, you know... when Razo let her out," the kid continues. "But then you showed up. I wouldn't have eaten our last can of spaghetti if I'd known she wasn't going to eat at all. But she ordered me to eat..." The boy looks down, a guilty expression on his face. "I should have said no. Made her eat some, too."

Shit... Mason wearily scrubs a hand over his face. "Okay, okay. Just tell me, when did you eat that can of spaghetti?"

"Two days ago..."

Well, fuck me...

Mason heads for the still open door.

"Where you going?" the kid calls after him.

"To get some food for you and your mom," Mason calls back over his shoulder.

Then it occurs to him to say, "And kid, just in case you're thinking about running while I'm gone...don't. I'll find you way before you can find your way out these backwoods."

It's a threat. A clear one.

"Name's Jordan." The kid shakes his head. "But June's not my mom. And we'll definitely be here when you get back."

He folds his arms across his small chest in a way that makes Mason revise his earlier impression about the boy being clueless. "It ain't like we got anywhere else to go."

3

JUNE

*S*he opens her eyes to an all too familiar scene. Jordan, seated in a chair beside her bed, watching a soccer game while he waits for her to come to. If he'd been dealt different cards, June thinks there might've been a chance he'd grow up to become a medical professional. Maybe a paramedic —or a doctor or nurse. Because Jordan's always there after the incidents with Razo, wielding ice packs, pain killers, gauze bandages—you name it—like a pro. Taking care of her, so she can take care of him.

But...something feels off. She feels...off. Jordan is in his usual position, but...

It's been so very long, June has to search long and hard for the word to describe her current state: fine. Better than fine, even.

She still has the Band-Aid on her chest where Razo burned her, but she's not aching with bruises. Her head is clear, and her stomach—well, for the first time in months, it doesn't have the awful clawing feeling inside...that ever-present sensation of hunger.

This more than anything confirms she's not in the cul-de-sac anymore.

"What's going...?" she begins, slowly propping herself up on one arm. Her voice sounds croaky and dry from disuse.

"June! Hold on, let me get you a drink," Jordan says, hopping up from the chair.

June pushes into a seated position and takes a good look around. *No, I'm definitely not in the Cul*, she thinks, blinking at the room. In the Cul, she and Jordan slept on a bare mattress in one of the otherwise empty pre-fab houses that dotted the neighborhood. But if anything, this room seems overstuffed. With heavy wooden furniture, and not one, but two beds. She glances down at the coverlet she's under. It's thick and covered with palm trees, so yellowed with age, she has to wonder how long it's been on the bed. Decades not years, she suspects.

The room reeks. Of cooked meat, sweat, and smoke...

But not the same pungent-scent that overlays the Cul. Not weed. More like...Razo's cigarettes—

Razo.

The previous night comes back to her like a bucket of icy water, cold and clear. The biker. The gun. The *sale.*

Oh, God. She remembers it all in stomach-churning detail. Razo sold her. He *sold* her! To...

A white supremacist. Razo sold her to *a white supremacist.* And she suddenly remembers everything in excruciating detail. The hand off. The drive. The moment when she finally realized what and who the biker is. The patches on his leather vest...

"Here, drink this." Jordan reappears by her side and pushes a huge, open bottle of Gatorade into her hands. "Mason said you'd need some electrolytes."

June takes a big gulp of the blue liquid. Just enough to wet her throat so she can ask, "How long have I been asleep?" without croaking.

"Almost a whole day," Jordan answers. "We fed you some soup, and you got up to use the bathroom a few times. But mostly...you slept."

They fed her. She's struck by a flash of memory. Of large hands pulling her up. Of a gruff voice ordering her to drink, to eat...

Strangely, it takes a full stomach and a day and night of sleep for June to fully grasp just how bad her situation is. How her and Jordan's luck has turned. From really awful to unbelievably shitty.

Razo *sold* her. The only reason she'd been with him in the first place was because she didn't know how else to take care of herself and Jordan after both their moms overdosed on a bad batch of heroin.

"I got a cousin..." Jordan said after the shelter didn't work out.

Unfortunately, his cousin turned out to be a small-time drug dealer and thug named Razo.

Better than the streets, June told herself when Razo offered her a position in his bed. Sleeping with Razo had to be way better than hooking, and it let her keep the promise she'd made to Jordan: that they would stay together, and out of foster care, no matter what.

That had been six long years ago. And her first two years in the Cul were a fairytale compared to the last two.

From the beginning, Razo hit her. Slaps for talking out of turn, backhands for accidently wearing a rival gang's colors. But then the slaps turned into punches. And the backhands into beatings that kept Jordan home from school, tending to her wounds.

By the time June realized she had to get them out of there, it was too late. She was a virtual prisoner in the Cul that Razo's rapidly growing gang called home. She was penniless with a growing kid to feed. And she was reminded daily by Razo's treatment of her that she was his to abuse, forever and ever. No amen.

The years dragged by. She and Jordan lived firmly wedged under Razo's thumb, and June disappeared further and further inside herself. Until the naïve high school kid she used to be disappeared, along with her teenage years, into the Arkansas night. June had found herself questioning her past, wondering if the teenage girl who'd once dreamt of becoming a graphic artist had ever really existed. Maybe June had only imagined that girl...read about her, or seen her on TV. Because the hell she lived in with Razo and his gang eventually felt like it was the only thing she'd ever known.

Then, during those last few months in the Cul, things came to a head. Razo had moved on to younger, barely legal girls who were either too naïve or too dumb to see through his dangerous charm. And that wouldn't have been so bad. Any real feelings June ever had for Razo—and there weren't a lot there to begin with—had withered and died years ago, and her body welcomed the respite from his sexual attention. But unfortunately, just because Razo had moved on sexually, did not mean he had any plans to let her go, or relax his "rules" where she was concerned.

No touching Razo's girl. No talking to Razo's girl. No looking at Razo's girl for too long. Only he was allowed in the house she and Jordan occupied, and only he could bring takeout or groceries when he arrived to fuck her. Those were his rules, constructed out of sheer pettiness and not remotely influenced by any feelings of affection or love on his part.

Even after he'd tired of her, Razo enjoyed keeping June as his prize. The nice, middle class girl he'd corrupted and now owned. Another notch on Razo's belt.

But it hadn't been so bad. Well, not at first. Jordan still had access to regular meals at school. And he filched cans of food from charity boxes whenever he could. But then the school year ended, and their food supplies started dwindling fast.

When they were down to their last few cans, June was forced to get creative. She went to the main house to meet with Razo.

They didn't discuss food or the lack thereof. Razo liked power games too much to just give them what they needed. Asking him for something he hadn't offered could result in him starving them for longer, or worse, earn her a beating. And given how weak she was from lack of nutrition, she wasn't sure she'd be able to recover from one of Razo's attacks.

Instead, June showed him her notepad with the design she'd been thinking about for his back. It was a beautiful sketch and she knew he'd be impressed although he would work hard to downplay it. The image consisted of two Dias de los Muertos-style Virgin Marys on opposite sides of an ornate cross, praying over a field of skulls. Skulls that could be interpreted as fallen Hijos or fallen enemies. Unlike her previous torso work, this image was further accented by two blood red rubies. One for each of the Hijos the gang lost in a recent skirmish with their enemies, the 2nd Streeters.

Razo liked the drawing. Of course he did. June worked hard to design a tattoo worthy of the future cartel leader he wished to become.

"There's just one problem, though. See, I've never worked in color before." June kept her eyes downcast, attempting to look as deferential as possible. As always, she found it much easier to talk with him—with anyone, really—as long as they discussed tattoos.

Then she mentioned Greco, a master tattooist from that TV show, *Lost Angels Ink*. She told Razo he'd be at a nearby convention center on Thursday night, teaching a free master class on coloring techniques.

In the end, it didn't take much convincing for Razo to decide she could go—so long as she left Jordan behind, of course. Collateral in case she might be entertaining ideas about taking off.

June agreed to his terms. After all, she didn't have a choice.

Plus, she and Jordan had a plan. Jordan would kick soccer balls in the front yard like always so Razo wouldn't suspect anything. He'd stay out there until someone eventually complained about the noise and told him to go back inside. Then he'd hop over their back fence. Meet June at the food bank closest to their house.

They'd pick up something to eat. And after that...

Well, she hadn't planned that far ahead. Her number one focus had been on getting them fed. And she'd hoped a full stomach would shed light on ways they could get out of this mess without breaking her promise to Jordan about staying together, no matter what.

But then the racist biker happened before they'd been able to implement any part of the night's plan.

"Where's our backpack?" she asks, setting the Gatorade aside on the nightstand. Like all the other furniture in the room, it's well made but from at least four decades ago, if not more. "We've got to go," she tells Jordan, swinging her legs to sit up on the side of the bed. She's relieved to find she's still dressed. "We've got to get out of here."

No head-spinning, even though she sat up real fast. Wow. She hasn't been able to make any quick movements without feeling dizzy for months now.

But Jordan doesn't move from the chair he's already sat back down in. "We can't leave," he says. "He paid a lot to get you off Razo. And we don't got any money."

June curses inwardly. It's true. About them not having

money. Also, about that guy buying her...and probably expecting something in return for his investment.

With a chill, she recalls the previous night. When she got her first real look at him in the full light of the cabin. Oddly enough, she found him even more intimidating inside the decently lit room than he'd been back at the Cul. Maybe because now she could see him clearly. He was huge, at least a foot taller than she was and wide. He had long, coffee-colored hair...longer than her weave, even. And his mustache was so thick and heavy, it was impossible to tell where it stopped and his bushy beard began. Long hair and beards may be in style, but this guy is definitely no plaid-shirted, man-bun wearing hipster.

He's a wall of leather, denim, and muscle. A biker. And obviously so. Not like the ones on TV shows like *Sons of Anarchy* and that reality program, *Hell Riders*. More like the kind you see in old seventies films. Not anti-heroes or fascinating character studies, but villains who exclusively steal, rape, kill, and sell illegal goods as a way of life.

And the way he'd looked at her. Those unsettling crystal blue eyes, staring down at her, intent, frustrated, angry. Like even though he made the decision to purchase her, she's the one who'd done something wrong.

This guy looked exactly like what he was. A death dealer. Like Razo. But way, way worse.

Last night, while she stood there trying to digest the overwhelming presence of her new "owner," she spotted the patches on his leather vest. The Hijos had patches, too, and most of them were subtle to the point of being difficult for a non-member to decipher.

But you definitely didn't have to ask for the meaning of the patches on the biker's leather vest. Because it was loud and clear to June...from the Sgt at Arms patch with the old-style German cross, to the diamond shaped "1%" overlaying the confederate flag, to the round WHITE POWER patch with a tight fist square in the middle.

Those patches told her all she needed to know about the man standing in front of her.

And now....

Now she's wide awake with a full belly and a very alert brain. So she's more than capable of understanding just how bad their situation is. White supremacist biker. Cabin out in the middle of nowhere. *Oh God, oh God...*

What was he going to do with them?

June looks around for their backpack, her mind in a panic. She needs to figure out a way for them to get away.

"We don't need to run," Jordan informs her as if he's reading her mind. He sounds calm, like he's the voice of reason and she's crazy for wanting to go. "He's okay, this guy. I think we should stay here with him."

But June knows he's not okay. He's totally *not* okay. She thinks once more about the patches on his jacket, and has to swallow down the bile rising in her throat.

"June, he didn't hurt you when you stepped in front of his gun to protect me," Jordan points out. "And he's been feeding us. He went to the store and bought soup, and now he's picking up a pizza. He's okay!"

June looks at the little boy she's sworn to raise. She has no idea how to clearly explain their current situation without scaring him. Because this guy might be acting nice now— feeding them, giving them a safe place to sleep—but she feels certain it's for reasons she doesn't even want to imagine. Razo fed them at first, too. Made sure they had what they needed. That's what bad men do...lower your guard, lull you into thinking everything's going to be okay, and then strike.

But Jordan is stubbornly oblivious to the gravity of their situation. "He helped take care of you while you was sleeping. And he came back, June. With food!" Jordan makes his case with the fervent conviction of a child. "He don't look it or talk it, but he's a good guy. You'll see!"

For a moment, June can only stare at Jordan, feeling sorrier for him than she's ever felt for herself. She knows how easily he falls into hero worship: Razo, the other Hijos—when any of them showed him even a sliver of kindness, he'd attach to them like a puppy. How many times did they have to kick him before he could see them for who and what they really were?

June is going to have to work hard to convince him not to trust this latest man in their lives.

"Jordan..." she begins.

The door crashes open with a huge bang.

June jumps, only to freeze in terror when she sees the biker standing there, arms loaded with two large pizza boxes and some plastic bags. He's swapped his long sleeved t-shirt for a Henley, but other than that, he looks exactly the same. Big. Angry. Dangerous as hell.

He stops short when he sees her upright on the side of the bed. His jaw ticks once or twice, before he growls, "You're up. Good."

The man's voice is low and gravelly. As if his vocal chords are located deep in his gut rather than his neck like everybody else. He stares at her. The same as last night.

June casts her gaze away. From him and from his patch-laden vest. Unable to form an answer, because it seems like his crystal blue gaze is eating her alive.

She hears him grunt irritably. Then there's the sound of pizza boxes landing on the table, and his feet stomping over to a window. She dares to peep up at him. Watches as he stalks around the room, yanking curtains apart and shoving windows open, until cool, tree-scented air fills the space.

It's actually not a new day at all, she belatedly realizes. It's late afternoon, early evening. Crickets, not birds, chirp in the background, warning of the soon-to-be-setting sun.

Again she curses silently. Not morning.... too late to run, unless they want to get stuck in the backwoods overnight.

"Told you to keep those windows open," the biker growls at Jordan, who's now at the table opening the two pizza boxes. The room is suddenly filled with the smell of warm bread, meat, and cheese.

"It got too cold," Jordan explains with a shrug as he grabs an entire box of pizza and brings it over to June.

He hands it to her. "Lookit, he got you sausage and pepperoni! *Your favorite.*" Jordan stresses the last two words, as if they prove his point that the white supremacist biker who bought her from Razo, is really a good guy.

For a moment, June is completely overwhelmed with a desire to scream and cry.

"Eat," a voice says, as if offering her a third option.

She looks up and sees that the biker has seated himself at the table. He seems calmer now that every window and door in the room is open. "But go slow with that food," he warns. "Eat too fast, and it might come back up."

June's eyes widen, surprised at his gruff but thoughtful warning. But then he turns his back to her and grabs a slice. Leaving her with nothing to look at but the huge patch on his back, the one that declares him a member of the SOUTHERN FREEDOM KNIGHTS MC

She quickly looks away, shivering. And not because of the cool summer breeze drifting through the room.

As if by mutual agreement, Jordan and the man settle into chairs on opposite sides of the small wooden table, the other pizza box between them. Jordan is back to his usual non-stop conversational stream about soccer. He's telling the biker about the soccer game he watched while June was asleep. Out of the corner of her downcast eyes, June watches the biker—what had Jordan called him? Mason? Yes, that was it. Mason folds a large slice of the pizza in half right down the middle, neatly ensuring the generous pile of toppings and melted cheese stay put as he raises the warm triangle to his mouth. It disappears in four bites, before Jordan has even figured out how to eat his slice without his toppings sliding off onto his paper plate.

"Eat," the biker growls at June again, shooting her a quick angry glance before he reaches into the box for another piece.

So she does. Because he told her to, because she needs to keep up her strength, because she knows she can't afford to be hungry and weak again. If he tries anything...if he pulls a gun on Jordan like he did last night, or tries to hurt him in any way ... she has to be ready.

So she eats the pizza, even though it tastes like warm cardboard in her mouth. For Jordan, she eats—even if his response, when he catches her worried gaze, is to roll his eyes with a look that clearly says "stop acting so scared!"

Jordan has seen many things he shouldn't have. *So* many things, thanks to Razo. But in spite of that, his worldview is impossibly small. He doesn't understand. Can't understand what they're dealing with.

Yeah, they've escaped Razo who sometimes beat her in front of Jordan, and occasionally starved them while he was off fucking other young women. But she can't help but feel like they've gone from the proverbial frying pan and into the fire with this white supremacist biker who could very literally be fattening them up to...

Well...truthfully she has no idea why he's going through the trouble of feeding them. Or what he plans to do next.

Which is why she ignores her queasy stomach and eats slowly. Exactly like he told her. She has to stay alive. For Jordan, she has to stay alive.

4

JUNE

*J*une stays braced for anything. But after they're done eating, Jordan simply picks up her half-empty pizza box, closes it over the leftover slices, and takes it to the little kitchenette on the other side of the room.

"Me and Mason going to watch some TV. Want your paper?" he asks as he puts the box into the fridge.

June thinks about it, then nods. Drawing will help her think. Maybe even calm her mind enough so she can figure out a decent exit strategy.

"Here you go," Jordan says, handing her the backpack that she now realizes was on the kitchenette counter the whole time.

She unzips it and looks inside. Razo hadn't allowed them to take anything that couldn't fit into the backpack, so this back-pack is all she and Jordan have in life right now. Relief fills her when she sees everything's still there, including her ink and tattoo gun, plus a few changes of clothes for Jordan. She pulls out her drawing pad and a black Sharpie.

June expects Jordan to settle back into the chair beside her bed, but instead, he climbs into the other bed with the remote control and says to Mason, "Soccer's done, but *So You Think You'd Survive* is on. Want to watch that?"

"That'll work," the biker answers.

June starts when he suddenly drops into the chair beside her bed with a tall Shiner Bock in one meaty hand.

She's terrified to have him this close. But he doesn't so much as glance her way. Just leans back in the chair to watch crazy people doing crazy stuff in some crazy reality show competition.

Eventually, she somehow manages to pull her attention away from him and settle against the headboard, folding her legs up underneath her drawing pad. Usually she gives a little thought to what she wants to draw before putting her Sharpie to a precious piece of sketch paper. But tonight, there's no advanced planning. She just starts drawing. Black birds with thick wings. Ravens in mid-flight. Her Sharpie skitters frantically across the paper as the show drones on in the background. She's thinking... *thinking*...but can't come up with anything that doesn't end with her and Jordan lost in the woods.

After an hour or so of this, June has to stop. She's filled up one whole side of the paper with ravens and she's rapidly losing the light to the setting sun. She could turn on the bedside lamp, she supposes, but that would mean moving an inch closer to *him*. She thinks about doing it anyway but finds she can't so much as move a finger in his direction.

That's okay, she decides. It's not like she's getting anywhere with her escape plans. Also, the sketch pad Jordan stole for her the last time the Hijos took him on a Cal-Mart run is down to its last few sheets. She'd only been letting herself draw on half pages for weeks now, and she has no idea when she'll get another pad.

Or if.

Yeah, June thinks, her full stomach churning, *drawing definitely isn't helping me out tonight.* So she starts to set the pad

aside, only to notice something. Something about the birds she's
sketched...a pattern or—

She stops, frowns, turns the pad sideways. No, she's not
imagining it. The ravens form a familiar shape...a motorcycle. A
dangerous-looking motorcycle made of black, ominous,
wickedly intelligent birds. June notices that her stomach is
mimicking the wheeling, circling, twisting of those birds.

She quickly flips the pad shut and puts it next to her on the
bed, turning her attention to the program on the room's ancient
20" Emerson TV. It's something about custom cars, a topic she
couldn't care less about. But she watches anyway. And then
another show comes on, one where two brothers go around the
country finding old cars, which they haul back to their shop in
Long Beach to restore. June watches without really watching,
faking interest while trying hard to ignore the increasingly
piercing call of her very full bladder.

Night eventually shrouds the room in darkness, and after a
few more episodes of the car restoration show, Jordan drops off
to sleep in the other bed.

Meanwhile, June's bladder is screaming at her. But she
doesn't move. Can't move. Due to fear of the man sitting in the
chair beside her bed. She's sure he's staring at her, even though
each time she's dared glance his way, his eyes are planted on the
TV. Face stony in the screen's flickering light.

But the feeling won't go away, hasn't gone away since he
entered the cabin. There's something about him.

Even when he's not looking at her, it feels like he is.

And even though his eyes remain intent on the 1959 El
Camino currently being restored on screen, it feels to June like
he's waiting. Waiting to pounce. And now Jordan's asleep.

How is this going to work? she wonders, glancing over at the
boy now sleeping peacefully in the other bed. Jordan used to be
so well-trained. He'd leave any room she was in as soon Razo

entered their house. But their cabin only has one room. Would he really fall on top of her here? Right in front of Jordan?

Her stomach twists at the thought, making the matter of her bladder that much more urgent. She can't ignore it any longer, she realizes with a sinking heart. She has to pee. She glances forlornly at the room's only bathroom. The one that feels impossibly far away on the other side of the kitchenette.

Carefully sliding out of bed, she creeps through the darkness. Past Jordan's bed, through the kitchenette area, making as quick and quiet a beeline toward the bathroom as possible. But before closing the door behind her, she risks a quick glance over her shoulder.

He's still in the chair. Eyes so glued to the TV, there's a good chance he hasn't noticed her departure. But it still feels like he's watching her, even after she closes the door and turns the lock.

After relieving herself, she looks forlornly at the threadbare hand towels stacked on the cracked green sink. She wouldn't mind a shower after everything that's happened. Too bad she doesn't have anything to change into.

Yet, she still can't regret her decision to use the allotted space for Jordan's clothes and not any of the outfits Razo had bought for her. They were ugly clothes. Tasteless and totally without any purpose other than cheap titillation. A waste of opportunity to sew beauty into an art-starved world, her mother would have said... back in that other lifetime when they did normal mother-daughter things together like back-to-school shopping.

June settles for washing her face. The faded make up comes off with a towel and water, but her sadness is a lot harder to get rid of. And the woman staring back at her from the oval mirror above the sink looks about a thousand times older than her twenty-three years. So weary, June can't help but wonder if she'll find gray hairs when she finally gets around to taking out her old weave—

The door opens behind her, as easily as if she'd never locked it in the first place. And just like that, she's no longer alone in the bathroom.

The biker's there. And he's got a knife in his hand. Bigger than a switch blade, but smaller than a sword, it sports jagged teeth on its blade. And it puts her in mind of those horror movies where villains hunt and kill humans like animals.

June freezes, her hands tightly clasped on the rim of the sink, too afraid to turn and acknowledge him face-to-face. He slips the knife inside his leather vest, and shuts the door behind him with a definitive click. Then he studies her reflection, his eyes brighter than anything else in the small room.

He's terrifying. She clings to the sink, more afraid of him than she's ever been of anything or anyone else in her life.

"Turn around," he says, his mouth barely moving beneath the large beard.

June squeezes her eyes shut, fighting back tears she didn't know she still had. *How's this going to work?* she'd asked herself earlier.

Now she has her answer. In the bathroom, where Jordan won't see.

I guess I should at least be grateful for that, she thinks as she grips the sink one last time before turning to face him.

She's immediately overwhelmed. The bathroom is on the small side and now that he's in there with her, it feels impossibly cramped. Like he's taken over every inch of space, his scent—leather and motor oil—overpowering every molecule of air. She can't move. She can't breathe.

"Hey, *hey*," he says, bending at the knees into an almost-crouch.

Then his face is level with hers. "Hey, don't do that."

Don't do what? June wonders, trying to look anywhere but at him.

But his head follows her eyes, his blue gaze chasing her darting brown one. Steady but insistent, until she finally gives up and meets his stare.

"You actin' so scared of me. That's got to stop." His voice is gruff but hushed in the small space.

I'm not acting, she thinks back at him.

"You're with me now, and that means you got to stay where I tell you to," he continues. "But that don't mean you have to be scared of me. I came in here to tell you that."

Her eyes drop to his disgusting patches.

"Yeah, I know..." He draws himself all the way up. And for some reason, this makes him seem like he's the one on the defensive, even though he's towering over her like a leather clad skyscraper. "But I'm telling you, I'm not going to hurt you or the kid. And I won't be forcing anything on you. It won't be like that..."

Bullshit. She doesn't believe him.

"I'm telling you the truth," he insists. "I mean, I ain't no monk. When you get the itch, come find me. But until then...I won't touch you unless you ask me to."

"Then you won't *ever* be touching me."

The sentence slips out. Somehow pushing past the air-tight seal she keeps on her words before she has a chance to stop them.

Oh no she didn't. Appalled at herself for challenging him, June holds her breath, waiting to see what he'll do next.

He visibly stiffens, shoulders going tight in a way that lets her know the animal standing in front of her is barely keeping himself in check. And for a moment, his expression slips. The careful curtain coming down so suddenly, she doesn't have to guess at the emotion in his eyes. It's hunger. Naked and raw... and on full display.

This time, she doesn't think first. Can't think first. She takes an involuntary step back, only to be stopped short when her butt hits the unyielding sink behind her. A not so friendly reminder that she's trapped in here with him.

He knows it, and she knows it. But in the end, he's the one who finally steps away—from her and the tension between them. "Like I said, when you get that itch, come find me. *Only me.* That's the one rule I got as far as relations between us are concerned."

June can only blink in response. She can't even imagine having the kind of itch he means—actually wanting, and not just enduring, sex. Much less seeking him out to scratch it. That will never, ever happen. Not in a million years, and especially not with him.

"Picked you up a few things while I was getting the pizza," he says, interrupting her thoughts.

He lifts a Cal-Mart bag she hadn't even noticed until now, and hangs it on the door knob. "In case you wanted to shower and change. Bugs will eat you alive you go outside wearing that."

June looks down at her current outfit, an unexpected burst of shame souring her stomach. Even though the clothes are pretty much standard wear back in the Cul, and probably what led the biker to buy her off Razo in the first place. Still, she folds her arms over her chest, unable to mask how self-conscious she feels in the skimpy outfit. Or say thank you for the clothes he bought her.

The seal's back on, and all she can do now is wait, silently broadcasting the *Please go!* she can't say aloud.

He must hear it, because after an awkward beat, he dips his head and grunts, "Okay, leaving you to it."

The door opens and closes and just like, that he's gone.

Leaving her with a lot of questions. Mostly for herself.

·   ·   ·

WHEN JUNE EMERGES from the bathroom, freshly showered and dressed in a Beaver Lake t-shirt and sweatpants, the room feels much different.

He's gone. She knows this even before she notices that the doors and windows are closed, and the curtains drawn. Or that the palm tree coverlet on the other bed has been pulled over Jordan's sleeping form.

And there's another surprise: her drawing pad isn't where she left it. But before she can descend into a full-fledged panic, she spots it across the room, on the table where Jordan and the biker ate pizza—no, where Jordan and *Mason* ate pizza. His name is Mason, she reminds herself. After the shared moment in the bathroom, it just feels weird to keep referring to him as "the biker"—or worse.

As she nears the table, she notices her most prized possession is flipped open to a new page...a page that's covered in handwriting. June lifts the pad to get a better look. It's a note, she realizes. Hastily scrawled with a ton of misspelled words. "Poorly written," her father would have said in that other lifetime, when she was the daughter of a high school English teacher with exacting standards. But in spite of the bad spelling, she gets the gist of it.

Mason has gone to a meeting. Read: *another gun sale*. She and Jordan are to stay here. Get some sleep. And he'll be back with breakfast tomorrow morning.

So he's on another gun run. For the night.

She and Jordan should plan a run of their own. Away from the cabin. Away from Mason the biker. Now, while they have the chance. The thought beats inside June's head for a few hopeful seconds, only to lose momentum when she looks up from the note toward the beds.

The sight of Jordan, sleeping peacefully, kills the plan before it's even fully formed.

It's completely dark out. And June honestly has no idea where they are. Maybe Beaver Lake like it says on her t-shirt, but really, they could be anywhere. Also, there's still their money problem. As in: they don't have any.

Going to a shelter is out of the question. They'd tried that in the early days after their mothers died, and had immediately been flagged to meet with a social worker. She and Jordan had snuck out before the woman arrived. Because June had promised Jordan, *promised him*, that she wouldn't let anyone split them up. That she'd do everything in her power to make sure they stayed together.

June sets the sketch pad back down on the table.

No, she can't pull Jordan out from beneath his warm covers to drag him off into the cold night. Not without a plan. A good plan that will allow her to keep the promise she made to him six years ago.

Rest, she thinks. Rest and think about how to get them out of this.

She ends up doing exactly that. No solutions come, but there are also no nightmares. Just the complete blank of a much needed, surprisingly deep sleep.

When June wakes the next morning, she feels refreshed and even a little, dare she say it, at peace. It's as if her subconscious mind has decided to take Mason at his word, even if her waking one hasn't—

Her blood stops cold. Not because he's opened the door and all the windows again, but because he's now seated at the table...*flipping through her sketch pad*.

She sits up in the bed, mouth opening then shutting over a protest. The seal on her lips won't budge, so she can't tell the huge man to stop looking at her sketches. What he's doing feels like trespassing in its worst form. As if he's reading her diary right in front of her. June feels violated, even as she sits there in silence, not daring to say or do anything as he casually glances at sketch after sketch.

"How much?" he suddenly asks. Even though he hasn't looked up once from the drawings, he somehow knows she's awake.

June shakes her head, not understanding the question.

"How much? For one of your tattoos, I mean," he clarifies, flipping to yet another page.

She shakes her head again, still not understanding. And he keeps looking through her pad. It feels like he's staring at her soul. Turning it this way and that under his curious blue gaze, before going on to the next page, and the next.

As if granting her silent wish, he finally stops. Only to ask, "You did Razo's tattoos, right?"

Not all of them, she thinks.

"Not all of them, right?" he says, seemingly pulling the words out of her mind. "Just the good ones."

His grin is truly shocking. It changes his entire face. Lighting up his eyes, almost to the point that he doesn't look completely terrifying. Almost.

He opens the pad again, and flips forward to a specific sketch, holding it up for her to see the raven motorcycle she drew the night before. Her visual interpretation of that new feeling in her stomach.

"This one," he says, tapping it with a huge index finger. "How much to get this one on the inside of my arm?"

*I...*she starts to think. Only to realize she actually has the words for this topic. It's her favorite subject, after all. The only thing she ever really speaks comfortably about with anyone.

"I've never charged anyone before," she admits quietly. "I'm still learning."

Also, Razo would never pay her. No matter how many hours

she put into making his tattoo work seem like less like a prison job, and more like works of art.

"Alright, let's see..." Mason pulls a smart phone from his inside vest pocket. Thumbs the screen a few times before announcing, "Internet says $150 an hour. How many hours you think them crows going to take?"

"Ravens," she corrects without thinking. Then she rushes to paste over her small insubordination with the answer to his question. "About four. Maybe three." June had become a pretty fast inker over the years. Razo wasn't the world's best sitter, and if she took too long, he tended to lash out at her, rather than tell her he needed a break.

"So you're okay with that number?" he asks. "One-fifty's cool?"

She has to try a few times before she's can nod. The truth is, she can't imagine actually getting paid for a tattoo, much less $450 to $600 dollars. That's more money than she's ever been paid for anything in her life. Enough money to run away on, maybe...

"It's a deal then," he says, standing. He nods at something else on the table. A sack from Hardee's she hadn't noticed before. "You two eat up. I'm going to grab some shut eye. We'll start with the raven bike after I'm rested and showered, alright?"

He waits. Obviously expecting some kind of answer. So she gives him another nod. Confused, but unable to say no to the promise of money. To the hope of FREEDOM, written in big block letters like the ones on his jacket.

With a nod of his own, he leaves again. But this time he doesn't shut the windows, only the door behind him. And a few seconds later, he reappears in front of the small cabin.

She rises up further in the bed, craning her neck so she can watch him crawl into a sleeping bag situated just a few feet from the open door. He seems more at ease outside than in, despite the increasing brightness of the rising sun and what looks like an uncomfortable sleeping arrangement on the hard ground.

"I like him."

June starts and then looks over her shoulder at Jordan, who's now sitting up in the other bed. "He messed up," he says on a yawning stretch. "And maybe he bad. But he got you talkin'. I like him."

God...

June doesn't know how to feel about that. About any of this.

He *is* messed up. He is truly a bad man. Just like Razo—but not like Razo, she's starting to sense. And she can only wonder what will come next.

5

JUNE

The first tattoo goes well. Mason is, as it turns out, a really good sitter—or in this case, layer downer. The inner bicep can be one of the most painful places to get a tattoo, due to the especially sensitive ulnar nerve that runs below the skin and, in Mason's case, a complete lack of cushioning fat.

Razo hadn't been able to bear the shading process on his bicep for more than twenty minutes or so. But Mason is a tattoo artist's dream. No complaints or asking over and over again how long before she's done. He's perfectly content to lie on the bed with his face turned toward the open window while she works. The install only takes three hours over a period of two days. Followed by a few hours with gauze for healing.

"Cool!" Jordan proclaims when June removes the bandage.

Mason isn't as quick to respond though.

The flock of ravens inside June's stomach go completely still as she watches him turn his bicep back and forth. He flexes it a few times, before saying, "Yep, let's go'on ahead and make it a sleeve."

A sleeve! He likes her work so much he wants a full sleeve. Not just that, but he's willing to pay her to do it—which, at $150 an hour, will result in at least a thousand dollars on top of the $450 she's just made. Maybe even more. June glows under the unspoken compliment, choosing not to think too hard about who it's coming from.

Mason heads out the next day for a "meeting" in Oklahoma. What she can only assume is another gun run. He tells her he'll be gone for four days, even though she rarely, if ever, bothers to respond to anything he says to her.

And in a very literal case of "teach a man to fish," he's hooked Jordan up with a pole and fishing lessons. Just enough groceries and know-how for them to survive without him. *But not enough for us to leave*, June thinks to herself as she walks Mason out to his delivery van. Not to be nice, but because he grunted, "Hey, walk me out to my van," a minute ago.

"I'll pay you when the sleeve's done," he says when they reach the driver's side door. "So let's make sure you get your money."

She doesn't respond, just glances away.

Only to have him chase her eyes again, insisting she look at him.

"I won't hurt you. That's a promise I'll keep," he says, voice as soft as it can get, considering its timber.

However, his gaze darkens soon after. "But I can't promise not to hunt you down if you try to leave. No..." He shakes his head as if it's a fact, beyond his control. "I can't promise that. So like I said, let's make sure you get your money."

It takes June nearly a full minute of eye chasing and awkward silence to realize he's actually expecting an answer.

She nods, silently promising not to bolt while he's gone. And only then does he climb into the van.

She watches him go, not feeling so much threatened by him as she is understanding of his motivation. Men, she'd discovered over the last six years, used whatever they could get their hands on to control you. Money, food, violence—whatever tools they had available.

Mason is a man. A bad man. And he's probably afraid she'll run off as soon as his back is turned if he leaves her with more than the promise of money, a kid who can fish, and a fridge full of groceries.

Normally he'd have been exactly right. But in this case, Mason didn't need threats, because he'd already managed to disable her with a direct hit to her biggest weak spot: the opportunity to do the thing she loves most.

As it turns out, the prospect of designing an entire sleeve for a naked arm interests her way more than Mason scares her. June still plans to run as soon as she and Jordan have the chance and the funds, but she spends nearly every waking hour of the next four days mocking up the design for his sleeve on several precious sheets of her sketch pad.

The final drawing, just like the raven bike, comes directly from her subconscious. A mixture of what she knows for sure about Mason (gears and engines), along with things she only suspects: a strong raven for his shoulder, a desolate but huge tree. *Somewhere for the flock of ravens inside his mind to rest,* she thinks. And beneath the tree, a score of skulls intertwined with its gnarled roots.

She sketches and re-sketches while he's gone. With so much emotion and so little "real intention," as her mother would have called it, she is half afraid to show the final drawing to him when he returns.

Afraid he'll laugh at her or call her crazy. Razo had done that a few times, before June learned to only show him mock-ups with death and/or religious themes.

It's possible, she thinks as she hands her pad to Mason, he might even be angry at what she's created. The tree might not be masculine enough, the huge raven too poetic.

So she waits, her heart buzzing worse than her tattoo gun, as he studies the drawing for a full three minutes.

And when he finally ends his examination with, "That'll work," it feels like an explosion of light in her chest.

In the weeks after that moment, they fall into a routine. Cereal for breakfast. Morning tattoo sessions (in the chair this time, since she doesn't need to get to the underside of his bicep) while Jordan fishes. Sandwiches for lunch, and depending whether or not Jordan catches anything, fish, chili, or pasta for dinner. Mason rarely stays in the room past eight or nine o'clock at night. He goes on runs or sleeps outside. Sometimes, when a nightmare wakes June in the middle of the night, she makes a cup of tea and takes it to the window. Peeks through the curtains to watch Mason sleep out there under the stars, stars she never saw back in the Cul.

Strangely enough, watching him sleep relaxes her. Calms her pulse and lulls her back into a deep sleep.

It only takes a couple of weeks of him keeping his promise not to touch her before she relaxes. Before the quiet between them goes from tense and fraught, to borderline nice and steady.

Which is probably one of the reasons why Mason looks so surprised when she asks him to remove his vest on the final stretch of the sleeve she's installing. "Your jacket vest thingy...can you take it off?"

His rotator cuff muscles tense under the leather opening of his SFK vest, which is all he's wearing up top today. "I thought the raven head was just going to be on my shoulder," he says.

"I know, but I've been thinking..." June takes out her sketch pad and Sharpie, editing what was supposed to be the final mock-up as she explains, "This raven isn't big enough to do its job. It should be larger. If it's going to guard you, it needs to extend a wing out over your heart. It should be ready to fly, to protect..."

She trails off when she sees the look on Mason's face. Ducks her eyes down to the sloppy edit she's made over an otherwise precise drawing. "I know it's not the best rendering. I can redo it, show you..."

"Those are more words than you've ever said to me all at once, sweetness," he says, interrupting her offer. "Your voice—it's different than I expected it to sound when we first met. More..."

He doesn't have to say the words he's reaching for, because she already knows. Her black classmates back in Bluebriar would have said "more white." But the father from that other lifetime would have congratulated her for sounding like the girl he'd raised to speak proper English.

June doesn't fill in the blank for the huge man in the chair, just fiddles with the drawing.

"I like it," he says.

She looks up at him and he answers another unspoken question. "The bigger raven and your voice. I like them both. Wish I could hear more of the voice, actually."

A wish not a command. So she doesn't answer, just picks up her tattoo gun. Her unspoken signal that break time is over and she's ready to start working again.

"Hold up," Mason says, glancing out the window.

June follows his gaze over to where Jordan sits on the dock. Fishing with earbuds tucked in, soccer ball perched beside him like a faithful pet. Then he asks, "Just the shoulder? You don't need to see my back?"

She shakes her head, then finds she needs to add more words to the daily record she's already broken. "And some of your neck. But...if you don't want me to look at your back, I won't."

More words, like he requested. But he still doesn't look all that happy.

"I don't," he grits out. "I don't want you to look."

She wonders if this means he won't take off his vest. But after another almost furtive glance toward the window, Mason moves from the chair to the bed. There, he pulls off his leather vest, revealing a wide and well-defined torso. Far as she can tell, there's nothing at all to be embarrassed about on his chest. But he shifts so he's sitting up against the headboard, his back all but plastered against the wood.

"Okay," he says. And this time, he's the one averting his eyes.

She has to shift to accommodate his new position. Climb up on the bed with him to reach the places she needs to in order to finish the raven.

Unfortunately, this requires moving his vest aside. Actually touching the thing, in order to place it in the chair he abandoned. It's shockingly heavy. Pounds not ounces, and all the gun and knife metal inside it winks in the light as she drapes it over the seat of the chair.

Mason watches her handle the vest. Neither of them say a word.

And then she starts back on the tattoo, her silence concreting over that slight bit of progress they made before she had to touch his disgusting piece of outerwear.

It takes another few days to complete the tattoo. And almost as if he's been waiting for her to finish, he announces the morning after she's done with it that all his guns have been delivered and/or sold.

"It's time for me to get back home," he says over breakfast, soon after Jordan leaves for his morning ritual of "kick the soccer ball in the direction of the forest."

Back to your gang, she silently fills in for him.

She shouldn't be surprised. The tattoo is done and it's been over a month since they arrived. It makes perfect sense Mason needs to return to his previously scheduled life.

"I'm going to pay you," he tells her, picking up his bowl and carrying it over to the kitchen sink. "Every dollar. Plus a tip."

He promises her this, even though she hasn't asked.

June only stares at the back of the vest he puts on every morning like preacher's robes. No, she still doesn't believe he's serious about paying her fifteen hundred dollars for the tattoo. But then again, she's still having trouble believing Mason let her cover an entire arm with her design in the first place.

"I got your money out in the van," he says. "But first I need to drop you and Jordan off someplace. So go ahead and get your things. All of them."

She does as instructed, curious and afraid as she follows him out to his van. Especially after he calls out to Jordan, "C'mon kid, we're heading out. Bring the pole and your goddamn soccer ball."

Jordan asks all the questions about where they're going as they leave the camp. But it's June who Mason looks sideways at when he answers, "Hold on, you'll find out soon enough."

6

JUNE

*T*he someplace turns out to be a house. Not a one-room cabin in the middle of nowhere, but an actual house, sitting on several acres beside a county road just outside Eureka Springs.

June feels like a participant on one of those house buying shows as she tours the cute contemporary ranch. It has two bedrooms, rosewood floors, and a deck which runs the entire back length of the home. The deck overlooks a backyard so huge, Jordan could kick his soccer ball as far as he wants without ever going over the property line. And she can barely see the neighbors, the next house is so far off in the distance.

Jordan immediately abandons her when he sees the yard. June watches from the deck of the master bedroom as he tries to kick his ball over a small barn sitting kitty corner to the house.

"The school district's only a six," Mason says, almost apologetically as he joins her a little later. "But Eureka Springs is just a couple miles up the road. They got an art store there. I saw it online. Noticed you were running low on paper. Not just the green kind, but the other kind, too."

He grins underneath his huge beard, and it humanizes him.

Makes him seem like less of a monster, even as the wind whips his long hair back, uncovering the patches on the leather vest he only ever takes off to shower, and receive tattoos.

He watches Jordan try to conquer the old barn with his foot for a few minutes before asking, "So...what do you think of this place?"

What does she think? She loves it. How could anyone not love it? It's everything she and Jordan never dared to dream of.

She's thinking this so hard, it takes her a few moments to realize he's waiting for her to answer. Out loud.

"This place is really yours?" she asks, carefully pushing out non-tattoo related words. "You own it?"

He nods. "My cousin's always saying I need to think about my future. Invest my money more wisely." For some reason, the mention of his cousin casts a sad shadow over his face. "So yeah, I decided to buy a place out here. Better than them cabins at Beaver Lake anyway."

"So you'll be staying here, too? With us?" she asks. Not that it matters what his answer is. This is the kind of house where any kind of future could be possible for Jordan. She'd do anything to have it. Let him go on top of her any way he wants if it means they can stay here.

Mason looks at her for a long time before answering, "Nah... that wouldn't be a good idea." He shrugs his humongous shoulders. "But it's all yours and the kid's if you want it."

If she wants it. This time June doesn't hesitate to use her words. "Yes, please," she says. "We want it."

"Good." With another grin, he pulls a huge envelope out of the vest and hands it to her as if she's earned a prize.

June takes it without counting the money inside. Suddenly trusting him in a way she couldn't have even imagined less than an hour ago. She's sure it's all there.

"Also got you this..."

He brings out a shiny new phone and hands it to her. "If you need anything, call me. My number's already plugged in. It's a pre-paid deal, but it came with internet and I'll put money on it every month. Okay?"

Again he waits. Expecting an answer.

"Okay," she says softly, not knowing how else to respond.

"Okay," he says with a little smile. Then he says, "C'mon, walk me back to my van."

So she does. And that's it. There should be more. It feels like there should be more.

But with a rough nod and an "Alrighty then," Mason turns and steps into the delivery van. He backs out of the dirt driveway, then peels down the same road he drove up to drop her and Jordan off. And as the van recedes into the distance, June wonders if he only invited her to walk him out so she could watch him leave.

She doesn't know how to feel about that. How to think about the strange sadness that lingers over her like a cloud for the next few days, although this house—this life he's left them to—is more than she and Jordan could have ever asked for.

She doesn't understand this feeling, doesn't know it's a sort of missing until the phone rings a week later.

"Hey, June," Mason answers her silent pick-up.

She has to work her throat a few times before she can say, "Hey."

"You doing all right out there? Need anything?" Then he says, "You got to answer my questions out loud, sweetness. Can't hear you thinking over the phone."

"No," she answers. She almost wishes she had more to say. So she can stay on the phone with him. Just a little longer.

"Jordan okay?" He also seems to be fishing for something to talk about, or maybe something to get her talking. "You get him registered for school and all that? No paperwork problems?"

"No, no problems." She got his old school to send over all his records with only a few emails. And since his mother's death isn't exactly on record, there hadn't been too many questions about her guardianship. As far as this new school district is concerned, she's just another single mother who got pregnant way too early.

"Good, good," Mason says. But he sounds a little disappointed.

And for the first time ever, she feels bad for him. She knows she's not easy to talk to. Knows it's a little like pulling teeth.

"The problem is, she's got a lot of art in her but not a whole lot of words," her mother told her first grade teacher in that other lifetime, when she'd called June's parents into a meeting about getting her switched over to Special Ed. Because she could draw for hours, but couldn't express her thoughts with words. Because she could write and read at a sixth-grade level, but had trouble stringing basic sentences together.

Her other lifetime parents, she vaguely remembers now, had loved her. Had wanted to talk to her, to nurture her. They'd wanted what was best for her. Just like she wanted what was best for Jordan.

But as June and her parents had eventually discovered, wanting something doesn't guarantee it will actually happen.

And she was still very, very hard to talk to. Mason should stop trying. Hang up.

But he doesn't. "So, uh, you got any summer plans?"

This question surprises her, because actually...she does. "I've been checking out local jobs," she tells him, reflexively reaching out for her new sketch pad and starting to doodle with her Sharpie. "The Cal-Mart Superstore in Berryville is hiring for some stocking positions, and they have a GED program..."

Her words are met with silence. One that stretches on for so long, she eventually stops doodling. Sets her Sharpie down on top of the pad while she waits for him to ruin her idea. To tell her she can't. Or say she's too retarded to work anywhere but on her back. Razo's assessments of her chances of making it out in the real world ring in her ears.

But all Mason says is, "Sounds good."

And June remembers something else from that other lifetime. How a speech therapist once told her if she wants to carry on a conversation with someone, all she has to do is reflect their questions back at them. "How about you?" she asks carefully. "Do you have any plans?"

Pause. "Kind of," he answers. "I'm in West Virginia right now, trying to sort some shit out with my cousin. It's not going the way I want it to."

"How do you want it to go?" she asks, not having to try so hard with that question.

"Fuck if I know," he answers with a heavy sigh.

"I'm sorry," she says, not really knowing how else to answer, but for reasons she can't explain, wanting to say something.

"Ain't your fault." His voice is sharp now. Brusque. Not quiet and intimate like before. Back to nails and gravel.

Nails and gravel, she thinks. *If he ever lets me work on the other arm, that's what I'll give him...*

"Anyway, I need to go. Like I said, use this phone if you need anything, but I probably won't be calling again. It ain't a good idea...for obvious reasons."

This time June doesn't answer. There are too many conflicting thoughts in her head to speak. Including, *will I ever see you again?*

"Okay, bye," Mason says after a few awkward beats.

The line goes dead, and June looks at the silent rectangle in her hand, heart stretched tight. Because that "bye" sounded pretty damn permanent.

Why did he do it? she wonders now that he's gone, maybe for good. Why did he walk into her life, change it for the better, then walk right back out?

And why...?

Why can't she convince herself that this ending is a good thing? The best possible ending for her and Jordan. Her ravens are quiet now. So why does it feel like something is dying inside her?

7

MASON

*H*e'll never see her again. Mason knows this. Knows he has to accept it, like he accepts breathing. Who he is. Who she is...no, he can't never see her again. It would only compound a terrible fucking impulse decision. Maybe even get her and the kid killed.

But that doesn't mean he can't buy her a birthday gift.

Jordan mentioned the date in passing, and Mason has time to kill while waiting for his seat and pedal adjustments at the motorcycle dealership. So he walked over to the mall to get a bite to eat with the two Knights who decided to accompany him on his "field trip." He hadn't planned on looking for a gift, but as it turned out, the mall still had one of them old CalsonBooks stores.

"Wait here," he'd told his SFK buddies outside the store.

And now here he is, scanning the aisles, panning for present gold. Searching, searching...until he sees it. The perfect gift. A slow, lop-sided grin spreads across his face. *Yeah, that'll work*, he thinks, picking up the thick, floppy book.

There's a bored teen behind the register. She's aggressively reading a *Doctor Who* graphic novel, the living picture of, "I don't get paid enough to do this job." And she doesn't look up from it, even when Mason drops the book on the counter between them.

He'd bet money she's a college student. Pining away in retail until she finishes college and some company magically offers her the job of her dreams. It's pathetic, but not for the first time since he left June behind in Arkansas, he wonders what life would have been like for him if he'd done that. Took schooling seriously and gone to college instead of stepping into his old man's former position as SFK enforcer after Fred got promoted to VP. D always said he was smarter than anyone gave him credit for, and that he'd been hiding his brain beneath a cloak of violence—or some shit like that. D had a way with words, and Mason had a way of rolling his eyes at those words whenever D got to talking about Mason's "wasted potential."

But lately, things were different. Lately, he'd been thinking a little too much about what might've been in ways he hadn't before D disappeared.

Finding his cousin's leather vest when he searched the campsite where D last stayed but never returned to—well, it had shaken him.

They'd vowed to wear their vests with pride during their swearing in ceremony, but there the damn thing was. Casually tossed across the front passenger seat of the delivery van D left behind when he took one of their restored bikes on a joy ride. Mason liked to do that, too. Bring a bike along in his van so he could get in some open road time between runs. Only in D's case, he never came back.

Not only did D leave his vest and van behind at that West Virginia campground, all his missed deliveries were still sitting there in the back of his van, too.

Mason knew something had happened to D. But more and

more, he was beginning to suspect his cousin hadn't been jumped and/or kidnapped. For one, there weren't any ransom demands. For two, every gun in the back of that van had been accounted for. In fact, D had only made one delivery: to The New Rebels, a mid-sized gang with a home base only twenty miles or so from D's camp. But those fuckers claimed, and kept on claiming, not to know jack shit about D's disappearance.

"We did the exchange and he left with the money..." the New Rebel prez told him. And he stuck to his story, even after Mason offed two of his prospects.

Mason gave the New Rebels a month to come up with some kind of additional information regarding D's whereabouts, and he planned to return in a few days to interrogate them some more. But hell if he really believed he'd get anywhere with it.

If those panties disguised as a gang knew anything about his cousin, they'd have definitely told him the first time he carved up one of their prospects and put a bullet through his head. So D's disappearance was starting to look more and more like something Mason didn't want to believe. Could hardly fathom. But nowadays he strongly suspected D might have disappeared himself. Run away from the SFKs and everything they stood for.

And if that's what happened, Mason knew things would be way worse than if D had been kidnapped or killed. As Fred was fond of telling newly-leathered SFK's, "The only way you'll get rid of your leather now is if we take it off your corpse."

So yeah, if D ran, if Mason doesn't find his remains in a ditch on his next recon to West Virginia, shit will well and truly get ugly. Because that'll mean his cousin is still out there some-where, but in hiding. And once the club reaches the same conclusion Mason has, they'll send him, their best tracker, after his own cousin. He'll be expected to bring D back. Not dead, but wishing he was. Then Fred would do to his own nephew what he'd done to the few other Knights who'd decided to opt out of their "SFK for life" vows. But he'd do it even worse. Because D was not only legacy...the board had also pinned a bunch of their future white hopes on him from the get go. He was the club's golden child, meant to lead them into a great white future. And their disappointment in D's betrayal would take on a life of its own.

As Mason thinks about his next and last trip to West Virginia, it feels like the huge raven wing that extends across his chest and up his neck is casting a dark shadow over his soul. Try as he might, he can't get those damn birds to rest in the tree June made for them.

Yet in spite of the pending shitstorm, here he is. At fucking CalsonBooks. Buying a gift for the black girl he really shouldn't be keeping back in Arkansas.

"You guys do shipping?" he asks the bored girl after damn near a minute of watching her pretend not to notice she's got a customer.

"We look like Amazon?" Bored Girl asks without glancing up from her book.

True, CalsonBooks has seen better days. Back when he was a kid, they had stores in every mall across America. From what he's heard, the last Calson executive damn near ran the company into the ground until his son took over a few years back. With all them Cal-Marts to save, this chain of bookstores was probably pretty damn low on the new leader's priority list. So Mason can't really blame the girl for not giving two fucks about her job or her customers in a dying bookstore. But still...

He looks down at the GED book on the counter. The present he plans to send June, despite knowing a store as big as Cal-Mart probably has a fancy computer program or something like that to help her out. Truth is, he doesn't even know if she actually followed through with her plans. Mason has forced himself not to call her again after that first time, and for all he knows, she wasn't serious about getting a job. Or about going after her GED.

And June had no way of knowing when she told him her plans...no clue about the buried memory she triggered inside him.

"MASE, *come here, honey. Come here. Lookit...*"

This was a good morning. At least it was good in the way ten-year-old Mason had come to define it. His father had returned from the clubhouse late last night, too drunk to hit. And now he was too hungover to do much more than silently stew in his morning-after misery at the breakfast table.

Usually his mom watched Mason leave with little to no fanfare. Smoking a cigarette while she and Fred listened to conservative talk radio and finished off the pot of coffee she made each morning. They didn't have a TV. Nobody at the compound did anymore. Too many coloreds on it these days, the board had declared. Bad for the club. Bad for their impressionable youth.

But this morning was different somehow. Mason could feel it, even if he couldn't explain it as he sat across from his parents at the little table. His mother seemed...lighter. Happier. Even if she wasn't smoking her usual cigarette.

She'd run out of them, he soon discovered, when his mother told his father she'd be walking out with Mason to pick up some more. So they'd left the house together and headed toward what passed for a school on the compound. A sad little home schooling co-op a few houses over, run by Edna Brayton, an old lady whose only connection to the club had died over a decade ago. Miz Brayton didn't really care about teaching, and Mason didn't care much for learning. But anywhere outside his house was better than inside it. And Miz

Brayton sold overpriced cigarettes out of her kitchen cabinet, so if you ran out, school drop off was the place for SFK parents to be.

But this morning, his mother pulled him aside as soon as they cleared their front door. "Mase, come here, honey. Come here. Look-it...," she whispered excitedly.

Like a drug dealer revealing his most illegal product, she opened her purse and out peeked out two bus tickets.

"We're leaving tonight. Soon as you get back from school and that waste of skin you call a father goes to the clubhouse. Talked to your aunt last night. She said we could stay with her for a few weeks in Mississippi. Plus, the Cal-Mart near her is hiring, so I could work there for a little bit. Maybe even go back to school. Get my GED! Dixon's mom is always telling me I'm smarter than I think."

Yes, D and his mom were alike in that sense. Optimistic about their Fairgood relatives against all proof to the contrary.

Mason's mother had been so excited. That was what haunted Mason the most. He'd never seen that look on her face before. Heard that note in her voice. It would take him years of watching forbidden TV during gun runs to eventually pin down the emotion. Hope. She'd been hopeful. And he'd allowed himself to get caught up in her hope, to the point that he could barely sit still while waiting for the bullshit school day to be over...

Stupid, stupid kid.

AND NOW HERE HE IS, years later, trying to figure out how to get a GED prep book to June. It wasn't like the SFK compound was the type of place you wanted to be sending books from. Especially ones addressed to nig—

Jesus, he can't bring himself to call her that. Not even in his head. But the main point is, it ain't safe. To buy this book for her, or send it. None of it is safe. Just like calling her wasn't safe. Or sending her that one postcard from West Virginia. Or the other one when he got back to Tennessee.

Mason knows all this, but still pulls out his wallet to pay for the book. Asks the girl, "Mall got some kind of mailing store? UPS or whatnot? Anyplace will do, so long as they take cash."

This time Bored Girl actually spares him a short glance, but only so she can huff, "Do I look like a mall directory to you?"

"I think you need to check your tone when you're talking to this one, girl!" a voice says behind Mason.

Well, shit.

The clerk finally looks up from her comic book. But this time her mouth falls open when she sees the wall of leather and denim standing before her. Mason is flanked by two shorter, but by no means small, SFKs on both sides. Bonner and Dietson. The bikers who'd insisted on coming with him to get an interim bike to replace the one that had been "stolen" back in Arkansas. Apparently, the men had gotten tired of waiting for him outside.

Dietson's statement accomplishes what basic courtesy couldn't. Suddenly, the young woman isn't nearly as belligerent. In fact, she looks like she's fixing to shit her black skinny jeans when she registers the significance of the patches on their leather vests.

"S-s-sorry!" she blurts, before meekly ringing Mason up.

Mason tells Bonner and Diets to wait outside for him. Again. And when they've left, he slips the clerk the GED book along with two twenties and a post-it bearing the address of his secret house in Arkansas. "June" it says simply at the top, because he still don't know her last name. *Fuck, what is he doing*?!?!

But that doesn't stop him from intimidating the fuck out of the entitled college girl behind the counter. Telling her he'll be back if that package don't get delivered exactly as he asks.

Yeah, he feels like shit for a number of reasons when he leaves the store.

"S-s-sorry!" Bonner mimics Bored Girl with an exaggerated wide-eye look as they leave the mall and head back to the dealership. "Did you see the look on her face when she saw our patches?"

These men are his brothers, Mason reminds himself. Guys who'd grown up in the compound, same as him. Well, a little worse than him. Because their dads weren't on the board, so they had no pull within the club. And these days, the board was almost completely hereditary. So Bonner and Diet had the SFK equivalent of dead-end jobs.

Which explains why they are just trying to get in good with a board member. Mason understands. He really does. And it's not like he can't do with a couple of trustworthy suck ups to help out with the gun runs after that near as fuck miss with the Hijos. So why does he want to punch both of them in the teeth right now?

"Bet the bike still won't be ready for us when we get back," says Bonner. "Goddamn service ain't worth shit these days."

"Specially out here in the city," Diets agrees, spitting at the concrete. "So you got a girl now?" he suddenly asks out the blue.

Mason doesn't answer, but he must look consternated because Diets responds to his unspoken question with, "No offense, but you don't exactly look like the GED type."

Again Mason doesn't respond, but Diets and Bonner don't let it go.

"You pick somebody up in Arkansas?" Bonner asks, like a gossipy old lady. "Wait, is it the same girl who did your new tats?"

Mason grits his teeth, and Diets says, "Oh shit, you gonna bring her back to the clubhouse? I could use some quality art. Been thinking of getting a wolf-head or something...right here." He points in the general direction of his left shoulder which sends him and Bonner off into a discussion about the artwork they ain't never going to get from Mason's girlfriend. First of all, because the woman living in his house in Arkansas isn't his girl-friend. Second of all, because he'd never let either of these assholes get close enough to June to receive so much as prick from her tattoo gun.

A memory of lying in her bed at the cabin while she installed the first tattoo comes back to him. The sunlight in her hair. The joy in her eyes as she worked...

One of his phones ring inside his vest, yanking him out of the memory.

"Dad," he says, after checking the caller ID.

"You're late," Fred answers, voice still strong, and laced with violence despite his advanced years. Or maybe because of them.

Yes, it's true. He's late for yet another bullshit board meeting. Or, should he say, "bored" meeting. That shit had become damn near intolerable ever since D disappeared. Without D around to keep the meetings organized and on topic, it was nothing more than a coven of old white men talking about their glory days, and wishing for stuff that would probably never happen. Especially without D there to lead them.

"Figured you didn't need me there for the vote," Mason answers. "I do whatever gets decided. You know that."

"Yeah, and I also know ever since Dixon pulled his disap-pearing act, the board's been a little jumpy. And tonight we're deciding what to do if you don't find him on your next trip to West Virginia. So humor me, Son. Get back here. Now."

Humor him.

More like feel a sudden murderous rage towards him. One for which Mason had no explanation, since he'd supposedly stopped feeling much of anything a real long time ago. And yeah, Fred was a shit dad who cared more about the club than he did about his own family. But hadn't he always been?

Still, Mason hadn't lied about his good soldier status, so he replies, "Copy that."

"Club's calling," he tells the other two. "Handle the rest of it with the bike."

He tosses them a roll of large faces and doesn't wait for an answer. They know and he knows what he's done to others with his serrated bowie knife and his gun. Knows he's the kind of crazy motherfucker who will do the same to them if they fuck him in any way on this deal. They know and he knows he's a natural born killer, and that gives Mason the confidence to walk away without fear of them not following his instructions to the letter and bringing back his change on top of it.

No one ever fucks with Mason Fairgood and lives to tell the tale. Well, no one except...

Another vision of June pops into his head. This time, she's standing in front of his gun. Eyes wide and terrified, but her gunless stance is braver than anything he's ever seen.

Terri.

He grabs on to the name like a lifeline. New SFK groupie. Raised right. Thick hips and large breasts she's not afraid to show off under crop tops and low-ride jeans. No butt to speak of, but if he closes his eyes, maybe he can...

With a shake of his head, Mason climbs into the delivery van. Revs the engine just because he can. The point is, Terri has made it clear every time he's stepped foot into the clubhouse that she'd like to audition for the part of his old lady. And tonight he's going to let her do just that.

He can't have June. He knows this. Can't see her again. He knows this, too. So tonight, he's finally going to start acting like it. Stop turning down the pussy women have been throwing at him left and right. Fuck Terri until he doesn't have any more visions of that damn black girl with the sad eyes. Until June is so far gone from his memory, he remembers who he is again. Who she is. And why they can't ever be together.

It's a plan. A good one Mason has every intention of following to the letter.

But he doesn't.

Because that night he gets a call from The New Rebels about D's whereabouts. And as it turns out, this call will change his life forever.

8

JUNE

Three months later

"June! Hey, June! Need to talk with you before you go. Wait a minute, please!"

June pauses in the middle of unlocking her bike. Considers pretending she doesn't hear her supervisor, Mr. Patel, calling out to her even though she clocked out at work ten minutes ago. But then she figures with only a month left until the GED test Cal-Mart so generously paid for, she'd better not risk pissing off her boss. Lord knows when and where she'd find another decent paying job with her limited social skills and lack of high school credentials.

So she turns around with her best version of a polite-but-in-a-hurry face.

However, Mr. Patel doesn't seem nearly as adept at reading her expressions as Mason.

"Hi, June. How did your shift go today?" he asks, sticking his hands in his khaki pockets. As if he's settling in for a long gab.

"Fine," she answers.

"Noticed you're getting pretty speedy with the price gun out on the floor!" He tilts his head to the side and crinkles his eyes. And June, who's never seen Mr. Patel read anything but bright-covered self-help books on his breaks, gets the feeling he might have read that positioning his head in this way makes people feel more relaxed when talking with you. "We might have to try you out on the register next."

June doesn't respond. Doesn't say what a bad idea this would be. Because while she's just about reached the point where she can tell parents with screaming toddlers where the booze aisle is located, the thought of having to deliver the sunny type of customer service required to work on a register gives her hives.

"How did you end up in our GED program again?" Mr. Patel asks, tilting his head the other way, threatening the imminent collapse of his aggressively gelled comb-over.

"I applied," June answers. "You said I could. So I did."

"Yes, yes, of course. That's great," he says, stroking his Cal-Mart shift supervisor lanyard like it's a cat. "You know, I just got word from headquarters that our CEO, Mr. Holt Calson himself, has tasked me with recommending one associate from our store for a new online marketing initiative. I haven't decided who it's going to be yet, but, ah..."

He finally un-tilts his head, crinkling his light brown eyes just like the book probably said to do. "Maybe we can talk about it over dinner at my house? Say, tonight around 8:00 PM?"

It takes June a split second to realize her boss is coming on to her. It's completely out of the blue, but not entirely unexpected. One of the other stock clerks warned June that their middle-aged supervisor had a habit of coming on to the new girls.

"I can't," June answers, eyes dropping away from the conversation. For once, she doesn't have any trouble whatsoever coming up with the right set of words.

However, Mr. Patel mistakes her dropped gaze for an indication of obstacles. And you know what every self-help book says about obstacles, right?

"If you lack proper transportation, I can come by your house and pick you up," he offers. Then, as if having second thoughts, adds, "Provided it's in a safe neighborhood."

Wow. Neighborhood assumptions aside, she could think of at least a thousand things she'd rather do than spend even a minute of her unpaid time with Mr. Patel: study for her GED, work on her tattoo portfolio, clip her toenails—seriously, the list stretches on for days.

But in the end, June decides to pull her ace card, the one that a few of her single-mom colleagues grumble works best when it comes to turning off men. "Sorry, but I don't have a babysitter," she tells him.

"Oh!" he says, the aggressively kind expression falling right off his face. "You have a child?"

"I do," she replies, hating that she has to use so many words to extract herself from his poorly disguised, pervy come on.

"I just...well, you look so young and you never mentioned a child."

No, she hadn't. Because when you're only twenty-four, you get worried about what might happen if someone starts asking too many questions about the ten-year-old boy you're claiming as your own.

"Can I go?" she asks, feeling nervous about discussing her guardianship of Jordan. She glances pointedly at her watch. "I need to meet his school bus."

"Yes, yes, of course," Mr. Patel says, shifting from foot to foot in a way that almost makes her feel sorry for him.

Almost. She is so over men who abuse their power to get women into bed.

When you get that itch, you come find me. Only me.

But that's not the only reason she turned Mr. Patel down. June shakes yet another stray thought of Mason out of her head as she bikes away from the store. Telling herself again that his declaration means nothing. She never itches like that. Probably she's incapable of itching like that after those miserable six years with Razo. Besides...

You probely wont be seeing me agin, but wantd you to know Im in WV.

That postcard with a pretty forest and mountain scene on the front arrived just a week after their first and only phone conversation. A few days later, another postcard with a Tennessee farm on the front and, *"dont know why Im bothern with this shit, but im bac in Tennessee."* Then the arrival of the GED book a couple weeks later.

Really, it was the GED book that threw her for a loop, and continued to do so over the long summer. Because the day before it arrived, June had given into the demons in her head. Until then, she'd spent her birthday month going back and forth in her head. She needs a GED to be taken seriously for a possible tattoo apprenticeship. She knows this is the first step towards making her dreams come true. But...

Razo spent the last six years telling her how dumb she is. Calling her retarded, joking to his men that she was lucky she was so fine, because fucking and gang tats was all she was good for.

And he obviously believed it. He beat her because he thought she was worthless. Sold her to the first guy who came along with an offer. Not caring about Mason's patches, or what he might do to her or Jordan.

So yeah, after six years of that, it was hard for June to believe in herself. Hard to believe anyone, outside Cal-Mart, would give her a job. And what seemed so clear a few weeks ago at the start of her stay in Mason's house, suddenly became murky. Making it hard for her to imagine she could ever start down the path to the dream she came up with while working on Mason's sleeve.

June asked for a GED application on her third day at Cal-Mart, only to ball it up and throw it away by her third week. She should feel lucky she could even get a job. Call it a day, focus on raising Jordan now that they finally had a safe place to live...and a declaration from Mason that he won't be coming back. The balled up application had just hit the rim of the kitchen waste basket when a brown-and-yellow carrier truck pulled into her dirt driveway.

And despite her doubts, when she saw who sent the package and what it contained, something fired up inside her. Propelled her forward as she went into work the next day and asked for another application. This time, she filled it out during her lunch break, and turned it in to Mr. Patel before she could second-guess herself again. Mason believed in her, so she believed in her, too. And this carried her through her studies for the rest of the summer.

But other than a few more postcards—one from Los Angeles, and another from Seattle, both bearing similar poorly written messages: *Howz it? Still dont get the fuckn point these things. But fuckit here you go*—June hasn't heard from the man responsible for her current frame of mind.

And she has no idea if or when he'll ever be back. *Not that I want him to come back*, she reminds herself as she bikes home down I-62 West.

There was that incident in L.A. soon after she got the GED book. The one that made the news, and had Jordan calling her over to their shared laptop to take a look. She'd been surprised but, you know, not surprised to see a picture of Mason brawling with a man who turned out to be his cousin with the headline

RACIST PENTHOUSE SHOWDOWN plastered above the torrid, gossipy-sounding news article.

Even Jordan had trouble believing Mason was a good guy after reading a handful of the reports.

Not that he let it stop him from liking him, however. Instead, Jordan simply stopped visiting internet news sites and watching TV gossip shows for a while.

So yes, it was unequivocally a good thing Mason Fairgood wouldn't be coming back. June doesn't want him to return. Obviously. But for some reason, this doesn't stop her from thinking about him. Like, all the time.

Ravens and skulls. She thinks about their days at the cabin. The heavy, but somehow gentle, weight of his stare as he watches her install his sleeve. *Nails and gravel.* Sometimes she dreams about being back in the cabin with him. Filling up his other arm in all that quiet, with nothing but cricket song to let them know when the day is done.

Apparently, Jordan still thinks about him, too.

"You think he coming back this week?" Jordan asks as they walk home from the school bus stop. She's pushing her bike, he's using his knees and feet to keep his soccer ball aloft, with occasional breaks in his never-ending dialogue to run after it when he misses.

Most kids would balk at having a parent or guardian pick them up from a bus stop in a small town where most kids walk home. But Jordan isn't most kids. If June isn't out there right when he gets off the bus, he usually sticks around and waits for her so they can walk home together.

Like her, he's having trouble taking this new life for granted. Like her, he knows all too well what not having a safe place to go after school feels like. And unlike the other kids who insist they aren't babies and don't need to be picked up by a parent, any kind of parental figure is a sort of treasure for Jordan. He appreciates June. And she appreciates him right back.

Which is why she doesn't pretend not to know who he is talking about when he asks about Mason's possible reappearance in their lives. And why she doesn't bother to sugarcoat her answer. "Probably not."

"He might. It's been three days since the postcard from Seattle. He might be on his way. I looked it up on the laptop. It only takes three or four days to get from there to here," he pauses, then asks, "Can I go kick the ball in the back when we get home?"

His change of subject is so abrupt, June nearly says yes. But then she remembers to respond with, "Not until after your homework is done."

"Come on, June!" Jordan begs, tugging her arm. "Practicing soccer is the only homework that really counts for me. The Youth Soccer Club tryouts are in two weeks. Please?"

"Jordan..." she answers wearily. Never mind her thoughts about him being more appreciative than other kids. It's clear to June that she's the only one remotely concerned with what Jordan's academic evaluations have revealed. As personable as he is, his reading is only at a second grade level, and he's just managing first grade level math. He was supposed to start fourth grade in the fall, but reviewing his test results, the school decided it was best for him to be placed in the third grade.

But that's neither here nor there to Jordan. All he cares about is that his new school has a soccer team.

Lately, June has found herself in the unenviable position of using more words with him than she's ever had to before. Strong words. The kind that might have come out of her own mother's mouth in that other lifetime. "Homework first, Jordan, or there won't *be* any Youth Soccer Club tryouts."

"Aw, come on! That ain't even right!"

They end up arguing about it all the way home, which is probably why it takes both of them a lot longer to see him than it should.

But they both stop when they finally notice the enormous man standing in their dirt driveway, leaning up against an even more enormous Ford 250 truck.

Dressed in jeans and a simple t-shirt, he's an all-American classic. But not really. Though his hair is long at the top with short sides slicked back ala James Dean, he's got dark brown stubble that keeps his face a couple steps away from clean shaven.

And he doesn't appear so much cool as patient. His hands are stuffed in his pockets, like he's been waiting for June and Jordan to arrive for a while now.

Even after this long observation, June doesn't get it. In fact, she wonders who this stranger might be and whether or not she should be worried until Jordan shouts, "Mason!" and starts running towards him like a long lost friend.

It can't be him. For a second, June wants to call Jordan back. Tell him he's got it wrong.

The Mason she knows is a large and intimidating hulk who never takes off his SFK vest unless he has to. But this guy isn't wearing the familiar vest, and he's intimidating all right...but not in the way he was before. This man is downright handsome. And he allows Jordan to all but knock him over with a tight hug around the waist.

Then June gets near enough to see the familiar tats running up one arm, and the raven feathers peeking out from beneath his collar...

His blue eyes rise to meet her brown ones over Jordan's head, and there's no mistaking who this is when that gaze chases her, his chin dipping and eyes following until her eyes are finally brought to heel.

Forced to acknowledge him.

Then, and only then, does Mason say, "Heya, June. Good to see you again."

And that's when she knows for sure. It really is him. Mason Fairgood. His *probably not ever* has turned into *right here, right now*.

9

MASON

*M*ason hates most shit and most people. But he can't say he hates the way the kid runs up to him when he sees him. Or the way June looks more surprised than scared when she spots him for the first time in over three months.

She doesn't respond to his greeting. But she doesn't throw any shit at him, either, which is maybe more than he ever hoped to expect after what went down in L.A.

"That a new truck?" Jordan demands, unlinking his arms from around Mason's waist and scrambling over to the Ford he picked up in Seattle.

"Sure is," Mason's answers, his eyes still locked on the woman standing in front of him. *She did it,* he thinks when he sees her familiar uniform. "So you got the job at Cal-Mart! Just like you said you would."

June nods.

"And what about your GED? How's that going?"

She seems to be flipping through her arsenal of silent responses before finally giving up and answering, "Good.

Thanks for the book. I'm taking the test next month. Paid for it with my own money. Not yours."

He hears the pride in her voice. He's proud of her, too. But he feels compelled to remind her, "It's *all* your money, June."

"I mean...the money I earned."

And Mason wonders how long it's going to take before she finally believes him when he says, "You *earned* the money I paid you, June. I didn't give it to you free. You earned every damn cent of it."

She looks away. Obviously embarrassed by his words. Mason might call it blushing if her skin was lighter.

"Let's go for a drive!" Jordan's voice lifts both their heads from their conversation. The kid's already parked himself in the passenger seat with nothing but a seatbelt between him and the open road.

"Homework first, Jordan," June says like it's an old conversation.

"Tell June I don't have to do my homework," Jordan says to Mason. "Then we can go for a ride right now."

Mason squints at the kid...notices, for the first time, that he and June aren't all rose petals and Sarah McLachlan songs. It's pretty clear to him that Jordan equates "man" with "someone who controls June." Mason understands why this is. But that doesn't mean he's going to put up with it.

"She's in charge of *you*, kid," he decides as the words leave his mouth. "June says "do your homework," then that's what you better do."

"But—"

"I said git, kid! Don't make me tell you twice."

And...cute reunion is officially over. Jordan grumbles his way towards the house, only stopping to shout from the front porch, "Welcome back! You stink by the way. You need a bath!" Then he yanks the door open and slams it hard behind him.

It's true, Mason does need a shower...real bad. He drove balls to the wall from Seattle for three days straight, only stopping to get gas and some sleep in the rear of his new truck.

But he forgot about his soap-free journey when he saw the two of them coming up the drive. Talking animatedly like normal folks nearing the end of a normal day. She'd changed her hair, he noticed. It's wide and curly instead of long and straight. And she's gained a little weight. Plumped out some likely as a result of eating regular meals. It suits her. He likes her big hair and Cal-Mart uniform. Likes that she no longer looks like the girl he bought off Razo.

Though strangely, June now strikes him as even younger looking than before. Back at the cabin, he'd guessed her to be around his age. Twenty-seven, maybe older. But now, scrubbed clean with a few months of decent sleep removing the bags from under her eyes, she looks like the kind of girl who regularly gets carded at bars.

They stand together in front of the house for longer than he intends. Him taking her in. Her staring up at him like he's a ghost come back to haunt her. Which in a way, he sort of is.

"So..." he says, breaking the silence between them. "What you guys eating tonight?"

"Leftovers," she answers. "Chicken and rice."

"Sounds fuckin' delicious. Can I come in?"

He's serious, but she still squints up at him. Obviously suspicious about his arrival and wondering what he really wants. But she doesn't say no, either. Just nods and turns to go up the front steps. Leaving him to follow. Wondering, same as him, what'll happen next.

10

JUNE

"Got something I need to talk to you about. In the bedroom."

These are the first words he says to her inside the house, his head dipped low, his voice a gruff whisper. Mason glances towards the kitchen table where Jordan is grudgingly doing his homework, his face set in the resigned and miserable look of all kids who would rather be doing anything but this.

In the bedroom...

He's waiting for her answer, and June's stomach drops. She thinks of that first night in the cabin at Beaver Lake. He promised he wouldn't. But he also said she probably wouldn't ever see him again. And here he is. The monster who bought her from Razo. The animal who made the news this past summer.

Without a word, she walks into her bedroom. Not wanting Jordan to see. Not wanting to disturb his newfound peace.

Mason follows close behind. Too close. She smells him, just as clearly as Jordan must have when he hugged him. And Jordan was right. Mason stinks. Of sweat and dirt and the faint scent of leather, even though his awful leather vest is nowhere to be seen.

Then she discovers the ravens aren't dead. They're flapping in her stomach like birds caught up in a cyclone.

As soon as he closes the door behind them in the bedroom, he strips off his shirt. "We need to do this in here," he says, confirming her worst fears. "Don't want the kid to see."

Oh, God...something in her chest cracks, and her throat dries up, even though she *can* do this. She can. Look how often she did it with Razo. It was simple. All she has to do is escape to the quiet place in her mind while Mason does his business. *That's all I have to do*, she reminds herself, even as she starts to hyperventilate. *All I have to do—*

"I want you to cover this up."

Mason's gruff voice pulls her back from the abyss. June blinks when she realizes he's standing with his naked back to her. Then she blinks again when she sees the tattoo.

It takes up nearly all of his back, and the image—well, it's similar to the logo on the back of his missing vest. But it's way worse. A crude shield with "SFK" in military-style font. Double lightning bolts underlying all of it.

The image squats there on Mason's back. It's a toxic looking thing, vile and rough. Also, it's definitely one of the worst tattoos June's ever seen. And she's spent the last six years of her life covering and embellishing a ton of crappy prison tattoos.

I don't want you to look, she recalls him saying back in cabin.

Now she understands why. And though he's holding perfectly still, she senses her answering silence is causing him all kinds of anxiety.

"Cover it up," he repeats, his voice more gruff than before. "Please."

June swallows. Her stomach churns at the thought of

touching the thing on his back. But because they are discussing a tattoo, the words come easy for her. "Can I ask why?"

"I ain't Razo," he says, glancing over his shoulder at her. "Ask me whatever you want."

He turns all the way back around then, but his typically direct stare finds the floor instead of her eyes. "But I got to take a page out of your book on this one, June." He shakes his head. "I really don't want to talk about it."

"Okay, um…" she struggles, then falls back on the question she used to ask before inking new Hijo recruits. "Do you have any special requests?"

"Nope. Don't give a fuck what you do so long as you cover it up."

June's mind is a blank. She has no idea what to put on top of it. Or how she can bring herself to even touch it.

But, she realizes after a few seconds of panicked thought, she has to try. She has to at least try. "When do you want to me to start?" she asks.

"Right now."

June calculates the time they have until dinner. "Okay," she says. "But you need a shower first."

"That's cool," he agrees with a hard nod. "Can I use your bathroom?"

It's his bathroom. *He* owns this place. She wonders why he acts like she has any choice at all.

But as it stands, he can't use the shower. "No. It's not working. But you can take a bath," she tells him. "I was waiting for my next day off to call a plumber."

"Why didn't you call me?" Mason asks, his intense blue gaze back on her. "I told you to call if you need *anything*."

She doesn't have an answer. So she says nothing.

And eventually, Mason sighs. "It's probably the diverter. I'll fix it later. And a bath don't sound half bad. Mind running one for me, sweetness?"

An awkward beat passes. And once again, they stand together in silence. Him waiting for an answer. Her trying desperately to ignore the flock of ravens chittering in her stomach. Then a strange thought suddenly appears in her head. That yes, he needs a bath so his skin will be clean for the new tattoo. But she also doesn't mind the smell of him now. Why is that?

June agrees to run his bath with a sharp nod, interrupting her strange thoughts. Her dark, dangerous thoughts. Then she all but sprints to the bathroom. Mostly as an excuse to get away from him.

*E*xcept it's not far enough. The bath is ready before she's ready to stop staring at the water. She's flipping through the mental rolodex of her current sketch pad, of all the sketch pads before that one...but nothing is coming to her. Nothing she's drawn or thought to draw seems to be the right choice. And now she's only a hot bath away from covering up that awful thing and she's fresh out of ideas.

June turns the handle to switch off the water. Tests it for warmth. Wonders if he wants bubbles like Jordan did when he was little...

"Bath ready?"

She looks up...only to have her brain stutter and come to a screeching halt when she sees him in the doorway.

He's naked. Completely. And his body—well, there are no words to describe it. A large slab of stone onto which two huge muscled arms, and legs as big as tree trunks, have been carved. And between those enormous legs...a long, heavy piece of flesh, hanging lewd and shameless.

Mason's naked body is a shock. June only ever saw Razo from the waist up. She inked his top half. His bottom half was something he thrust into her in the dark, while his voice whispered, *"Take it,* puta. *Don't even think about fighting."*

Not that she could. Even if she wanted to. He always came to her in darkness, when she was most vulnerable. And in those later years, he most often took her after a beating. He'd give her just enough time to fall asleep, to relax, before he'd fall on top of her and enter her bruised body without warning. June didn't fight. She'd been too dead inside to bother.

"June, can I take my bath now?"

Mason's voice pulls her out of those terrible memories, back to his impossibly large... everything.

It's going to hurt when he's on top of me. Her body, which has grown strong and filled out over the past few months, suddenly feels weak again.

"You okay?" Mason chases her eyes, but this time she doesn't let him. Instead, she keeps her gaze locked on the floor as she rises from her perch on the edge of the tub. Her body braces. Waiting. To pay the price for everything he's given her and Jordan. Because June knows: everything comes with a price. *Everything.*

Mason steps closer. And she puts all her effort into staying calm. Into being brave while she quietly endures what's to come. After all, she's going to do what she has to so she can provide for Jordan.

But all she feels is the soft bump of his body passing by her in the narrow room. Then a splash as he steps into the tub. By the time she dares to raise her eyes, he's gingerly lowering his massive body into the warm water.

He takes a few moments to settle in, then looks up and asks, "What's up, June? You okay?"

This time, his blue gaze grabs on to her and won't let go.

She nods. Slow. Unsure. The ravens flapping like crazy as she realizes.... she wants to look at him again.

June settles for shifting her gaze to the artwork on his arm. "You've taken good care of your tattoos," she says.

"Yep," he answers, plunking a large arm on each side of the tub. His head falls back to rest against the back rim, eyes closed. "Did just like you said," he tells her. "Kept it covered the first few weeks, made sure to put that ointment on, and became besties with SPF 50, even though wearing that shit makes me feel like a pair of panties."

"Good," she says with a small smile. The ravens are beating their wings like they might burst from her stomach any second now. June can barely think, much less figure out what to do with herself now that he's in the tub.

Leave. The answer is obvious. She glances back down at Mason. He's breathing evenly, eyes still closed. He might even be asleep. He's so large, he has to bend his legs in half to fit in the tub. Which means the thing between his legs is hidden, tucked away from sight, making her feel safe again. Well, at least safer than she felt a few minutes ago.

June's body shifts. It's time to go. But then she spots the linen closet next to the bathroom door. Wash cloth. He needs a wash cloth. And soap.

She opens the narrow door and takes out a folded yellow square, along with a fresh bar of soap. *I'm not lingering*, she tells herself. *I'm making sure he has what he needs.*

But when she turns back to the tub, instead of placing the items on the ledge, June gingerly lowers her bottom to the thin piece of acrylic, and seats herself only a few inches from where Mason's draped one of his tan, muscular arms.

Without giving it any thought, she bends to dip the wash-cloth in the water. It's very warm, almost hot. June figures after so many days on the road, the liquid heat probably feels real good on Mason's aching muscles. Real, real good...

She places the bar of soap in the center of the wet square of cloth and wraps it up tight. Then she takes the soapy washcloth and places it on his chest. It's all muscle—a steel-like construct —with barely any give other than what's provided by the springy dark hairs scattered across it. Her eyes follow those dark hairs as they trail down to his navel. She struggles to breathe as a warm bolt of electric heat travels up her arm and into her chest.

Mason's breathing also stops abruptly, the damp cloth June clasps in her hand no longer rising and falling with the rise and fall of his chest. *Oh, God!* she thinks, hand freezing.

But the man in the tub stays silent. He doesn't even open his eyes to ask what she's doing, or why. And eventually...

He's breathing again, taking in slow, deep breaths as if he's concentrating real hard on staying calm. June cautiously watches the up and down motion of his chest, waiting until she feels it's safe to move the washcloth again.

She drags it gently over his upper torso and down each of his arms. Hesitating for a split second, before running it across each of his huge legs. Mason slowly parts them, just a little. And his breath quickens once more as June tentatively places the washcloth between them, careful to avoid looking at or touching the thing nestled in the "v" where his upper thighs and hips meet.

Aside from his rapid breathing, he doesn't respond, doesn't talk. He simply lets June do what she wants with the cloth, which she eventually drags down over his ankles, his feet, his toes. Then back up again to his top half where she runs the soap-slickened rag over his broad shoulders, neck... Finally, June removes the bar of soap and sets it aside. Then uses the washcloth to wipe the grime off Mason's face. She's mesmerized by the way the excess water trickles down his newly revealed cheekbones.

He's definitely clean now. But she doesn't want to stop.

After another moment of hesitation, June stands and grabs the shampoo bottle from the hanging shower caddy, and an empty rinse cup from the sink counter. Then she drops back down to the edge of the tub, scooting herself back towards the tiled wall where Mason's head rests.

She squeezes a large dollop of pearlescent shampoo into the palm of one hand, then places both hands on his head, fingers moving rhythmically over his scalp as she lathers up his hair. This, out of everything she's done so far, is what finally breaks his silence.

"Fuck, you're killing me," he says, his voice sounding low and gruff.

From June's new vantage point, she can see that the thing between his legs has transformed from passive flesh to steel, and stands at full attention. She abruptly stops lathering.

Then he says, "It's okay. It's okay. Go ahead and finish."

So she does. Trusting him for reasons she still can't explain. When she's done, she nudges his back a little to indicate he should sit forward.

He does, giving her just enough room to scoop a few cups of bath water over his hair, without getting it everywhere.

Soon she can check Mason's hair off the list. Clean. But there's still one very important item she hasn't attended to...

June reaches down for the soap and washcloth and, with every ounce of her inner strength, forces her gaze towards Mason's back and the awful tattoo. Looking at it makes her feel sick, as if she is staring at a writhing pile of maggots. But she resolutely soaps up the rag and uses it to scrub his back. There's nothing gentle about the way she's touching him now. She can't help it. The only way she can stomach any of this is if she scrubs hard.

But she knows no amount of scrubbing will remove that hateful image. Yet she presses down on the soapy cloth as she drags it up and down the skin of his back. So hard, his skin begins to redden until it looks like it's on fire. And though he doesn't say a word, by the time she finishes "cleaning," she knows she's upset him. Mason is hunched over his knees, back muscles tense, biceps twitching as if it's an effort to stay still.

June taps him again to let him know she's done. It feels like she's giving him a sort of reprieve.

And now it really is time for her to go. She has to start work on Mason's tattoo. And Jordan is no doubt wondering where they've disappeared to, what's going on. But June doesn't want to leave things like this. With Mason's ugly tattoo still in her mind's eye. With him probably feeling worse now than he did back in her bedroom.

She touches him once last time with the cloth, running it over the raven's wing on his chest. Reminding him, reminding them both, to pay attention. Pay attention to the here and now. She drops the washcloth and closes her eyes...covers the dark wing with her bare palm. His heart beats thunderously beneath it.

The water is beyond dirty now, and barely lukewarm.

Her senses finally restored, June moves to leave. But Mason's hand shoots out of the water and grabs hers. Holds it in a vice-like grip, the way Razo used to hold her in place so he could deliver a sure hit.

But that's definitely not what's going on here, she soon realizes.

Because he's the one who looks scared. He's breathing hard, and sounds a lot like he's begging when he croaks, "Don't go. Stay here with me. Just...please stay with me for a little bit..."

Mason's voice gives out, and his breath comes in shorter and shorter gasps as he rocks forward into her trapped hand. He's not crying, exactly. Instead, he's making some kind of keening noise somewhere between a sob and a scream. It's as if he's having a heart attack, or a mental breakdown, or both.

Panic attack. The term floats into her head unbidden, maybe from a TV program or a book. Either way, June knows something happened to him. In the time they've been apart, something wrecked him. She doesn't know what, and she's not like other women...able to provide comfort with just the right words.

Instead, she tentatively reaches out her other hand and strokes the side of his face. This time, she's the one chasing his eyes, reigning him in with her gentle but persistent stare.

"Oh fuck, June. D-don't look at me," he chokes out. "I don't... I don't deserve..." The panic attack or whatever is going on has stolen his words. But she understands what he's not saying, and can fill in the blanks. *Sympathy*. Mason doesn't think he deserves her sympathy.

Deserve it or not, he has it. She continues to look at him. One hurt person to another, letting him know she's sorry for whatever or whoever did this to him.

His eyes squeeze shut, only to helplessly pop back open a moment later, still pleading with her to stop looking at him.

But June isn't going to stop. Instead, she stays with him and waits. Then waits some more. Until his breathing calms. Until he stops rocking and keening. Until the bath water goes from barely lukewarm to downright cold.

Eventually Mason finds his words, and his stubble-covered jaw moves beneath her hand. "I can't stop thinking about it. Him running up to me like that."

It takes June a moment to realize who he's talking about. *Jordan*.

"It made me feel good." His voice is quiet, hushed. She absently notices that the light is dimming in bathroom window, and realizes it must be near sunset. "Made me feel worth something to have him greet me like that. Nobody's ever..."

June more than gets it. Jordan has kept her from going into some pitch black places. Made her feel like her life was worth more than the little value Razo assigned to it.

Mason continues, "Him welcoming me like that. Like I'm some kind of fucking hero...I've never felt like that before."

At first June thinks he must be feeling a good thing. Pride, or friendship maybe. But then he squeezes his eyes shut again, as if he's fighting off another panic attack. And the water splashes as he angrily kicks the front wall of the tub. "Fuck, June. How soon can you cover it up?"

His bath took longer than it was supposed to. So... "First, I need to make dinner," she replies. "But after that, I'll work on your back for as long as it takes."

Never mind the fact that she just pulled a full shift at Cal-Mart. June makes the promise without a second thought. Because, surprisingly, she suddenly knows exactly what to put on his back.

"I have two requests for you, though," she says, her free hand dropping from his face. "I want to design it as I go along, so no mock-ups before I start. You just have to trust me. Which is hard, I know, but—"

"Okay. No problem," he interrupts, squeezing her other hand still trapped beneath his. "What else?"

"You can't see the final product until after it's healed."

Mason stares at her for a long time. Then says, "Yeah. I can do that."

"Okay," she says, unable to contain the smile that spreads across her face.

"Okay," he repeats with a solemn nod. Her still-trapped hand feels his heartbeat—slow and steady. She notices his breathing is back to normal, too. Which is good, because June has things to do and she really needs him to let go of her hand...

"Mason..." she says.

"Yeah," he answers. Hand gripping hers.

June opens her mouth...to ask him to let her go, to remind

him she's got to make Jordan's dinner before he gets the low blood sugar crazies. But instead, she leans forward.

Brings her face close to his...

And then gently presses her lips to his mouth. Pushing forward into an official kiss.

She lingers. Waits for Mason to make the moment more than she thinks she's ready for. But he doesn't kiss her back. Doesn't move at all.

She leans back. Ends the kiss and opens her eyes. His gaze has changed. It's softer, not so intense. "How was that for you?" he asks. As if she just took a sip of wine rather than a sip of him.

"Good," she replies on a whisper.

It's the simple truth spoken with a minimum of words. But to June it feels more like a complicated confession.

Mason smiles, his blue eyes caressing her face. "Good."

Then, and only then, does he let her hand go.

12

JUNE

This isn't happening, June thinks when she sees the empty bus stop. *This is not happening!*

But it is.

She's nearly an hour late thanks to her second-hand bike breaking down in the Cal-Mart parking lot. Lucky for her, Cal-Mart has two dozen or so loaner bikes for employee use.

"These are usually reserved for associates to use in-store," Mr. Patel pointed out. "But I suppose I can loan you one so you can pick up *your son* on time."

He says "*your son*" like her motherhood status has somehow deeply inconvenienced him. Not for the first time, June is grateful she almost never speaks unless she absolutely has to.

Ironically, Mr. Patel's sulky insistence that she sign a ton of non-indemnification papers before taking the loaner bike is why she's late to pick up the boy her boss assumes is her son.

And that boy is now nowhere to be seen. June curses. Pulls out her phone, and once more tries to call Jordan on the cheap flip phone she gave him in case of emergencies like this...

"*Hey, what-up! This Jordan. Doing big thangs, so can't come to the phone. But leave a message. You know I'll get back at ya!*"

Voicemail. Again. *Where is he?* June knows Jordan. Knows he *always* waits. And for him not to answer his phone...

She takes a few deep breaths, hops back on the bike, and tries not to worry as she pedals home...

Only to hear his familiar shouts and laughter before she even reaches the front door.

She walks around the house to find Jordan and Mason in what has become a familiar scene since the older man's arrival.

They're playing soccer, using Mason's sleeping bag (he refuses to sleep indoors at night) as a sort of defacto goal while Mason—the goalie—attempts to slap the ball away before it can get past him. Under the circumstances, the sight of them would be a huge relief. And maybe even a little heartwarming.

Except for one thing: Mason's not wearing a shirt.

June stops short, as if she's run right into an invisible wall. Her ravens start revving up again.

Mason misses Jordan's next ball. Not because he doesn't see it, but because he spots June watching them from the deck.

"Hey, you okay?" he calls out, heading toward her. His large strides eat up the ground, and he jogs most of the distance between them before she can even take a few steps in his direction.

"Went ahead and picked Jordan up when you didn't get back by the usual time," he explains, coming to a stop in front of her. "We thought maybe you'd been held up at work or something."

June nods. "I did. And I'm fine," she answers, then tells him, in as few words as possible, about the bike and how she borrowed one from the store to get home.

Instead of looking surprised or sorry for her, Mason's brow furrows. "June, why didn't you call me?" he demands. "I would have come and got you."

She stares at him, recalling the past six years with Razo. He was the last man she went to for help. Just thinking about what went down the few times she had makes her throat tighten so much, she can't even respond.

But Mason gets it without June needing to say a word. "Okay, okay. I get it," he mumbles, taking a step back. Giving her space. "But next time, call me. Okay?"

He expects an answer. But she doesn't have one. He's been there for a few weeks. Long enough for her to finish his new tattoo, and for it to be almost completely healed. She has no idea how to tell him she'd rather try to figure most things out on her own than depend on him.

Luckily, she's saved from a response by Jordan. "I didn't tell Mason about the tattoo, in case you were wondering," he announces. Then immediately follows up the good deed report with, "Can I go to Luke's house?"

Luke. The neighbor kid a half mile or so up the road. "How about your—?" she starts to ask.

"I'll do it there. You know, we're in the same class so we can work on it together."

Good point. "Well, okay. But please be back in time for dinner," she says. "I'm making your favorite."

"Lasagna?"

"Yep," she confirms.

"Yes!" he shouts, pumping his fist like he's won the lottery. "See you at dinner!"

He starts to run off, only to do an about face. "Oh wait, I need my phone." Jordan jogs over to the deck where he set his phone down. He glances down at the screen and his eyes go wide. "Thirteen missed calls!?"

He rolls his eyes at June and snickers. "Seriously, June?" Then calls out, "Okay, bye!" before dashing up the drive without so much as a backwards glance.

"Kid's a piece of work," Mason says as they watch him go. His gaze swings back to her. "Sorry about that. Should have had him call you when I picked him up—"

"Put on a shirt, please! That tattoo needs to stay out of the sun. I told you—" The words burst out without warning, way louder than she intended. And she breaks off abruptly, remembering...

Men don't like to be bossed around. She once risked telling Razo something similar after doing work on his arm and received a backhand for her efforts. *"Never, ever tell me what to do! You got that, puta?"*

Yeah, she definitely got it. But maybe she needs another reminder. Because here she is, telling another dangerous man what to do.

June holds her breath, waiting to see what Mason will do. But he only says, "Sorry, I forgot," before yanking at the thin t-shirt tucked into the back pocket of his jeans. "How long before I can see it?"

"One more day," she replies, her voice softer now. "It's healing real well."

Mason gives her his patented lop-sided grin. "Good. That's good."

Maybe he's not making a reference to the bath. Or to the one —and only—kiss they'd shared. But...it feels like he could be, and those damn ravens are flapping around inside her stomach again.

Mason's head dips down as it often does when he talks to her. As if he might otherwise have trouble hearing what she's saying from way up there. But today, his familiar pose makes her wonder: if she stands on her tiptoes, could she reach his lips?

Whoa! June stops herself right there, and without another word, hurries up the steps and into the house. She doesn't stop until she reaches the kitchen. Mason has left his mark on the room. All the windows are open, along with the door that leads out to the side yard where the old barn sits.

A few minutes later, she can see Mason standing in the barn's open doorway through her kitchen window. He's been working out there since he arrived. Hammering, sawing, and—best as she can tell—doing a full renovation. She has no idea what his plan is, and he doesn't volunteer any details. But June still enjoys watching him neatly place several dozen black-and-white floor tiles over the fresh concrete he laid a few days ago.

Mason's shirt is back on, but his muscles still visibly ripple as he makes his way around the barn. He presses a large white tile into place, the veins in his forearms popping so hard, they're easily visible from her vantage point in the kitchen. It's been unseasonably cool out. Most days, the temperature doesn't go higher than fifty degrees. But the weather hasn't had any effect on Mason's productivity. He seems to be in a perpetual state of hot and sweaty, constantly swiping his meaty forearms across his forehead. Sometimes June feels like she's watching one of those ads featuring a sexy but thirsty construction worker, the kind designed to sell a brand of refreshing beverage.

Enough, June. Make dinner! She needs to focus on prepping the lasagna for Jordan. With her newfound resolve, and a stubborn refusal to think about the man hard at work in the barn, she opens the fridge—only to swear out loud. She's out of ricotta.

Okay, spaghetti it is, she thinks, going over to the pantry to dig out the necessary ingredients. But before she can reach the box of dried pasta, her phone vibrates in her back pocket. She tugs it out and curses again when she sees who it is.

"Hi, Mr. Patel," she says, because Jordan has told her more than once that normal people "don't get" silent hellos.

"Hello, June. I'm outside the store, about to head home. And I notice your bike is still here."

"Yes, I know. Remember, it's broken," she responds, taking a few minutes to briefly explain the situation again. Even though her supervisor should be well aware of what happened, because he made her fill out all that paperwork so she could borrow the store bike.

Mr. Patel clears his throat. "Yes, yes...of course. But perhaps you do not know about our employee parking lot policy? All employees are expected to remove their vehicles—bikes included—from the store parking lot by the end of the day. Any vehicles left overnight without good reason will either be towed at the owner's expense, or otherwise impounded. I'm calling to ask you to please pick up your bike before closing hours. I would hate for you to lose your main form of transportation."

"Wait, what? But...you know who the bike belongs to. Can't you just leave it or store it in the breakroom and I'll get it tomorrow?"

"I'm afraid not, June. If we make an exception for you, then we risk every employee thinking it's acceptable to store their vehicles here overnight. And we simply can't bend the "no overnight parking" rule because doing so would turn our parking lot into a potential security risk for the store and increase the company's liability."

Mr. Patel says this as if the prospect of leaving her bike in the store until tomorrow morning is on par with someone waltzing in and releasing a jar of live cockroaches in the grocery section.

"Please, Mr. Patel," she tries again. "I don't even know how I'm going to fix the bike, let alone move it. There's a problem with the chain. And I'm in the middle of getting dinner ready for...for my son. I just need a little more time. Please."

"I am sorry, June. I really am," Mr. Patel says in the overly empathetic tone people adopt right before they say something that proves they don't really give a shit about you or your situation at all. "But rules are rules. And with Holt Calson popping in for surprise visits at a number of our stores, I simply can't be too careful."

"But—"

"Move it or we will have to move it for you. See you soon, June."

The line goes dead before she can protest again.

"What's wrong?"

She turns to see Mason standing on the other side of the screen door. Sweaty and impossibly big and...cue those damn flapping ravens, which she *really* doesn't need right now.

But Mason clearly does not get the memo. He pushes the door open, and walks into the kitchen, sending her ravens even further into overdrive.

"Saw you there at the window from the barn. You looked upset. Is everything okay?"

June knows she needs to figure out what to do about her bike. Instead, she's kicking herself for making Mason put his shirt back on. Because now the fabric is sticking to his sweaty torso like a second skin...defining every single muscle. Every. Single. One.

"Earth to June. You still haven't answered my question."

She raises her eyes from his chest. And she's pretty sure she must have a dazed expression on her face. Because now he looks worried, and his voice has taken on a more urgent tone when he asks for the third time, "June, what's going on?"

"It's my boss," she blurts out, resolutely ignoring the flapping wings. They seem to be getting more and more frantic every day. "He says I have to pick up my bike before the store closes tonight, even though he knows why I can't. He says," June drops her gaze to the floor to hide her growing frustration, "if I don't get it tonight, it'll be gone by tomorrow. Apparently, it's a company policy."

She's about to go into detail about the policy, when she sees the way he's looking at her, with anger blazing in his eyes.

"Wait a sec. You mean to tell me you're really not going to ask me for help?" he asks. "Again?"

June blinks. Because the truth is, it hadn't even occurred to her *to* ask.

And she thinks he must understand, because instead of staying angry with her, he simply shakes his head and says in a resigned tone, "Okay. Well, let me take a quick shower, and then I'll meet you at the truck."

Mason leaves the kitchen and heads to the back bathroom. He fixed her shower weeks ago—yet another thing he'd done without her having to ask.

This is...nice, she realizes. Nice to have someone around to help out. Especially someone who doesn't seem to expect anything in return. But it's becoming harder and harder for June not to get used to this. To not like it. Or like him.

HER WARM FUZZY feelings stick around all the way down US-62E, back to Cal-Mart. Only to increase dramatically when Mason takes one look at her bike in the parking lot and says, "Oh, it's just the chain. I can fix that. Got the tools back at the house."

He can fix it! the ravens twitter adoringly in her ear. *He can probably fix anything. ANYTHING!*

As she slowly wheels the loaner bike back into the store, June reminds the ravens who Mason is, reminds them about his missing vest...and what it represents. Then she resolutely turns her attention to the task at hand. She makes a quick detour through the grocery department to grab a tub of ricotta—might as well try for that lasagna after all. Then she heads over to the night manager to return the loaner bike. June is relieved she doesn't have to deal with Mr. Patel. The night manager is much more laid back and happily married. He takes the bike with a smile, and tells her to just take the ricotta. No need to pay. "It's on the house!" he says to her with a wink.

People can be kind. This thought suddenly occurs to June for the first time in years. Which explains why she's just about in the best mood she's been in for a long time as she walks back through the grocery section towards the main exit.

Which makes it doubly ironic when an unpleasantly familiar kissy sound erupts behind her.

June really doesn't know what she hates more: the way he uses the sound to summon her like a dog, or her Pavlovian response when she hears it: she literally stops in her tracks and turns towards him like a puppet on a string.

And there he is...just a few feet away. Honestly, whenever June used to worry about the possibility of him finding her, she never in a million years imagined it would be in the frozen foods aisle of a Cal-Mart. It would almost be funny if...well, if it just wasn't. Like at all.

Razo is dressed in his usual classy attire: a black wife-beater, baggy cargo pants, and a loose flannel shirt that all but shouts, "I'm carrying!" He's flanked by not one, but two Hijos, just in case his routine shopping trip turns ugly and requires backup. June might have rolled her eyes at his ridiculousness if he didn't completely terrify her.

The three men come to a stop in front of her, and coincidentally, the grocery department rapidly empties of all customers. Some primal flight or fight instinct, encouraging them to do the former.

June glances around and sees no other store employees nearby. Having worked the late shift a few times, she knows the floor staff coverage is reduced by two-thirds in the evening, which means a good fifteen to twenty minutes might pass before someone wanders over and thinks to call security.

Not that it matters. Even another minute is too long to spend with Razo.

She moves to get past him, but he darts in front of her, blocking her way.

"Hey, *mija*! I been missing you," he says with a friendly smile. God, how she hates that smile. She'd fallen for it at first. Actually thought he was friendly, generous, even if the offer to share his bed came less than twenty-fours after he'd invited her and Jordan in from the streets. "That's no way to treat your man. Come in for this hug."

To her utter horror, he reaches out and pulls her close. His pungent scent of stale marijuana smoke and sweat makes her want to gag. "Looking good, *mija*," he murmurs in her ear. "You gettin' an ass again. I like that. It was sagging toward the end there."

Because you were starving me, she thinks back at him. But June's not interested in arguing. She only wants to get as far away from him as possible. She quickly pulls out of the hug, and attempts to leave again.

But he holds her there, hands cupped tightly around her shoulders.

"Still not talkin', huh?" he asks, with that same friendly smile. The phony mask he wears outside the Cul.

But then his friendly smile is replaced with a look of surprise. Like he's just now noticing the Cal-Mart uniform she still hasn't changed out of.

"I heard he got you working here. I had to come see it for myself, *mija*. I can't believe it. I mean, I knew he was into that slave shit. But I didn't know he put you out in the fucking field for reals. Day-um!!!"

Right on cue, the men with him snicker like he's the funniest small-time gang leader on the planet.

"But I guess that figures," says Razo, schooling his face back into a sympathetic look. "He probably need all the money he can get now he ain't affiliated no more—what, you didn't hear about that?" he asks, when he sees real confusion on her face.

Then he nearly falls down laughing. He addresses the men by his side. "Oh shit! He got her turnt out—workin' at Cal-Mart, and she got no idea!"

There's another fake pitying look. Classic Razo. So sincere, so cutting. The cholo version of a mean girl.

June detests him in that moment. Hates the way he makes her feel. Like she's some piece of shit beneath his Timberlands.

"Okay, okay, no more jokes. Here's the deal," he says, like he's doing her a solid by breaking it to her. "Word on the street is that SFK fuck turned traitor on his whole crew. I heard he snitched them out like a straight bee-yotch to the Feds. Then the whole board, except for him and his cousin, got disappeared. There's a rumor going round he and his cuz shot them up and buried them where nobody'd find them."

He stops. Blinking as if a new idea has suddenly occurred to him. "Maybe you should come back home with me. I been missin' you, and I've come up in the world, you know. Used them guns of his to end this 2nd Streeters beef you got me into, and now I'm running all of Summerdale. I should do you a favor and rescue you from that asshole."

A chill runs up her spine at the thought of going back to Razo, of ever being under his thumb again. She won't do it. June pushes words out of her mouth, "I don't need rescuing," she tells him, practically spitting the short sentence in his face.

"You sure 'bout that?" Razo's friendly smile appears to be on the verge of laughter, and his head is bent in such a way that anyone passing might think he's flirting with her.

But they would be wrong. She's not some naive seventeen-year-old any more, and she can practically feel the evil radiating off of this fake-as-hell asshole.

June opens her mouth, feeling the strength of her new life surging through her. She's stronger than she's felt in years. Strong enough to tell Razo she is 100% positive she'd rather stay with Mason than ever, *ever* go back to him. No matter who Mason is, or what he's done.

But before she can get the words out, a voice behind her growls, "What the fuck is going on here?"

13

JUNE

"*M*ason—" she starts when she sees him standing at the entrance to the aisle, next to the frozen pizza and corndog section. His expression is beyond pissed off.

She quickly steps away from Razo. But Mason is already moving toward them. Then he's getting between Razo and her. "Why are you here? Why are you even talking to her? What the fuck do you not understand about the terms of our deal?"

"Mason…" she tries again, because this is her place of business. Only for Mason's voice to bark, sharp as a punch, "Stay right the fuck where you are, June."

"Hey, hey! No need to get swole, man," Razo says with his easygoing smile. "Me and June was just talking. You know, catching up."

A pause. Then Mason takes another towards Razo, coming in so close that the toes of his motorcycle boots touch the rounded tips of the smaller man's Timberlands. "You do not talk to her. You do not look at her. She's mine now. Do I make myself clear?"

Razo's smile stays, but his eyes narrow and shift to his crew.

The ones who stand by, watching him get schooled by a white biker, in front of his ex-woman.

Having firsthand knowledge of Razo's extremely sensitive embarrassment button, June is terrified, but not at all surprised by his next move. There's a non-subtle shift of his hand, and Razo uses it to pull the bottom edge of his black tank top up just enough so his other hand can come to rest on the gat tucked neatly inside his waistband.

Fear nearly blanks June's mind. But Mason doesn't even flinch

"Think I give a shit about your little gun?" he asks, towering over Razo. He tosses a

dismissive glance at the two Hijos. "Or these panties you brought with you? Hear me now, Razo. If I see you *anywhere* near June ever again, I'm going to end you right where you stand. Understand, this is me being respectful...giving you fair warning. Next time, all you'll get is dead."

For the first time ever, June sees real fear in Razo's eyes. His inner mean girl has fled. And his gun seems about as threatening as a water pistol in the face of Mason's zero fucks.

Again, Razo glances over at his crew. Which is funny. Because he brought them for back up, but now they're a liability. Razo probably expected Mason to back down after he flashed his gun, but the huge man called his bluff instead. And now there are two witnesses who saw Mason humiliate Razo in the frozen food aisle of a Cal-Mart. It's an untenable position. If he backs down, the rest of his gang will find out as soon as he returns to the Cul. If he pulls his gun, then he'll do time since there are security cameras everywhere in Cal-Mart.

Razo is a lot of things, but stupid isn't one of them. He already served time back before he met her. And as much as he brags about his stint in prison, she knows he has zero interest in going back. Not to mention, it's kind of hard to become a cartel leader if you're rotting away in an Arkansas jail. June can practically see his slimy mind turning the problem over. Trying to figure out the best way to get out of this situation without losing face or going to jail.

"Hey! There a problem here?"

Ed, one of the store security guards, appears at the end of the aisle, where Mason stood just a few minutes ago. He's clasping his taser and looks like he's ready for anything.

Saved by a security guard.

And just like that, the fake smile boomerangs back on Razo's face. "No, no problem here," he says in an overly friendly tone.

His beady eyes shift back to Mason and in a much lower voice he says: "You know what? I already got your bike...and your guns. That's all I need...for now."

Razo jerks his chin up in a sort of nod towards June, then leaves with his two men.

She watches him go, relief filling her lungs with long-delayed oxygen. June hadn't even realized she was holding her breath until now.

"Thanks, Ed," she gasps.

"Sure thing, June," he answers. "You okay? I swear we get more thugs like that in here every day. They should let us start carrying real guns while we're on duty." He frowns at June. "What are you doing here anyway? I don't think you're on the shift list for tonight."

She holds up the small tub of ricotta by way of explanation.

"Oh, I see." Then his eyes go from her to Mason, who's still standing in the exact same place as before. Face stony, eyes tracking Razo and his boys as far as they can before the trio disappears from sight. June knows he's livid. With them. With her.

"You okay?" Ed asks June, head tipping toward the towering guy in front of her.

June nods.

But Ed doesn't look like he believes her. Even without his leather vest, Mason still has that biker air about him. Still reads dangerous no matter how often he shaves these days. "Are you sure—?" Ed starts to ask again, only to get cut off by Mason.

"Hey...maybe instead of standing there flapping your jaws, you ought to follow those three out to the parking lot. Make sure they ain't harassing other customers outside."

It's a dismissal. And also a reprieve. Ed seems relieved he won't have to deal with Mason on top of everything else. "Yeah, okay," he says to Mason. "June..."

With a tip of his security cap, he walks off.

Leaving her alone with Mason.

As if sensing the danger has passed, customers begin to slowly return. June sees them out the corner of her eye, but in spite of the growing number of people around her, she still feels very isolated with Mason.

At first he stands there, watching the scene unfold outside the store's sliding glass doors. June's too short to see over the shelves but she assumes Razo and his crew are on their bikes and about to head off into the setting sun. She wonders if Razo's riding the bike that used to belong to Mason. The one he traded for her.

But even though the Hijos are gone, June can still feel their oppressive presence. Even after Mason's finally shifts his gaze from the front entrance back down to her.

"What were you doing talking to him?" His crystalline gaze blazes with rage though his tone sounds calm. "Letting him touch you? What part of "you belong to me now" do you not get?"

He's not yelling, but he might as well be. June's shifts her eyes from side to side, narrowly missing the redirected stares of a few customers. And a few don't even bother to pretend they're not staring. They've stopped in their tracks, elbows propped up on the red handle of their shopping carts, watching her get chewed out by the huge white guy in the frozen food aisle.

June has no words. Only shame. Along with an all-too-familiar cocktail of dread and fear.

Mason jerks his head toward the entrance. "They're gone," he grunts. "C'mon..."

For a second, she doesn't move. She doesn't want to go anywhere with the angry man standing in front of her. She wants to stay right here. At work. Where she's safe.

But then he says, "June, it's getting late. The kid's going to be home any minute expecting dinner."

Is it a reminder or a threat? She has no clue. But it works all the same.

She follows him out of the aisle and through the sliding glass doors into the parking lot.

14

JUNE

The silence on the car ride home is way worse than if he screamed at her. It vibrates with the promise of bad things to come.

A memory swims to the forefront of her mind.

That fateful meeting with the 2nd Streeters.

It was supposed to be a friendly get-together. A discussion about merging the two smaller gangs so they could cover more territory. Things were going well until the 2nd Street leader made a critical error and miscalculated June's status in Razo's gang.

It might have been because Razo didn't introduce her as his. Instead, he kept calling her over with that horrible kissy sound, issuing orders like, "Hey, *puta*, get my boy another Tecate," and "Hey *puta*, we low on blunts. Keep 'em coming."

She thinks this is why the 2nd Street leader looked her directly in the eyes, touched her arm, and thanked her after she brought his third beer. June was so stunned by the unexpected show of good manners, she actually smiled back. Then...disaster.

"Hey," he called out, "This bitch like me! Bet I'm up in her pussy before the night's through." He laughed loudly at his own joke before taking a long pull of beer from the bottle June had given him.

Razo laughed right along—up until he stood and shot the gang leader at point blank range through the chest. Then he turned his gun on the three other 2nd Streeters who'd come to the meeting, shooting them before they could avenge their leader.

"Look what you made me do!" Razo's words echo in her mind as Mason drives them back to the house.

Because of her everything was ruined. And instead of merging with the 2nd Streeters, the Hijos went to war with them.

Razo ordered his men to remove the bodies and then get the fuck out. That's how things usually worked with him. See, he didn't mind punching or slapping her in front of others. But for the real beatings, he preferred no one else see him like that. Crazed and damn near foaming at the mouth. Unable to control his rage. Like a child throwing a temper tantrum with his fists.

But make no mistake, it was a grown man beating. Thankfully her mind blanked out during the worst of it, because all she remembers is waking up on her mattress nearly two days later. Jordan seated in his familiar position beside her bed. Tending to her injuries with a little help from Google: "how to fix broken ribs without a doctor."

The results of the beating were so bad, Jordan risked injury and begged Razo to take June to a hospital when he showed up to fuck her just a few days later.

"June is having a hard time breathing," she heard the boy say from the mattress. Jordan explained to his cousin that she might die if a broken piece of bone punctured her lungs, liver, or spleen.

June watched their conversation through her less swollen eye. All the while thinking, *Stop, Jordan. Stop.*

But in the end, it was her stench that saved her. While she'd been unconscious, June had peed on the mattress at least twice, and some of it leaked out onto the surrounding floor. Jordan tried to clean up after her but he struggled to do a thorough job given the extent of the damage. After about a day or so, June and her room began to smell like a back alley.

Razo must have realized he'd beat her past the point of being fuckable. But of course he refused to allow Jordan to take her to the hospital. Instead, he threw a pack of oxy at his little cousin and, switching to English, said, "If she die, she die."

Then he ruffled Jordan's hair and walked out of the house.

Jordan skipped an entire week of school to tend to her. He prayed and begged her not to die, reminding her of the promise she'd made back when he was only four. That she wouldn't ever leave him. Ever.

June struggled to keep that promise. It wasn't easy. The pain was unbearable, the kind that turned a human into an animal—an animal who wanted to crawl into a hole and die.

But she held on. And she somehow survived the worst beating of her life. For Jordan.

However, Mason is twice as big as Razo. His fists ten times as large as Razo's.

Her ribs ache at the thought of what might happen when they get home. She fishes her phone out of her purse. Texts Jordan: *"Are you home?"*

"Yeah."

"Go back to Luke's. Right now. Stay there tonight."

She doesn't give away much at all, but months of the good life hasn't completely erased Jordan's memory.

"He not like that." The response comes back instantly, emphatic in its speed.

"Just do as I say. You promised, too."

Desperate to make sure he's nowhere near the house when she and Mason return, she references the promise she forced him to make after the first and last time he tried to get between her and Razo during an assault. That bit of bravery ended with them both getting beaten, barely able to nurse each other back to health.

"Be practical, Jordan," she explained afterwards. "We can't both be injured. I need you to stay in one piece so you can take care of me."

She's pretty sure he remembers his reluctant promise because there's a brief pause and then another text, *"Okay. Going now."*

With no small measure of relief, June slips the phone back in her purse. Glances over at Mason. His eyes are intent on the road, his thick knuckles white on the steering wheel.

It feels like millions of years pass by as she watches him drive out of the corner of her eye. But then they're suddenly back at the house. And it feels way too soon.

"Where's the kid?" Mason grunts when they get inside.

From the state of the living room, June can see Jordan helped himself to her stash of chips and cookies—something he definitely would not have done had she been there. The couch and surrounding floor are covered in crumbs. He also forgot to turn off the TV, which is why it sounds like there are two British men in the middle of the room shouting excitedly over a roaring crowd. She glances at the screen and sure enough: soccer.

Mason grabs the remote from couch and switches it off. "Jordan! Jordan!" he shouts.

"He's at a friend's," she admits, just to keep him from going through the house, calling Jordan's name.

He swings back around, his expression stone-like. "You told him to be back for dinner."

June doesn't answer, just looks at the rosewood floors she'd so admired when they first moved in.

She feels Mason's eyes on her for several long, hard seconds before he says, "That's who you were texting in the car."

The words hit her like truth-filled bullets. The ravens have stopped flapping, and it feels to June like they're frozen in place... waiting to see what Mason will do next.

His blue stare goes glacier cold, and he takes a step closer, dipping his head so he's almost at eye level with her. "June, what exactly did you think was going to happen here?"

"Answer me, goddammit. I am not in the mood for this shit, June. Not tonight."

She blinks back against the rapid sensation of tears. She will not cry. That will only make it worse. Crying only ever feeds the beating. Drama only ever feeds the beating. Fear only ever feeds the beating. She has to stay calm, dead inside. Act like it doesn't take everything she has to choke out, "An argument."

"Fuck yeah, *an argument!*" he replies, emphasizing the last two words. "I don't care what kind of history you got with that motherfucker. *He sold you to me!* That means you don't talk to him. You don't let him touch you. You don't let me catch you looking that little prick in the face or there will be consequences. That clear?"

A pause, then a weary, "For fuck's sake, June, I need an answer. Do you hear me on this?"

She nods. Giving him what he wants, even if she knows what she says won't matter. This is just the pre-show, a prologue to the drama yet to come. Then she waits.

And waits.

Nothing happens. Nothing, that is, aside from the sound of him moving away. And when she dares to look up, June sees he's bustling around the living room in that now familiar way. Throwing open windows with additional force like they, not she, did something to piss him off.

When he's done and sees her still standing there in the

middle of the room, he says, "What are you waiting for? You said you were making lasagna tonight."

Without a word, but with a few very careful glances over her shoulder, June heads into the kitchen.

She pulls the tub of ricotta from her purse and sets it on the table. Feeling as if the soft Italian cheese has morphed from an everyday dairy item found at most grocery stores, to a hard won prize...evidence of a dangerous journey she undertook and somehow managed to survive.

After an Odyssean journey, I have returned from the store— triumphant!! She almost smiles, recalling the hyperbolic statements the father from that other lifetime used to make after her mother dared send him on a domestic errand. He was a good man. A good father. But from a different era when men did not go to the grocery store.

But alas, he'd often faux-lament, *I've made the great mistake of marrying an artist, and must therefore resign myself to being sent out on last-minute quests for milk.* Like many artists, June's mother was both flighty and forgetful, and she refused to make lists. But it wasn't a big deal. Because her father loved her mother. In that other lifetime, he'd teased June's mother mercilessly and acted put upon, but it was usually in good fun and almost never mean spirited.

This all plays out in her head as she pulls the blue box of large lasagna noodles down from the top pantry shelf with trembling hands, only to drop it on the counter.

June clasps her hands tightly, balling them into fists until the trembling stops. Then she turns on the tap and places a large pot directly beneath it.

A moment later, Mason storms into the kitchen, whipping open all the windows and doors she'd shut before driving to Cal-Mart. She waits at the sink for him to finish, hoping he'll leave and continue his work in the barn until dinner is ready.

But she doesn't hear him go out. And when she finally works up the courage to look over her shoulder, she spots him leaning against the back wall of the kitchen. As close to the side door as a person can get without actually leaving.

Unsure of what else to do, June lifts the now full pot from the sink and carries it over to the stove. She turns on the burner, and prepares to literally watch water boil, trying hard to pretend she doesn't feel the weight of Mason's eyes boring a hole in her back.

This tactic only works for little while. After about five minutes, Mason lets out very loud huff of air and says, "June, shut off the damn stove and turn around." His voice sounds a lot louder than she thinks it should. She almost immediately realizes it's because he's standing directly behind her, so close, she can feel his words on the back of her neck.

June turns and lifts her eyes to meet his. She's tired of him chasing her gaze every time he wants to talk, and she really wants to get whatever's about to happen out of the way.

"You didn't answer my question," he says.

Question?

"What did you think was going to happen here? What were you expecting?"

June's voice is stuck somewhere between her rapidly beating heart and the flock of ravens, cowering in her stomach.

"Did you think I was going to hit you?" he asks.

June presses her lips together so tightly, she's not sure she'll ever be able to speak again.

15

MASON

*A*ll Mason can do is stare at the woman in front of him. He wants to shake her, and he wants to wrap her in cotton wool like she's a goddamn piece of fine china.

He's confused as hell.

Mason knows he's a scary motherfucker. Not quite as bad as before, but still pretty damn intimidating. Yet he's still surprised and distressed June could think he'd ever try to hurt her under any circumstance.

Especially after that bath.

Especially after that kiss, the one he'd used all his goddamn willpower to hold himself back from for fear of scaring her off.

He wants to howl with rage and despair. He wants to go out to the barn and rip apart everything he's built.

But worst of all is what he *doesn't* want. Mason does *not* want to remember. But he's as capable of stopping the onslaught of memories as he is of stopping a speeding train. And he's finally forced to give in.

He comes home from school. Finds his mother on the floor, slumped like a broken doll against the kitchen wall. Beaten so badly, he knows—even as a child—that something inside her is broken, and she really needed that something to stay alive. Torn up and scattered on the floor next to her are the tickets she'd shown Mason that morning. The ones she'd been so excited about.

Later, Mason found out his mother had confronted his father after her morning meth hit. Had waved the tickets in his face, no longer able to keep them a secret. Wanting him to know. Wanting to hurt him even more than she wanted to escape.

According to Mason's father, she came at him with a frying pan. And he was trying to defend himself. His father told him, told anyone who would listen, that his wife always gave as good as she got.

"She was," his father mumbled, drunk and sobbing at her funeral, "a fucking firecracker. A real goddamn woman."

But not anymore.

"I guess your daddy won this one," his mother told him through blood-stained teeth.

Mason arrived home too late to save her. And she was already dead by the time he returned with D's mother, the compound's nurse, in tow.

They buried her, same as they buried everyone else in the compound: deep in the woods without a marker. The official reason was to protect the privacy of the deceased in case the Feds ever managed to get that warrant they'd been threatening the SFK with. But Mason was pretty sure the real reason had more to do with making it hard for the law to use forensics to find out how many of the SFK dead were victims of drug overdoses, unlawful torture, and—like his mom—physical assault and battery. As Frank always said, "The government is always looking for any excuse to shut us down, so we got to be extra careful."

Afterwards, Mason lingered in a state of shock for some time. Less than twelve hours after his mother introduced him to hope, his father took it away. Leaving him to forever wonder if she'd really been serious about leaving the compound and starting over, or if it had just been another of the sick mind fucks she and his dad frequently indulged in.

But that was the past.

And the present...? Well, the present stands right in front of him. Suspects him of being as bad as his father was.

Thing is, Mason's really been trying with June. Holding himself back. Tiptoeing around her, and handling her with the softest gloves he could find inside himself. Because he understands she's damaged and working her way back to normal. But right now, he's not so interested in tiptoeing.

He flat out tells her, "Look, my dad hit my mom. Too much. That's how she died. I found her in the kitchen after school. And I been carrying that around with me since I was as old as Jordan."

Mason raises his large hands, wanting to grab June by the shoulders so she understands how serious he is. But he realizes this would be a bad idea. So he lowers his arms and puts all his pent up feelings into his voice instead.

"June, I would *never* hit you. Never lay hands on either of you," he says. "You could pull a gun on me, and I'd let you shoot me before I'd harm you or Jordan. If we're going to go on like we have been, I need you to understand this. Do you?"

She looks down at the floor, and he thinks he's going to have to chase after her eyes again. But she surprises him and boldly raises her face to his. Gives him a small smile that nearly breaks his heart. Then nods.

It ain't enough. And hasn't been enough for a while now. "No, sweetness. I need you to say it. *Say it,* so I believe you believe me."

Another surprise: she answers almost immediately. "I do believe you." Her soft voice is barely above a whisper but he hears her loud and clear.

But it still isn't enough for Mason. That weird, panicky feeling is building up in his chest again. The same feeling he had that time in the bath. He realizes what he needs from June is an absolution. He takes her hand. Places it against his raven feather tattoo before he even fully realizes his intention. He needs to feel her there while she tells him he's not a goddamn monster. "Say it, June. Say you believe I will never, ever lay hands on you."

June glances to where their hands are clasped over his heart.

"I believe you will never, ever hit me. Or Jordan." She sounds breathless, like the truth of her words are a kind of shock to her.

The surprise in June's voice does it, though. Mason's panicky feeling starts to fade.

Then she says, without him having to force it out of her, "I'll stop. I will try my best to stop being so scared. I promise."

And just like that, he's back to seeing her as a fragile piece of porcelain. He doesn't want to make any sudden moves or do anything else that might break her. "Good," he says, forcing himself to let go of her hand. "Now please get back to making dinner. I'm starving and I fucking love lasagna."

16

JUNE

*G*et back to making dinner.

June turns to do just that, her hand reaching out to switch the burner back on. This time she doesn't have to glance over her shoulder to know Mason is heading for the door. She can hear the soft thud of his booted feet walking away. But instead of feeling relief, a surprise surge of anger suddenly rises up inside her. She turns to see him about to walk out, and his name slips past the seal of her lips, "Mason."

He stops, spinning back around when he hears her voice. June averts her eyes to the stove, blinking rapidly at the pot of water, like she's asking it for advice. *What do I do???*

"Yeah?" he asks, his tone curious, cautious. Probably because this is only the third time she's ever called out to him. And the first two times had been at the store earlier this evening, when she'd been afraid he was fixing to make the news again.

She opens her mouth to answer with "nothing."

But ... other words, *stronger words* slip past the seal. Coming out before June even knows they're there, or what they are. "Don't ever do that to me again. If you want to talk, you don't need to raise your voice. And definitely do not speak to me ever again like that at Cal-Mart. *That's where I work.*"

Mason is silent for so long, she begins to wonder if she should reconsider her newfound trust in him. But then he says, "Okay."

Okay. Great, conversation over. But no, not yet, because she's not finished, "And Mason...?"

"Yeah?"

This next thing. It's way bigger than telling him not to yell at her. So big, she actually has to step forward to ask, "Did you really kill your whole gang like Razo said? Even your dad?"

His eyes shutter. And for the first time since the bath, Mason looks away from her and won't meet her eyes.

"It was the board, not my whole gang. And no, I didn't kill them," he answers. Before June can respond, he confesses, "My cousin did. And I went along with it. I helped him come up with a plan. Then I helped him execute it. It was the only way we could put a stop to the SFK, to weaken and disband the organization forever. It was the only way I could help D keep his woman safe. But..."

Mason lets out a long shuddering breath, and June realizes they've reached the heart of the matter. That he's about to tell her what's been haunting him well before he made his way back to her and to Jordan.

"See, grown up Mason understands his parents were fucked up people who fought like cats and dogs until things went too far. But ten-year-old Mason couldn't ever wrap his head around it. Could never put the SFK before his feelings the way he was supposed to. I thought I was doing okay. I thought all that shit from my past was buried and gone. But then I met you. And then D needed my help. And," Mason pauses and takes another deep, shuddering breath, "I helped D kill my dad. Because he needed me to, because it was the only way to stop more bad things from going down...but also for a whole bunch of other reasons that are way too fucked up for me to reconcile. Not now. Maybe not ever."

Mason's eyes shift again. Not back to her, just to another square of the kitchen floor. "I understand if knowing this makes you not want to live together no more—"

Probably no one's more surprised than June when Mason is forced to stop talking. Not because he's run out of things to say, but because she's blocking his mouth with her own.

And this time, she takes way more than a sip of him. With the ravens circling like a tornado in her stomach, June curves a hand around Mason's muscular neck, pulls him in close. Presses her soft body into his hard one, as she finally realizes...

...her ravens and that itch he'd mentioned? They're one and the same.

June wants this kiss. And she desperately wants him. Wants him like she's never wanted any man before. She kisses him, and kisses him some more. Demanding he believe her. Demanding he trust her.

But instead of responding to her kiss, Mason cuts it off. He draws back, his eyes wide and intense, his huge chest heaving angry, panting breaths.

"I'm sorry," she whispers, mortified. All the ways she might have misread this situation suddenly pour into her head. The last thing he probably wanted after sharing the horrible circumstances of his mom's death, was for her to decide this was the perfect time to let him know how she felt. That both she and her ravens wanted him to do things to her that she'd only ever endured before.

Mason doesn't acknowledge her apology. Instead, he very deliberately steps around her. Then walks stiffly over to the stove and shuts it off, before turning around, crossing his big arms in front of his chest, and asking, "Are you serious?"

Oh God, oh God. How many times can June feel humiliated in a single day?

"I'm—" she begins. But the words escape her, flapping just out of reach. She tries again, "I'm sorry, but I like you...I think. You make me feel like I've got a flock of ravens in my stomach. And you have from the start. I know it might seem like I would have a lot of experience with this sort of thing, because of- of where you found me. In fact I don't—at least not when it comes to real emotions. But my ravens...they're telling me I want to be with you. But I'm not...," June spreads her palms wide and places them on either side of her burning face, "...good with words. This is hard for me to say. I want you. And that's why I kissed you. And...I'm sorry. That's the best I can do."

Mason stares hard at her for a very long moment, his expression unreadable. Then he surges forward and...pushes past her. Like he's got somewhere else to be. Anywhere but here.

Oh God...a deep shame, like none she's ever felt before, crashes over her in tsunami-sized waves.

But instead of walking out, Mason reaches out a big arm and sweeps the items on her kitchen table to the floor.

What the—?

Before June can finish that thought, he strides back across the room and grabs hold of her, covering her mouth with his. And his kiss...it's nothing at all like hers. This one is rough, unchecked, demanding. For what seems like a lifetime, Mason lays siege to her mouth, both calming her ravens, and stirring them up into a fever pitch.

"Alright, sweetness, alright..."

He turns her around, face forward, and pushes her onto the table, her breasts pressing into the wood as he places a firm hand on her back. Mason yanks her Cal-Mart-issue khakis down, and the next thing she expects to feel is the full length of him entering her from behind. Hurting her, invading her...

But no...the next thing she feels is...

Oh. Oh!

His mouth. On her pussy.

June knows what this is but only in the vaguest sense. She's seen men and women perform oral sex on each other in the pornos Razo sometimes put on for background entertainment at parties. She also recalls reading florid descriptions of the act in the romance novels she sometimes snuck past her father in that other lifetime, way before she stopped believing in romance completely.

But watching it and reading about it are very, very different from having the actual experience. At first it feels strange and more than a little invasive. But it doesn't take long before it starts to feel good. Mason makes a rough sound in the back of his throat, and it feels like he's drinking her pussy. His tongue flipping a switch on and off at the top of her mound, one she didn't even know she had.

And then... And then...

She claws at the wooden table as a sensation unlike anything she's ever felt comes over her. It's as if a bolt of lightning hits her and floods her entire nervous system with a feeling somewhere between unbelievable pleasure and pain. *Pleasure...* June grabs on to the word. There's so much pleasure, and then she's no longer the silent one. She moans, as the new sensation fills her entire body...building, building until—the ravens take off, only to explode in mid-air, their dark feathers floating down into a soft pile at the bottom of her stomach.

Somewhere in the distance, she hears Mason say, "Fuck, this ain't going to work. Need to see you. Enjoy you."

The next thing June knows, she's in his arms. There's the sound of clattering dishes, then he plants her butt on the kitchen counter where the tub of ricotta and other lasagna-related ingredients used to be.

His hands follow, ripping her khaki pants the rest of the way off, before his mouth captures hers in another rough kiss.

Back when he actually bothered with things like that, Razo's kisses were soft, almost gentle, and perfect for luring young, unsuspecting girls like her into his spider's web. Mason's kiss is nothing like that. And it's at least ten times more aggressive than the one she'd tentatively given him.

He stops, fumbling with something between them. A condom, she dimly realizes, when she hears the familiar crackle of tearing foil.

June knows what comes next.

But then it doesn't.

Mason's forehead drops down...presses into the top of her head. "Put me in," he rasps.

"What?" she whispers, not understanding.

"Said I wouldn't ever touch you unless you wanted me too," he explains, his voice strained. Maybe because he's reminding himself of his promise as much as he's reminding her. "If you really want this. Really want me. You got to put me inside you."

Put him inside her...???

June's first thought is she can't. She's not capable of doing anything of the sort.

"You can do it," he assures her, as if reading her mind. "C'mon, sweetness...this can't happen unless you make the first move."

Mason kisses her again, gets in closer, his hard length pressing against her wet slit.

The ravens are back. Flapping, circling, demanding...

June takes him in her hand. His heavy thickness is shocking. He's hard, but covered in velvet...she runs her hand up and down his skin-covered shaft—only to nearly drop it when he inhales sharp and hard, ending their kiss.

"It's okay," he says with a hoarse chuckle. "Just like you

touching me there a little too much. I'll get over it. You take as long as you need, sweetness."

As long as she needs.

With a tentative tug, June pulls him forward. Puts the tip of him at her entrance.

The ravens go crazy. Cawing, urging her further...making her moan as she splits herself with his length.

"Mason..." she gasps when he's in as far as she can put him.

His chin is on top of her head again, pushing down. She can feel his breath, stirring her hair with each pant. "Fuck, sweetness, you feel so good on my dick. But I ain't gonna move. Not until you tell me it's okay."

"Move," she commands, more curious than afraid. Then in a softer tone, "It's okay."

Mason pushes inside her. He's so big, yet it doesn't feel like an invasion. June can actually feel the walls of her pussy gripping him, welcoming him. And it doesn't burn or hurt, it simply feels good. So good, she thinks maybe he's moving too slow.

"Faster!" she gasps, and begins to claw at his rippled back, the same way she clawed at the kitchen table. Demanding, needing, wanting something she still can't describe or explain. "Mason, please..."

"Fuck, sweetness..." He starts moving faster, as if he'd merely been waiting for her to ask. "Hold on, hold on..." He wraps her legs around his strong waist, his hands moving down to her hips.

June's body instinctively knows what to do. She leans forward, wraps her arms around his neck, and, oh God...! The pleasure is even more intense in this position. His chest hair feels amazing against her budded nipples, and the way he moves between her legs...each thrust touches a secret place inside her. Again, she experiences the bittersweet build of pleasure. The ravens flying...flying...until they combust, filling her with a warm light she's never experienced before.

She is dimly aware of her shouts. Of Mason's grunts. Closer and closer before—now it's her turn to curse. Because he swells even larger inside her. The hilt of him hitting her hypersensitive secret place, setting off another cycle, another hot stream of pleasure, as a third orgasm rips through her body.

Mason bucks between her legs, but then surprises her. He catches her mouth in another kiss, right before he releases into the condom with a guttural grunt that vibrates against her lips.

Then there's only the sound of heavy breathing. June holds him, and he pins his arms at her sides, keeping them upright as they float back down to earth together.

Eventually, Mason quietly pulls out, leaving her alone on the counter. But only for as long as it takes him to toss the used condom into the trashcan beneath the sink.

Then he's back with her.

They look at each other.

No chasing of eyes.

No words.

They don't need any.

Without any further discussion, Mason picks her up. Cradles her in his large arms as he walks to the back of the house. To the bedroom.

And June knows but doesn't remotely care, that they won't be having lasagna tonight.

17

MASON

*W*hen Mason first started dealing for the SFK in the small town surrounding the compound, he had regular interactions with a variety of folks—many of them full on addicts who'd as soon sell their mother, if it meant getting a much-needed fix. But of all the people he dealt with, the ones who troubled him the most were those who, through family or friends or plain ol' luck, somehow managed to get clean. To stay sober for a few months. Maybe even a few years.

Only to fall off the wagon.

And it was never just a little stumble. No, when they fell, they went all in. Wanting packets of heroin. Not one pack, but a fucking bag. Enough to binge on. Enough to silence the cravings...for a little while at least. Of all his customers, they were the ones most likely to OD.

Mason didn't touch the stuff, especially after seeing what drugs did to his mother, to his family. So he never understood why those particular clients seemed incapable of practicing more self-control. Buy a little heroin—why not take one bite of cake instead of eating the whole damn thing?

He never understood, that is, until now. Mason finally gets it.

When you've used all your will power to hold yourself back for a very long time, you're not going to want a damn cookie. You're going to want the whole fucking dessert platter.

That night, Mason is insatiable. As far back as he can recall, he's never, ever begged anybody for anything. That's not the Fairgood way. But with June, he sure as hell comes close, whispering, "Put me in, sweetness" against her neck with way more desperation than he intends.

And when he's finally too tired to get it up, he buries his face between her legs. Dragging orgasm after orgasm out of her. Just to hear her come.

With one taste, he's become addicted to June. By the end of the night, he's consumed with the need to either be inside her, or have some part of her in his mouth. Mason devours her pussy. Tongue-fucks her breasts, loving the sounds she makes when he conquers her with his lips. The way she pushes and scratches at him, hard enough to leave a mark when she's close to coming.

He can't stop making her cry out. Can't stop listening for the little gasps she rewards him with, as if everything he's doing to her is exciting and completely new.

She might have been Razo's girl when Mason found her, but it doesn't take long for him to realize she's never been fucked right. And knowing this makes his heart rev hard in his chest.

He loses count of how many times he makes her come. But eventually, he knows he's taken her past her breaking point when he tries to go down on her once more and she begs him to "please, let me sleep," her sweet voice raspy with fatigue.

That's when Mason discovers he really can't deny her anything. He relinquishes his new drug without protest, settling back on a pillow and dragging her limp body across his chest.

"Sorry I wasn't gentler with you," he apologizes as they drift off to sleep. "You had me out of my mind, sweetness."

"That's okay," she mumbles back. "I liked it. I never liked it before."

June's tired confession makes him feel proud and sad at the same time. The man in him likes being the best she ever had. Yet another part wishes better for her. Wishes she'd grown up entitled, like that college girl at the bookstore. Not vulnerable to the whims of losers and creeps like him and Razo. Wishes she lived the kind of life that would ensure she'd never have to give a piece of shit like him a second glance.

But he doesn't have the words to say all this, and she mistakes his silence for something else.

"Seriously, Mason. It's okay," she says with a sleepy laugh. "I'm not a princess, and it's not like I ever had it gentle before."

It's more words than she usually gives him. And he knows they're supposed to make him feel better. But they don't. Instead, he stays awake. Long after she's fallen asleep, Mason stares into the dark bedroom, thinking.

18

MASON

"So that's why she told me to go back to Luke's last night."

Mason stops short in the kitchen doorway. Surprised, but not really, to see Jordan at the stove, frying up bacon in a large cast iron pan, a bowl of eggs waiting their turn on the counter next to him.

During the last few weeks, Mason has sussed out how these two work. Most mornings, June takes care of Jordan like a doting parent. Unless she just worked the night shift in the stock room at Cal-Mart. Then Jordan handles breakfast duty and gets himself ready for school. They take care of each other, and probably have been doing so for years. So it isn't much of a shock to find the kitchen he'd damn near destroyed last night all cleaned up. And a fresh pot of coffee brewing on the counter.

If anything surprises him, it's waking up in an actual bed for only the second time in as many months. The first time was under extenuating circumstances, when he was stuck with D's fiancée in a big city and reluctantly checked into a hotel. It had been a strange, ugly sensation to wake up in that particular bed, in that particular place.

But waking up here, with June's soft body stretched out across his chest...

Well, he doesn't have the words to describe how good it feels. He'd probably still be in there with her, if he hadn't smelled bacon frying while taking his morning piss. In any case, he's grateful he decided to throw on a pair of boxers before coming out to investigate.

"I need to leave for the bus stop in about fifteen minutes. You taking me, cool?" Jordan says in that way of his. Making a request sound like something the two of them already agreed upon.

"Yeah, sure," Mason answers, padding over to the coffee machine. He hadn't realized he needed a cup until the toasty, acrid scent of it hit his nostrils.

He's grateful to the boy for making a pot in the first place.

Maybe his gratitude towards Jordan is what leads him to address the elephant in the room. "You know I'd never hurt June, right?" Mason says as he sits at the table with a steaming cup of coffee. "Or you."

The kid's thin shoulders stiffen, but then he shrugs casually. "Yeah, I know," he says. "Otherwise, I would have stole your wallet a long time ago."

Mason nods, taking a small sip of the very hot coffee. After all, he's been in this kid's shoes before. He understands the desperate planning that goes on in the head of a child who has found himself in a very shitty situation with someone he loves but can't protect. If Mason's mother hadn't been a meth addict and his father's punching bag, he might have considered taking similar action, too. But even back then, Mason knew he couldn't save her from his father...or herself.

"Here you go," Jordan says, setting a paper plate of perfectly cooked bacon in front of him. "You want some eggs, too?"

"Yeah, but let me make 'em," he offers.

Jordan looks surprised, but doesn't hesitate to take the seat Mason abandons as the older man heads to the stove.

That should have signaled the end of the discussion. But Mason feels oddly compelled to continue, even as he cracks two eggs into the frying pan, liberally sprinkling them with salt and pepper. "You know, I been where you're at, kid. Watched my mom get beat for years. It's a goddamn mind fuck."

Jordan is quiet for so long, Mason isn't sure he's ever going to respond. But eventually, he asks, "So you wasn't always big? You couldn't protect your mom?"

"Nope. My size comes from growing up, staying fit, and keeping the promise I made to myself that I'd never let anyone give me a beat down again." And that's where he really ought to end their little chat. But Mason adds, "Ain't no such thing as a kid big enough to stop the adults in his life from doing what they gonna do. That shit shouldn't be up to a kid to handle, anyway."

Another long stretch of silence. The eggs are done, but Mason takes his time sliding them out of the pan and onto the plate. He wants to give the kid a chance to chew on Mason's words, along with the bacon.

Jordan eventually says, "Last time Razo hit June...it was real bad. I thought she was going to die. She said she wanted to a couple times. Told me to let her go. But I begged her to stay. That's probably the only reason she still alive..."

The kid trails off. Then adds, "I should have gotten her out of there. I should have figured a way for us to leave."

Mason grips the wooden spatula hard, wishing it was his bowie knife. Wishing that slimy fucker Razo was here so he could hurt him worse than he hurt June.

But he holds it together. For the kid. Mason gently puts the spatula down on the counter. Then he brings the plate of eggs to the boy. Keeps his voice calm as he says, "Sounds like you kept her out of some dark places, kid. That's worth something. Giving someone a reason to live counts for a lot more than you might think."

"I guess..." the boy says, sounding unconvinced. But the room feels lighter now, like a shift has taken place, a weight has been removed. For them both.

He and the kid eat the rest of breakfast in companionable silence. After a bit, Mason says, "Tell you what, I'll drive you to school so you don't have to bother with the bus. Just let me get dressed..."

"Thanks!" Jordan says. Then he grins. "While you in there, take a look at your tattoo... it's all the way healed now."

WINGS AND TITANIUM. Mason adjusts the angle of the hand mirror so he can get a better look at the tattoo on his back. June covered the whole of back torso with a pair of thick, black wings...shaded so realistically, he can see the detailing on every single feather, the artistry in every stroke. And down the center of his back is a spinal cord. No, he realizes with narrowed eyes, not a spine, but a motorcycle drive chain made to look like a spine. Again, so finely detailed, she must have spent hours and hours looking at pictures and mocking it up on her sketch pad.

June gave him wings. And a mechanized spine to power them. *Well, fuck me...*

"She said you told her she could do what she wanted," Jordan reminds him when Mason returns to the kitchen, stone-faced.

Yes, that's true. Which means June chose to see him like that. Not as a dangerous white supremacist biker, but as a man capable of flight. A man capable of rising above his past...of leaving it way the fuck behind him...

Mason has shared a lot with Jordan today. So he's not about

to tell the kid the real reason for his expression. He knows he looks pissed off. But he's not. This is just what his face does when he's trying to keep his emotions in check. Because he grew up in a place, in a situation where men don't emote. Period. No matter what.

With a grind of his jaw Mason asks, "Who takes care of you when June needs to go out at night?"

Jordan sucks on his teeth. "I ain't never had a babysitter in my life."

"That's not what I'm asking you, kid."

"I'm ten!" Jordan says in the same tone a forty-year-old might use to get out of being carded.

"And...?"

"And I'm too old to have a babysitter."

"Alright, whatever," Mason says testily. "So can you disappear tonight? Maybe go back to your friend's house?"

"I'm good at making friends," Jordan says. "I got a lot of places I can go."

Though Mason suspects the kid's talent for finding places to go in a crisis was born out of need rather than natural inclination, it sure does sound like a brag. "So that means you can find someplace else to stay tonight?" Mason asks again, tone flat.

"Yeah..." the kid answers. But then he asks, "You trying to get rid of me?"

Jordan's tone is light and joking, but his eyes have gone old again. Mason can tell the boy is sitting on some fear. Wondering, like June wondered last night, if he can truly trust Mason.

Lucky for him, the answer to that question is yes.

"No, I ain't trying to get rid of you," Mason replies. "I'm trying to do something nice for your sister. To thank her for the tattoo."

"She's not—" Jordan begins, more or less confirming what Mason already suspects. But then the kid grins, as if just now processing the rest of Mason's sentence. "Well, in that case, if you trying to be nice to June, the new FIFA game just came out. If you get it for me, I'll go over to my friend Danny's house and play it on his system."

It's blackmail, pure and simple. But Mason doesn't care. Because June is worth it. "Alright, kid, it's a deal."

19

JUNE

Thank goodness I'm working a later shift this morning, June thinks as she rushes around her bitterly cold bedroom, trying to get ready for work. Not only did she not get Jordan ready for school, she has little more than an hour until she's supposed to clock in at Cal-Mart. And thanks to last night's...activities, Mason never did get around to fixing her bike.

"You got work today, huh?"

Speak of the devil. June looks up to see the man responsible for her late rise walk into the bedroom.

She nods, watching as he begins his strange ritual of sliding open the patio door, along with all the bedroom windows—the ones she'd only closed a few minutes ago after waking up in a freezing room.

"You don't have to rush," he says when he's done. "I'll drive you to work this morning since your bike's out of commission. Actually, scratch that. I'm going to drive you to and from work from now on. No, June. No...don't shake your head at me. It ain't up for discussion. Me taking a shower with you—that we can discuss. You biking to work by yourself anymore—that topic's closed."

Before she can protest again, he says, "Oh, and grab something to wear after work. We're going out tonight."

Which is how June ends up discovering the joys of shower sex...and then later that night, finding herself sitting across from him at a little French restaurant called Chez something or other.

Who knew she'd feel even more awkward around Mason now than she did night before, when he spent hours fucking her so thoroughly, she could barely stand at work. Or stop thinking about all the things they'd done together, all the things he'd taught her with just a few rough words.

Chez Whatever is a very romantic place, with small tables covered in crisp white linens, and twinkling fairy lights strung across the room's brick walls. June and Mason are surrounded by couples who look nothing like them. Those other folks seem relaxed and refined in their tailored shirts and chic dresses, their overly white teeth shining brightly as they laugh at anecdotes and smile knowingly at one another. In contrast, Mason wears what looks like his nicest black t-shirt under a black motorcycle jacket he bought after the weather turned cold while June wears a blue maxi dress she found on the sales rack in the women's section at Cal-Mart.

And if that didn't make her feel uncomfortable enough, the elegantly printed menu—on which she recognizes nothing but the prices—does the trick.

Mason orders a beer, she orders a water.

"Sparkling or still," the waiter asks.

"Still," she answers, hoping that means tap.

The waiter returns with their drinks. June is surprised to see her water comes in a very fancy looking sealed glass bottle that the waiter opens and ceremoniously pours for her. She wonders how much that's going to cost. But June interrupts her worries to focus on what the waiter is saying. He's running through an elaborate list of the daily specials—she thinks the dish descriptions would be mouth-watering, if only she recognized any of the food.

Mason appears to be having the same challenge. "How about steak?" he blurts out, interrupting the waiter. "I want steak. Can you do that? Rare?"

"Of course," the waiter responds in a gracious tone. He turns to June. "And for you, madam?"

Her confused look must be answer enough. "I'll give you a few more minutes with the menu," he offers, turning to leave.

But a few more minutes doesn't really do a thing.

June finally decides to order a steak, too. But when she raises her head from the menu to tell Mason, she can see he looks even more uncomfortable than she is. He's tugging at his t-shirt collar, casting forlorn looks at the tables next to the restaurant's huge front window. He'd asked for one of those spots as soon as they walked in, even offered to wait as long as it took for one to free up. But the hostess told him they were booked solid for the evening.

Mason tears his eyes away from the window. He takes a long swig from the glass of Chimay the waiter brought him, grimaces...then looks toward the window again.

"Mason...?" June asks.

"Yeah?" he answers, still staring towards the front of the room.

"If I pay for the drinks we ordered, can we go somewhere else?"

"Fuck yes," he immediately replies, whipping out his wallet like he's been waiting all this time for her to say the word. He throws down a couple of bills, as if he didn't hear her offer to pay for the drinks. "Where do you want to go?"

She thinks about it. "You prefer the outdoors, right?"

"Yeah," he admits with a sheepish half grin.

"Then let's go outside."

"This was a great idea," Mason says less than an hour later as they walk through Calson Botanical Gardens.

June can't take full credit for the idea. For two weeks straight, she'd spent her fifteen minute breaks in the Cal-Mart employee break room, seated across from a flyer advertising the annual "Drink the Garden" event at the botanical gardens, hosted by none other than Holt Calson himself. So, as that father from the other lifetime might have punned, it had been all but *planted* in her head.

But in any case, Mason seems fully at peace among the wildly mixed crowd of hipsters, business people, and senior citizens.

June had spent most of the day feeling nervous about their upcoming date. She worried Mason would expect her to talk with him again after all they'd shared the night before. But he seems perfectly at ease. Content to take a quiet walk with her around the garden while she nurses a bottle of water, and he takes deep swigs from a bottle of good old American pale ale (courtesy of the Ozark Brewing Company, one of the event's sponsors).

June is feeling content, too.

"What do you mean?" a harsh male voice cracks through the quiet evening, surprising them both. "What are you trying to say?"

She and Mason stop, listen. June doesn't want to eavesdrop... but the intensity of the tone sets alarm bells off in her head.

"Holt, I don't want to hurt you," a softer voice says. "I—"

"You thought you could keep this from me," the man interrupts before the woman can finish. "How long? How long did you plan to hide this?"

There's no response.

The man's voice comes again, sounding low and mean. "I will destroy you for this."

"Holt! Please, please try to understand—" the woman sounds desperate, and June's palms are beginning to sweat in anxious sympathy.

"Don't tell me to try and understand! There's no understanding what you've done."

Holt. June's eyes widen. Surely it can't be Holt Calson, the new Cal-Mart CEO. Then again, Holt isn't a very common name...and he is hosting the event.

"Holt, please calm down. Please listen to me...listen! I need you to—"

"Do you really think I give a good goddamn what you need? After what you've done? Save it. Anything else you have to say to me can go through my lawyers."

"Holt, please! Holt!" The woman sounds desperate, but her pleas seem to fall on deaf ears.

June hears heavy footsteps, and a figure storms around the corner. She feels a jolt of shock when she realizes that yes, that's definitely Holt Calson. He looks exactly like he does in all the photos she's seen of him in company brochures and newsletters. Clean-cut. Classic. Tall and lean. The Little Prince, all grown up and with a good fitness plan. The only thing that doesn't match the photos is the current expression on his face, darker than the raven she inked on Mason's chest.

She stares at him, but he pushes past them both without so much as an "excuse me."

"That was...dramatic," Mason notes in the brief silence that follows the incident. "But, c'mon, we don't have to let his drama ruin our good time."

He holds out a hand to her and she takes it, moving forward with him through the Japanese garden. Only to encounter the sound of weeping as they come upon the little red bridge arched over the garden's koi pond. On it is a woman, hunched over the railing, shoulders shaking as she cries into her hands.

She must hear them approach because she abruptly stops. And like a rabbit, she dashes off in the opposite direction, disappearing down the path before June can get a good look at her. She has no idea who she is. Or why the Cal-Mart CEO was yelling at her.

"Huh," Mason pauses, looking as perplexed as June feels with his deeply furrowed brow. "Any ideas what that was all about?"

She shakes her head and they start walking again.

"That was Holt Calson, right?"

June nods. That's the only part of the mystery she can definitively clear up for him.

They come to a stop on the small bridge freshly abandoned by Holt and the woman. She and Mason slip back into a companionable silence, the soothing sound of crickets filling the cool night air. June wishes it was still light enough to see the beautiful fish in the pond below. She has always loved the shimmering golds and whites and oranges of koi.

After a few minutes of silent contemplation, June says, "You don't just like being outside. Being indoors upsets you."

It's more of an observation than a question, but Mason answers like it's the latter. "Upset ain't the right word. It's...weird for me. But that ain't the right word either. I guess you could say I feel trapped. Being in closed up rooms makes me feel like I did that time in the bath."

A beat passes, and he starts speaking again, this time in a much quieter tone. "You know what Razo did to you...burning you with the cigarette? My dad used to do that to me all the time. Hit me, too. Especially after my mother died."

Mason chuckles, but there's no mirth in it. It's more like something he's doing to release or dismiss pain.

"His brother—my cousin D's dad—was just as mean. But he was also a survivalist. He could have been on that survival show Jordan watches, easy. My uncle even taught me and D to hunt. But my dad, well he had a cushy position on the SFK board. Never spent any real time outdoors unless it was to settle a score with another gang. I guess somewhere along the way, I decided if my dad was always inside, then I was always going to be outside. Where he couldn't get me."

June thinks about his story. About his past. "Mason?"

"Yeah?"

"What does the D stand for in your cousin's name?"

Long pause. Then even more quietly, "Dixon. Me and him were born in the same week. I guess our dads thought it'd be funny...naming us like that."

Old history lessons from that other lifetime come back to her, and June puts the names together. Wow. The silence between them becomes less companionable, more loaded.

"Mason?" she says again.

"Yeah?"

"Why did you buy me from Razo?"

June can barely see him in the darkened garden, but from the way he shifts and turns his head away, she can tell he's uncomfortable. Still, he eventually answers. "I can't say for sure. I kind of surprised myself when I did it."

June thinks about what Razo said during her confrontation with him at Cal-Mart. She has to ask, "Do you have slave fantasies? I mean, is this—"

"No! It ain't nothing like that," Mason cuts her off with a sharp shake of his head. "I really don't know what this is. Can't explain it. But it ain't anything to do with slaves. I just...I wanted you, is all. From the moment you stepped in front of me and my gun. And I knew the only way I could convince Razo to give you up was talking to him in a language he would understand: money."

He looks at her under the garden's soft lantern light, his gaze hungry and constrained. Like he's starved but doesn't want to bite her.

June turns her eyes back to the pond, mulling over his words. She decides she believes him. Mason's reasoning sounds a lot like her tattoos, deeply instinctive and frequently without a good explanation, or at least none that anyone else can understand.

The fact is, everything has changed in the last few months. For them both. She doesn't belong to Razo. And Mason's father —the man who burned and hit him the way Razo burned and hit her—is dead.

"Do you miss him? Your father, I mean," she asks.

Mason goes back to staring down at the water for a long time before finally admitting, "Yeah, but not the way you might think. It's... it's hard not to have somebody to hate. Somebody to direct all your anger at. When that goes away, you have to live your life, and you can't hide behind what fucked you up anymore. You have to deal with who you are, and the choices you've made."

June thinks about Razo again. About her recent struggles to move on and learn how to live without his tyranny. She nods, completely understanding.

"June?" he asks.

She looks up. "Yes?"

"You and Jordan. You real kin?"

June clamps her lips tight, but then thinks about all he's told her, all he's shared. And she decides to trust him. Again.

She shakes her head.

"That's what I thought. D might say you and I got to work on that. File some adoption papers, so the state don't try to get involved and split you up. I'll make a few calls. How old are you anyway?"

"Twenty-four," she answers. "How old are you?"

"Twenty-seven." He grins. "You're older than I thought. Mind you, I ain't complaining. It's good to know I don't have to feel like a pervert on top of everything else."

"You're younger than I thought," she admits. "I'm not complaining either."

He chuckles. She smiles.

They stand for a little while longer on the red bridge. Beneath the sliver of crescent moon. Above the brightly colored, non-native fish who are oblivious to their presence, maybe even drifting to sleep.

The silence becomes comfortable again. Until June says, "Mason, you almost done with your beer? Because I think I know where we should go next."

20

MASON

*F*uck. *Fuck, fuck, fuck.*

Mason has really been trying. Trying hard not to—

But when he sees where she's brought them, he can no longer deny what he's been suspecting since he came back to her and the kid.

He's falling in love. He knows it for a fact as soon as the huge drive-in movie screen appears over the horizon. And by the time the movie credits roll on *Shaolin,* the kung fu movie she'd taken him to see, he can't deny his feelings any more.

"Did you like it?" June asks, smiling up at him shyly.

Truth is, martial arts films have never really been his thing. But all that's changed. Mason will always love martial arts movies from here on out because they will remind him of tonight. Of sitting in the cab of his truck with June curled up under his arm.

"Yeah, I liked it," he answers, his words all but drowned out by the intensity of his feelings. *And I'm falling in love with you.*

But he stops himself from saying the words out loud, recalls his uncle's hunting advice: "Don't move too quick, boy. If you've got a critter in your sights, you got to be patient so you don't scare it away." Mason can be patient. He has to be.

He swallows and instead of telling June how fucking mind-blown he is by her thoughtful date night substitutions, he says, "I should have planned tonight better. I'm sorry for putting it all on you."

She responds with another of her rare smiles. One so shy and hesitant, it makes him feel like they're meeting for the first time. "Oh, it's okay," she says. "I never got to be in charge of plans like this. It feels like a real gift."

Jesus, she's killing him. Despite the wings on his back, he feels like he's plummeting fast and hard. He has to bite down on the inside of his cheek to keep from telling her how he feels.

Instead, he says, "You need to go to the doctor." The words come out way more emphatic than he means them to. She leans back in obvious surprise and not a little confusion.

"I mean, I been to the doctor." As he says this, he realizes how stupid he must sound. He knows he's not making any sense.

Mason shakes his head, forces himself to talk straight. "What I mean to say is, I'm clean. And...well I think you should get checked out, too, because of..."

That killing feeling comes over him again. His fists open and close. He wants his knife, just thinking of that Razo fuck.

"Mason?"

Her gentle voice pulls him out of the killing rage. It's the emotional equivalent of her taking his gun and dismantling it right in front of him.

"I already been to the doctor. Soon as I got my health insurance. I'm clear and..."

Her eyes dim beneath the dim overhead lights of the drive-in parking lot, even as she forces a smile to her lovely face. "Well, it doesn't look like I can get pregnant. My ovaries are in bad shape, according to the doctor. Which I guess explains why it never happened before. I mean, I tried to use protection but towards the end there...well," June stops and glances down. "Anyway, we can do it however you want tonight."

Actually, he hadn't been worried about her getting pregnant. But now that he knows the situation, it makes him a little sad. June's only twenty-four, and though she's obviously trying to put a nice spin on her situation, Mason knows it must be hard for her to deal with, especially after what she'd already been through.

He swallows, searching desperately for something helpful to say. "Then we really better get that paperwork started on Jordan. Make him your kid, officially."

Her face brightens and she smiles. Which makes him feel like he's getting some kind of medal pinned on his chest.

Until he recalls the last time he tried to do something official for her, sending her that GED book in the mail. "Uh, June. My source is going to need your last name, but you never told me yours."

She winces. "You're not going to believe me when I tell you."

"Why? What is it?"

"Mason."

"Yeah?"

"No, that's my last name. It's Mason."

He looks at her. Laughs out loud. "You're fucking with me."

June shakes her head. "I knew you wouldn't believe me."

But he persists, "Nah, come on June. You're fucking with me, right?"

She shakes her head gently.

He leans forward to cup her round face in his huge hands. "Cuz if you ain't fuckin with me, then this really is starting to feel a whole lot like fate."

"Serendipity," she murmurs.

"Seren-what?" he asks, thinking—not for the first time—that

his schooling wasn't nearly as thorough as hers. She's too smart for him. Too beautiful. Too everything.

"Serendipity. It's another word for fate," she answers.

Fuck not deserving her...Mason kisses her anyway.

Kisses the woman life branded with his name from the start. He could've spent the night with her in that truck. Might've done it, too. If a movie lot attendant didn't choose that moment to bang on his window and tell them it was time to leave. So they did.

21

MASON

"Fairgood love ain't nice. It's instant, relentless, and rough. 50 Shades of Hillbilly," his other cousin Colin joked, when they made up over beers after everything that went down in Los Angeles.

The new generation of Fairgoods is definitely an upgrade. They don't hit women or children. But in some ways, they're just as intense as their fathers before them. Because when it comes to love, they go all in. Fall harder than anybody else with a lick of sense would ever do. Mason guesses all that intensity has to go somewhere when it's not being filtered through a lens of hate. So...love it is.

That said, June is still healing. Six years with that little fuck, and it's going to take a while. He's got to keep things to himself for now.

That night, he places her on a bed covered in rose petals (he's proud he managed to make that happen while June was at work), and makes love to her in a room filled with the soft glow of candlelight. Mason gives her slow kisses, keeping his touch purposefully gentle. He treats June like she's something delicate and precious. Whispers sweet things in her ears without any cussing—a feat she probably didn't even know he was capable of.

The night before had been all about the consummation. About finally claiming her as his.

But tonight, it's all about the warm candlelight, the rose scented room, him kissing her all over, before asking her to open up for him.

She does so willingly. And then he drops his head between her legs. Lapping at her core. Gentle this time. Showing her he's not always set on "animal" mode.

"Mason, please stop..."

June pushes at his head, and he stops immediately, feeling confused. Climbs back up to ask, "Did I hurt you? Are you okay?"

She looks away, embarrassment shading her candlelit eyes.

"Tell me," he says. "Whatever it is, you can tell me. All I want is to make you happy. Tonight is all about you, June. So if I ain't being gentle enough..."

"No, no...it's not..." The words tumble out of her. Then trail off.

And here comes the panicked feeling again. Right on cue. The feeling that tells him he's in way over his head. That he's like a motorcycle that can't be fixed—a junk bike—no matter how many ravens, trees, and wings you paint on it. Mason hates himself for not being able to do this right.

And the shame...he's nearly overwhelmed with memories of who he was before. Along with the weird guilt of wanting her to be his more than anything else, but wishing better for her.

"Not like this." Her quiet voice brings him back from his personal brink. "I don't—I can't do it like this."

Mason stills on top of her, his soul taking on an intense new heat as he understands what she's trying to tell him. "You mean it's too gentle for you? You want me to take you rough?"

June nods, turning her head to the side. Maybe feeling ashamed.

"Thank fuck! Put me inside you..."

She does, one hand wrapped around his thick length as she guides him toward her wet entrance. Only now, he drives into her as soon as his tip hits her tight hole, filling her wet heat with one thrust.

All former gentleness goes right out the window, and now he's fucking her so heavy, both their bodies jerk upwards with every hard stroke.

Mason's hands run up the sides of her arms, lifting them up and over her head, before he pins them down with one huge hand on her wrists.

He's giving it to her rough, like she asked. But something comes over her.

Not fear. He knows when she's afraid, especially of him.

She bucks under him, tearing her wrists from his grip with a strength he didn't think she had in her. Cussing, scratching, pushing hard, even after he stops moving on top of her. Until suddenly, the sound of a sharp slap cracks through the candlelit room.

Mason reaches up to rub his face, his cheek stinging from her unexpected slap.

And she blinks, as if coming out of a trance. "Why did I do that?" she asks. Him or herself? He can't tell.

"Because you wanted me to stop?" he hazards, treading very carefully.

But she's shaking her head almost before the words are out of his mouth. "No, I liked it. I was really liking it. But then I just wanted to hit you. I can't explain it. I just wanted to fight back. I guess because I could? I'm so sorry!"

She looks up, her eyes sorrowful with apology. "And your face! Mason, I'm so sorry I hurt you! But you didn't do anything wrong. I promise. I wanted... I don't know what I wanted. Or why I wanted to fight you when you were just trying to please me... Oh God, I'm so messed up."

"Okay then...can I fuck you while you fight me?"

Her eyes saucer. Confusion overtaking regret.

"Um, what?" she whispers.

He tries to keep his expression blank, the way he always does when he's feeling too much. But she's tripped one of his secret wires, and it's taking everything he has to keep himself in check.

"You got my permission," he grounds out. "What I mean is, you can hit me. Hard as you like. It don't matter so long as I'm fucking you while it happens."

As so often occurs with her, he can hear her thoughts almost as clearly as if she's speaking out loud. *But it does matter! It's wrong, and—*

"Fuck, June, I'm trying. Really I am. But you got me so hot right now. I can't wait for you to think this out. Either tell me to get off you, or hit me again. But decide something. I can't, I can't..."

He grits his teeth, unable to finish.

And she slaps him again, even harder this time, without any restraint whatsoever. Like she didn't even pause to think about it.

Mason barely flinches. But something goes dark in him, revving his engine up well and good.

And when he drives into her the next time, it's like nothing he's ever experienced. Raw animal sounds come out of him as he moves between her legs. Mercilessly fucking her, even as she slaps at his thick shoulders, her fists pounding against his back, giving him all her anger, all her rage...

Until she can't hit anymore. Not because he stops her, but because an orgasm overtakes her. Wiping her out with its intensity. And as for the rutting beast on top of her...

Mason lets out a ragged sound, something between a growl and a keen, before his entire body shudders. His cock kicks, deep sensation shooting up his spine, right before he floods a hot river between her legs.

"Mason!" she gasps as another orgasm washes over her. This time, instead of hitting him, she holds on for dear life. Like he's her only port in an unexpectedly intense storm.

The silence that follows is way more intense, more charged than any they've ever had between them. And that's fucking saying something, considering how quiet things usually are with them.

June is weeping. Hot tears spill from her eyes.

Oh fuck...

"Ssh," he says. Mason pulls out of her, lifts himself off her body, and rolls her into his arms. "It's okay, June."

"No! It's not okay. I hit you! I *hit* you!" she sniffs. "Just like your father."

Fuck, this girl is trying to kill him. Thinking about him, when she really should be thinking about herself. He's falling...falling...

"Not like my old man," Mason insists. "You're nothing at all like him. You went through some shit, June. Now you're working it out with me. However, I'm not going to lie to you, sweetness. You fighting me like that—it's hot as hell."

June sniffs again. Then asks, "Have you ever done that before?"

"Nope. Never knew it was something I wanted to do. Most women probably wouldn't dare, and truth is, it never would have occurred to me to ask for it if you hadn't tried it first. But fuck, you took it to the next level, sweetness. Thank you."

His words seem to relax her. And when he looks down, she's smiling against his chest with an expression he hasn't seen on her face before: pride.

Even though he still has reservations about the guy she's decided to get mixed up with, he begins to think maybe this relationship of theirs could work. True, they got no business together, but they also got more going for them than a lot of other folks. Hot sex. Understanding. Maybe if he keeps this up, keeps doing for her, protecting her, and making sure she stays well-fucked, well, maybe one of these days she'll start falling for him, too.

22

JUNE

*I*t's a soul quake of a night. June falls asleep feeling like her relationship with Mason has entered a new phase. Not because of the sex, but because of the trust.

He trusted her to hit him. And she trusted him not to hurt her when she unleashed all her pent up anger and rage.

She wakes up in the morning feeling refreshed and brand new. Like a phoenix. Reborn from the ashes of her past.

Which is why she's surprised to find herself alone in bed. The open doors and windows are the only sign Mason was ever there.

She puts on her nightshirt and goes to kitchen.

He's not there either. The windows are closed and sealed up, like they always are before Mason joins her and Jordan for breakfast. Only the door leading outside is wide open.

Shivering in the morning cold, June pads down the short path between the house and the barn in her bare feet. She finds him in the barn, exercising. Chin-ups on an iron bar. Or pull-ups. She can never be sure of the difference. Only vaguely remembers not being able to do even one during her PE tests in that other lifetime.

But there he is doing them at a steady pace, only his sweat-glistened shoulders giving any indication it requires any effort whatsoever. She watches, completely mesmerized by the display of his muscles and stamina, until he sees her and stops.

"Hey," he says, dropping down to the barn's newly tiled floor. "Testing out the new chin-up bar I installed on Friday. It's holding up good. Barn's old, but not a total piece of shit like most buildings you see these days. It's got strong walls."

Yes, very strong walls, she thinks, her eyes floating to his pecs. No bruises there. But she still remembers what it felt like to push against his unyielding muscles, only to have his chest drop down on top of hers. Crushing her breasts flat as he fucked her into the bed.

Okay, okay...she thinks, her face heating up. She raises both hands with a nod. A clear signal that she's happy to leave him to it.

But before she can make good on her gesture, he says, "Hey... where you going? Get over here. I need you."

I need you. The words give her an unexpected thrill.

"Stand right there," he tells her, pointing to the wall right across from the chin up bar.

Confused but game, she does as he says.

Once she's in place, he does another pullup. But not as fast this time. Slow and deliberate.

He's asked her to stand very close to him. So close, his body brushes against hers as he slides down and back up again. His dick is thick behind his black gym shorts, hardening as it cruises up her nightshirt. It only takes three incredibly slow chin-ups for her to grow hot and bothered. For her breasts to swell, and her sore pussy to ache.

"Does it...bother you?" she asks.

He arches an eyebrow. "Does what bother me?"

"That you work out a lot." *Like a lot.* "And I...don't."

Mason comes back down. Shrugs. "Been thinking about putting a treadmill in here, too. You could start walking at least thirty minutes a day, now you ain't going to be biking to and from work. Lotta heart disease in the old gang, and that shit's a bitch. But as far as your body goes...I like fat chicks."

Uh, okay...wow...

"That ain't an insult," he says, reading her mind again. "It's a fact. And what else did I tell you?"

June doesn't respond. Though she does recall him saying something once about liking big women. It makes her wonder about his past. How many "fat chicks" has he been with? A sudden somber thought sinks her heart. How many fat chicks is he currently doing this with?

"That's ten—whoa, where you going?" he asks, dropping down in front of her again as she turns to leave.

June doesn't answer. Just looks away. And keeps her eyes averted when he gets in front of her face.

"Look June, I ain't trying to offend you," he says with a chuckle. "But you may have noticed I'm a big guy. And rough as hell. Sorry if I don't want to worry a girl's going to break when she's under me. What I'm trying to say is, I like your body just fine. More than fine, in fact."

"Okay. But what does that mean, exactly?" she asks. "Am I your fat chick in Arkansas? Do you have one in Tennessee, too? Maybe in West Virginia and California?"

June stops when she sees how hard he's grinning. "What?" she demands grumpily.

"Never had anybody get jealous over me before. Ain't going to lie. It's a good feeling having you actually spit a bunch of words at me because you're riled up at the thought of me with someone else."

"I'm not jealous—" she huffs, realizing what an obvious lie it is as soon as the words leave her mouth. "We didn't use protection last night," she points out instead.

"Yeah, that was a first for me," he admits, his grin turning sheepish. "I liked it. How about you? You like what we did?"

Obviously, she liked it. But she crosses her arms under her breasts. Not yet willing to give him the satisfaction of a reply.

"Yeah, me too," he answers her silence with another lazy grin. "And trust me, if I had any other fat chicks tucked away in other states, they'd all have gotten a break-up call this morning. Only you..."

Without warning, he steps forward, his large body trapping her between it and the wall behind her. He takes his hand in hers and brings it down to cup his large length. "Only you do this to me, sweetness. Make me feel this obsessed. Like I wanna be inside you all the damn time." He moves her hand up to his chest and asks, "You think I got room in here for anybody else, crazy as I am for you?"

He stares at her. Insisting on an answer.

June thinks about it. Really thinks about it, and the feeling she wouldn't admit as jealousy slowly fades as she shakes her head.

Mason's lazy grin returns, like a stamp of approval for getting the answer right. "Damn straight, there's only you. Now turn around, sweetness." His voice is muted, but it's an order.

Without protest, she does as he says, and sighs little inside when his large hand cups her sex, and two meaty fingers slip inside her. She pushes onto those fingers, already slick for him.

"Yeah, we're getting there," he says, rubbing, titillating...but then he removes his hand.

"Ten more of these, then I'm going to fuck you," he whispers in her ear. "Hard."

Ten more? What, no...!

June wants to protest as he lifts himself up again. His lengthy erection cruising over her butt and up her back this time. Before Mason, she wouldn't have considered her back an erogenous zone. But now it feels like her whole body is on fire.

One...two...

Her pussy's clenching and unclenching. Yearning. Helpless. It's a strange feeling. Like she could come at any moment, but still might never be satisfied.

"Please, Mason..." she hears herself begging, voice needy with desperation.

"Seven more, sweetness," he answers. His voice slow and lazy. He's teasing her, and it feels grossly unfair.

"No! You fuck me now," she demands.

"Sure, right after I finish these six—"

"No, Mason. *No.*"

She turns around, tugs at his shorts. It's only supposed to be an insistent pull, but the shorts are looser than she thinks. One yank, and they fall to his ankles. Exposing his naked cock. Long and hard. Mason freezes at the top of the chin-up bar. Just hangs there.

And then...

He's in her mouth, her lips wrapping around his shaft with unchecked curiosity. This is another thing she's never done voluntarily. Mason makes her want to...taste him, like he's tasted her. To explore her boundaries. He makes her feel...

Safe. The word hits her like a surprise downpour. But it's the right word. She takes more of him in her mouth. Loving his taste. The way he smells. Of sweat and denim and the faint whiff of the industrial soap he used hours ago before their date.

"Sweetness..." a growled warning. One she ignores.

Her head moves back and forth, taking in more and more of him with every push forward. Wondering how long he'll last if she keeps going.

"Fuck!" she hears from up above.

He roughly pulls himself out of her mouth, and drops down in front of her. Mason steps all the way out of his gym shorts, leaving them crumpled on the ground behind him.

His lethal blue stare lands back on her. He inhales. One angry animal snort, before huffing out, "I said five more."

He's huge. Intimidating. Strength and heat come off him in waves.

Unnerving. That's what he is, she thinks, remembering the first night at the cabin when he cornered her in the bathroom.

But that was months ago. This is now.

Something bold rises up inside her. Without fear, June reaches out, hands curling around his hard waist. Pulling at him as she answers, "And I said *fuck me now.*"

Mason tenses, head dipping the way it did when he told Razo he didn't care about his gun. For a moment, she thinks he'll go back to his set. Or worse, kick her out of the barn.

But instead he asks, "Is this the real you I'm seeing here, June? The woman who's been hiding under all that silence— that who I'm talking with right now?"

June nods, losing her words again for a moment. It's true, she realizes. This is who she was in that other lifetime. Confident, bold. Not meek and scared all the time. And she knows this is who she is now.

But maybe meek and scared is what Mason wants. Maybe he won't like the real her. Razo certainly hadn't.

A slow smile spreads across Mason's face. "Well, fuck me! I've sure been waiting a long time to meet you, darlin'!"

But then he turns her around, crushing her breasts against the wall as he growls in her ear. "If you want this dick so bad, you take me and put me in you."

She doesn't hesitate. Wraps her hand around his large cock, and guides it towards the back of her tunnel. Pulls it into her sopping wet heat—only to groan out loud when he pushes the rest of the way in.

Mason's thick forearm wraps around the front of her neck, while his other hand cups her pussy. *I'm trapped*, she realizes. Held so tight against his larger body that she can't move. The knowledge constricts her breath, panic closes around her heart like a tomb, because she has no choice. She has no choice...

But then he growls in her ear, "You like this? You like making me dominate you? Cuz I can't control myself when I'm with you. You like the way you own me when I'm supposed to be the one owning you?"

He provides her with another perspective of their current position, one that allows June to see the power she has. Over him. Over what happens next. She nods on low moan, unable to deny herself the pleasure of controlling a man rather than having him control her.

"Yeah, you fucking know I'd do anything for you, and you had to go and prove it, huh? You want me to keep going? Want me to dominate you? Fuck you into submission instead of finishing these pull-ups?"

Another helpless nod.

She can feel his mouth curve into a wicked grin at the side of her neck. "Alright, sweetness. Take this dick. Take all of it."

He begins fucking her for real now, trapping her more tightly against the wall. But she's not afraid. Can only feel the need. To be taken by him. Possessed by him within an inch of her life.

"Fuck," he curses behind her. "Can't hold out much longer."

The large hand on her pussy starts rubbing with malicious intent. "Come," he growls in her ear. "Come on this dick right now!"

She does exactly that, crying out as the orgasm shudders through her.

"Fuck, fuck, fuck..." he chants, right before letting loose. His cum load is so large, her pussy can't hold all of it, and she feels his warm seed run down her leg.

Mason's hands are in a vice grip at her waist. And he's cussing like she did something to him. Like she conquered him, even though it's his jizz streaming down her thigh.

When it's over, he pulls out. But only to turn her around.

"Good morning," he says with a wicked grin, then pulls her in for one possessive and extremely domineering kiss.

Just like it felt to him like he was finally meeting the real June, it feels to her like she's meeting the real Mason. Domineering as all get out, without a gentle bone in his body. June should be scared, but instead, she feels protected, cherished. She sighs even further into the kiss. Safe. Somehow, in spite of everything, Mason Fairgood makes her feel safe.

And that makes it a very good morning indeed.

23

JUNE

*U*nfortunately, the good mood of the morning is soon disrupted when Jordan returns home. Not because they aren't ready for him. They shower and dress ahead of schedule. So by the time Jordan arrives, Mason is back in the barn, working on another project, and June is removing the lasagna she'd promised to make two nights ago out of the oven.

Right on time, she thinks with a smile when the boy bounds into the kitchen.

"Lasagna, yes! Finally!" Jordan says as the smell of fresh baked pasta and melted cheese hit him. He must be really excited, because he goes to the silverware drawer and starts setting the table without having to be asked.

After he's done, he opens the side door, and yells toward the barn, "Mason c'mon! June made lasagna! Finally!"

The whole situation would have been amusing...if Jordan didn't take a seat at the table without removing his bulky coat.

"Coat," she reminds him.

"No way," he answers with a look like she's crazy for even suggesting it. "You been outside today? It's cold! And you know he ain't going to let us keep the doors and windows closed like normal people."

Yes, Jordan's right. June recalls her walk out to the barn earlier that morning. She'd definitely been cold...before a certain person warmed her up, that is.

And to think it's only October. Not even winter yet.

"Mmm, that smells good." Mason's gravelly voice interrupts her thoughts. "And right on time. I'm starving!"

She looks up to see him come through the side door—which he leaves wide open.

"June makes good lasagna. The best," Jordan, who she's fairly sure has never had anyone else's lasagna but hers, informs Mason. Then he launches into a list of all of June's other culinary feats. Including: peanut butter and jelly sandwiches, stovetop ravioli, and macaroni and cheese.

June barely listens to Jordan as she watches Mason open the windows. It's like he's on auto pilot. The slave of a compulsion he can't control.

She sets the lasagna on the table. "Do you mind dishing this up?" she asks Mason, handing him the metal spatula.

He seems startled. Probably because she rarely spares words for casual requests or asks him to do anything she can do herself. But he says, "Sure."

June holds back a tick, waits until he's slicing out a portion of lasagna, before she does something unheard of.

Back at the table, Jordan's eyes widen. June shakes her head at him before he can open his mouth to ask questions.

He clamps his lips shut, but his eyes follow her around the small room, watching her close all the windows.

Mason, for his part, must be as hungry as he claimed, because three pieces of lasagna are plated before he looks up and notices...June closing the side door.

He goes still. Very, very still.

Before he can ask, or even worse, get up. She sits back down and takes his hand, holding it as tightly as she can.

"Let's eat," she says. Ostensibly to the whole table, but really just to him.

Silence. The tensest pause yet in a relationship filled with tense pauses.

But she doesn't let go of Mason's hand. Resolute, even as she picks up her fork with her other hand.

"So how was Danny's?" she asks Jordan, her voice casual. Like small talk is something she engages in every day.

"Good," Jordan replies. Only his big eyes give away how disconcerting he finds the situation. "We played my new FIFA game, but then Danny made us switch to *Viking Shifters* because I kept winning. Kind of pissed, since playing FIFA with him was the whole reason I got the game in the first place. It's not like I got somewhere else to play it."

There's a sudden clang of metal against wood. Mason's dropped the spatula. His hand is reflexively opening and closing.

Without missing a beat, Jordan moves his chair from the other side of the table next to where Mason's seated. He wraps his much smaller hand around Mason's large clenching one. A second anchor in the man's rocky sea. Then Jordan begins eating with his left hand as if it's no big deal.

They eat like this for nearly a full minute, until Mason's whole body quakes, and he rattles the table with a sudden rise from his chair. Only to stop halfway to standing, because both she and Jordan are still holding on to his hands, refusing to let go. If he goes any further, he's going to pull the two of them out of their seats right along with him.

"You're safe, Mason," June says quietly. "Your father isn't here. Just me and Jordan. We won't hurt you. He can't hurt you anymore. You're safe, Mason. You're safe..."

Mason shudders, tugging at their hands. For a split second, June wonders if she made a mistake. If he might throw her and Jordan off like paper bags, and make a mad dash to open all the windows. It would take zero effort for a man his size to shake the two of them off.

But then the table rattles again when Mason falls back into his chair. A thin sheen of sweat breaking out across his forehead. His skin looks pale. And his body shakes, probably with the effort it's taking him not to hulk out and open the windows.

"I'm sorry," he says gruffly. "Know this is fucked up. Know I'm a fucking mess."

Jordan and June exchange a long look. Yes, he is. But so are they. And this right here, helping him when he can't help himself—it makes perfect sense to them. Even if it's not a thing they can explain out loud.

"It's okay, man," Jordan says for the both of them. "It's okay. Eat the lasagna. It's real good. Best one June ever made. I promise you."

To June, his words sound like something else. A promise to Mason that they've got his back. That he has nothing to fear here in this warm kitchen with her and Jordan.

Maybe Mason hears the promise. Because with one last look toward the side door, he removes his hand from Jordan's. And without another word…he eats.

Relief floods the room. But Jordan, being Jordan, simply picks up the conversation like nothing's even happened. "I don't know how much money we have for Christmas. But maybe I can find a cheap video game system online?" He throws June a hopeful look, "Or…maybe Cal-Mart will have a Black Friday sale? You can used your discount even on Black Friday, right, June?"

"*Viking Shifters*—that's my cousin Colin's favorite game," Mason says, voice shaking as he abruptly joins the conversation.

"Been meaning to check it out. Heard a rumor they're going to announce a Dragon Shifters game any day now."

"Yeah, that's what Danny said," Jordan replies, switching his fork back to his right hand.

Finally, June feels safe releasing Mason's hand.

And for the remainder of lunch, she returns to her usual quiet state while Mason and Jordan discuss the merits of various gaming systems, and what the next game in some *Shifter* series she's never heard of might feature.

"You still going to pick up that old motorcycle today?" Jordan asks Mason as he and June clear the dishes.

"Yeah. Got an appointment at 3:00 PM. Wanna come?"

Jordan's face lights up. "Yeah!"

"All right. We'll head out in a couple of hours."

June parcels the leftover lasagna into lunch-sized portions for work and school, and bigger slices for Mason. Meanwhile, Jordan places the plates and silverware in the dishwasher. She feels Mason's eyes on them both as they clear up. Like he finds their routine fascinating.

"I'm going outside to kick til it's time to go," Jordan announces after he's done.

"Close the door behind you," she says, trying to keep her voice as casual as possible.

As soon as the click of the door sounds, there's a huge figure at her back, reaching past her to turn off the tap at the sink. "C'mon," he says, tugging her arm.

June follows him into the bedroom. Nervous and afraid.

When they reach the room, she closes the door behind her. Then moves around the room, closing the windows like she did in the kitchen, and then slides the patio door closed.

"What do you think you're doing?" Mason growls in her ear after she draws the curtains shut, blocking the scene of Jordan kicking his ball outside. "With that stunt at lunch?

Telling the kid to close the door behind him? Shutting me up in here? You're pushing all my fucking buttons today, aren't you?"

"Mason, I..." she starts to explain.

"No, the time for talk is over, sweetness."

Tipping her face up with one large hand, he captures her mouth with an angry grunt. The room is much warmer with the windows and doors closed, but suddenly she's suffused with a different sort of heat as he knocks her head back with his hard, insistent kiss.

"Do you know how long I been dealing with that shit? Nobody ever tried to cure me. Nobody but you—fuck, I need inside you...you ready for me?"

June might not have been, but for the feel of his fingers at the V of her legs. Testing her to make sure. It does something to her, makes her want whatever punishment he's about to mete out. She's wet, the feel of his heavy chest on her back making her wild with need.

"Put me in," he whispers roughly.

She finds herself whimpering, "No, take me. Please, Mason, just..."

She doesn't have to ask twice. He pushes into her warmth. Then hooks one meaty forearm around her neck. Keeping her there as he ruts like an animal from behind.

June comes fast in this position, his relentless cock pulling the orgasm out of her in a keening wail. But for him, it's not nearly enough. He pulls out with a curse.

"I want in deeper. Want inside you like you've already wormed yourself inside me."

She has no idea what he means. But it feels like the most erotic poetry when he guides her over to the bed. Grabs her by the hips and all but slings her on top of him.

In this position, he doesn't have to ask her to put him in. Her pussy slides up his thick length, finding home without any guidance from either of them.

"C'mon, sweetness, c'mon," he grinds out. "Give me all of you."

She does and without any reservation. This is new for June. Being on top. Completely new. And he's right about it filling her deeper. He's so far inside her, it feels like their bodies are rolling together as one as she gets closer, closer. The pressure builds, and then...

"Mason!" she screams, unable to stay silent. The orgasm is so intense. And then he blasts into her, his warm seed bathing her insides with its sticky wetness.

"I thought you was supposed to be one of them quiet girls," he says when she collapses against his chest.

And June laughs because, "I was a lot of stuff. Before I met you."

"YOU GOT ANY THOUGHTS ABOUT CHRISTMAS?"

The question comes later that night. After they've gone to bed and enjoyed their second session of sex behind closed doors. This time with June biting down on Mason's arm, so as not to disturb Jordan in the next room.

The question is so out of the blue, it takes her brain a moment to catch up. "Christmas?" she asks.

"Yeah, it's coming up," he says. Voice casual but more gruff than usual.

"Yes, after Halloween....and Thanksgiving." Which reminds her, "I want to make Jordan a big Thanksgiving meal this year. And you, too...if you plan to be here."

"I'll be here. D's trying to get me to go to Seattle for Thanksgiving, but his old lady is fucking insane. And by fucking insane I mean vegan. I'll be damned if I will pass up a home cooked meal for tofurkey or whatever goddamn nonsense she got planned."

"Uh...okay..." June giggles. Actually giggles. "Then I'll get us a turkey."

"Sounds like a plan. And after Thanksgiving? What about Christmas? What you got planned?"

She laughs again.

"Why are you laughing when I'm asking you serious questions?"

"Because I didn't expect you'd be so into holiday planning," she answers honestly. "It doesn't seem like you."

June can't see him in the dark, but she's pretty sure he's smirking when he answers, "I was a lot of stuff. Before I met you."

The reminder of her earlier words tugs at her heart. June rises up on one arm, reaching between Mason's legs to take his soft length in her hand.

It's not soft for long.

"Sweetness..." he growls low in his throat.

It feels like a threat, sounds like a warning. But like this morning, she ignores it completely.

She wants him. Again. Like the slut Razo always claimed she was, even though she never wanted him. Not like this. She never even got wet for that creep.

Mason's hard now. June pulls, just enough to get him to turn towards her.

Then she puts him inside.

He responds with a sharp groan. Like she's hurting him...

Right before he gathers her in his arms, holds her tight as he pumps into her below. Taking back his power.

But soon they're both too far gone to care who's in charge. Who's dominating who. Who's controlling what. And the kiss, when it comes, feels like it's both their ideas.

"You're killing me, sweetness," he says. "Killing me..."

Mason's dick jerks, sending another warm flood through her. This is the first time he's come before her. It's her fault, she knows, because she practically molested him when he was least expecting it.

But it doesn't matter. Knowing she's undone him, stripped him of his control...it does something to her. Soon she's coming, too. Joining him in this weird new relationship they seem to be forging (and figuring out) together.

24

JUNE

*S*omething totally strange happens over the course of the next month. Something June never expected could happen. Not to her. Not in this lifetime.

Things start going *even better* than planned.

In October, she takes her GED test and finds out within three hours that she passed. They celebrate with a big camping trip—Mason's suggestion. Obviously. But as it turns out, sleeping outdoors in the back of a truck isn't nearly as bad as June thought it would be. Especially when she has huge Mason on one side, and the boy she loves more than life itself on the other, both keeping her warm as she drifts off to sleep.

Only to be gently shaken awake a few hours later.

It's Mason, standing outside the truck, and pressing a huge finger to his lips.

"C'mon," he whispers. "I wanna show you something. Don't wake the kid."

He gives her these commands, even as he reaches down and lifts her over the side of the truck as if she doesn't weigh a thing. As if whatever they're doing has already been decided.

They walk hand in hand through the woods, Mason seeming to know on instinct where he's going in the darkness. But then suddenly, it's not so dark. They emerge from the trees to a lake blanketed by a million, billion stars. A large reddish moon all but sits on top of the calm water, turning the blue black night an eerie purple.

"They call that a blood moon back in Tennessee," Mason explains behind her. "Rumor has it if you get scratched or bit by a wolf during a blood moon, you'll turn into a werewolf."

Of course, right then some night critter chooses that moment to rustle in the nearby brush. June jumps like a teenager in a horror movie.

"Don't worry, June. I got you," Mason says, wrapping his arms around her from behind.

She relaxes. He has her. With him, she's safe.

Are you falling in love? the ravens, who've now taken up permanent residence inside her, ask.

The question feels like way too much to ponder during a midnight field trip.

"Maybe we should get Jordan," she says. "He loves spooky stories and I'd hate for him to miss this—"

Mason puts an end to that notion with a kiss.

And soon after, June discovers how it feels to make love in a billion-star hotel, with nothing but a leather jacket beneath her, and Mason above her, framed by a blood red moon.

Pretty damn good. That's how it feels.

IN NOVEMBER, June discovers Jordan is doing well in school. According to his teacher, October brought a sea change to the quality of his schoolwork.

"Please let me know what you've been doing for him at home," the teacher says during the first parent-teacher conference June's ever dared go to. "I'm always looking for good ideas to share with other parents."

Mrs. Winder is round and kind and dressed in a long skirt paired with a hand-crocheted sweater vest. She's only one missed hair color appointment away from looking exactly like Mrs. Claus. So June isn't sure how to explain the magic Mason has brought to Jordan's world. How renovating the barn, and helping Mason restore a rusty old motorcycle they brought home like a stray dog, has improved the boy's ability to focus way more than his ongoing obsession with soccer ever has.

So June just answers the teacher's question with a shrug and a sheepish smile.

In any case, Mrs. Winder is ecstatic about his progress, even if it can't quite be explained by the extremely quiet woman she believes to be Jordan's young mother. "I'm going to put him on a more advance curriculum for the winter semester. And if this keeps up, and if he's willing to go to summer school, I'm pretty sure we can advance him to fifth grade next year."

"But what about Soccer camp?" Jordan whines when June returns home to share the good news. "You promised I could go!"

"C'mon, kid. Let's go out to the barn and work on our bike while June gets dinner done." Mason verbally heads Jordan off at the pass, as he often does when the boy tries to bully June into complying with his wishes. Then he gently herds Jordan out the door by blocking his view of June and moving resolutely forward until the boy is all but forced to leave the kitchen completely.

June watches them from the kitchen window. Although they both have their backs to her, she can see Mason doing most of the talking while Jordan either shakes his head or nods.

Later, when they finally return for dinner, Jordan says, "All right, I'll go to summer school."

"What did he say to you?" she asks him afterwards, when it's just the two of them washing up at the sink while Mason uses the bathroom.

He shrugs. "That it's the least I can do since it's important to you, and other than him, there's nobody else on this earth who really gives two shits about me."

She winces. "He said that?"

Another shrug. "Yeah. But it's true. You two are the only family I got."

Family...

June opens her mouth to deny it. Mason's past is always a factor that keeps her absolute trust in him out of reach. Jordan doesn't know about all the bad history between black and white the way she does. He's far too young, his friends far too open-minded. Plus, he watches way too much *Power Rangers* to know how skin color can make or break a person, depending on where they're from.

And as for them being a family...June wants to warn Jordan not to get too close, because in her experience, family has a way of dissolving right before your eyes. That's why she's never put a label on what Jordan is to her.

But then June closes her mouth. Truth is, that's *her* experience. Not Jordan's. Fact is—and here's what really makes her brain stutter—Mason has never let the boy down. Never raised a hand or his voice to him—even if he does need to work on all that cursing.

And try as she might to deny it...she can kind of see the three of them the way Jordan does.

A family. They may not necessarily look like one. But some-how, that's what they've become in the months since Mason moved in.

The next day, June nearly clears out the lifestyle magazine

section of Cal-Mart to find recipes for the perfect Thanksgiving dinner.

She spends the following week putting together a menu, then quietly spends just about all of Thanksgiving morning and afternoon preparing it while Mason and Jordan watch European soccer games via satellite. Or as Mason puts it as they sit down at the kitchen table, "Wasted damn near the whole day watching FC Barcelona fucking shit the bed against them Frenchies. But that's okay," he assures Jordan. "You know Roma won't let us down."

After subsisting on little more than corn chips, dip, beer (in Mason's case), and juice all day, the two barely give June's gorgeous dinner an appreciative glance before falling on top of it like hungry animals.

But later, when there's barely anything left but bones and a few sad dregs of cranberry sauce, Jordan declares it the best Thanksgiving dinner he's ever had, and Mason calls it a "damn sight better than fucking tofurkey."

"Mason, you need to work on not cussing around me so much," Jordan tells him with a frank shake of his small head. "I'm only a kid. I don't need to be hearing all that."

"Fuck you," Mason answers. "Eat your pie."

It's definitely not the most heartwarming scene many might witness that Thanksgiving, but June has to turn her head away to keep from crying.

Jordan's words, *"I'm only a kid..."*

Less than a year ago, he never would have said that, never would have even tried to defend his childhood status. His life has been so very hard...and his obvious contentment with his new life makes all her effort preparing dinner completely worth it.

Well, that and the "thank you, June" tongue down Mason gives her later that night. It goes on so long, and so relentlessly, she has to scream into her pillow when the orgasm overtakes her so as not to wake Jordan.

And even then, he's still licking at her folds, his strong shoulders pushing into the backs of her thighs as his tongue laps up her cream, punishing her clit until she feels her stomach clench with renewed electricity. That's the only warning she gets before a second orgasm wipes her out.

"I know you don't want me to ever just lie here while you're on top of me," she pants up at him. "But I don't think I got it in me to do anything else after that."

It's not a complaint, more like a joke than anything else. Because they both know June will rally. Tap into an extra energy reserve if it means doing by Mason as good as he's done by her.

But he doesn't laugh. "'S okay," he mumbles, coming up to drop down beside her. "Let's skip me tonight."

Now it's June's turn to go still. "Mason...what's wrong."

"Nothin'."

"Mason..."

"I said I'm fine," he snaps.

That makes her sit up, because there are two things Mason hasn't done yet in all the time they've been going at it: miss his turn, and snap at her for no reason.

"Mason. Tell me, what's going on?" she demands, her ravens flapping in alarm.

"Nothing," he insists, slinging a meaty forearm over his eyes.

"Mason..." she tries again. "You're scaring me. What's wrong?"

"Nothin'," he repeats—but then maybe realizing she's not going to let it go, he admits, "I want to open the doors. And all the windows." He lets out a shuddering breath. "Really, really bad."

He wants to open the windows...

At first she feels insulted. He doesn't want to have sex with her because she's no longer willing to live with him in a freezing cold house? But then she takes a breath and does what she's been trying to do a lot more of lately: give him some credit.

Instead of assuming the worst, June thinks about how Mason hasn't once complained about the windows and doors since that dinner back in October. In fact, this is the first time it's come up. She also can't help but notice how his usually obscene cock droops disinterested and fallow between his legs. Hmmm...

"Did something...?" she stops, searching for the right word. "Did something trigger you?"

"Yeah, I guess you could say that," he answers from beneath his arm.

June's not the talking type. Everyone knows it. And Mason's mental state—it's not her business to pry into his private inner world. She wonders if she should drop it.

Nonetheless, she says, "You want to talk about it?"

"No," he answers. Blunt. Voice little more than a rough scrape across the air.

She settles back into the crook of his arm. Plays with the hairs on his chest. "What would you say if I said you have to talk about it?"

"That it's bullshit."

"No, actually it's not. Thing is, I'm not sleeping in a bed with someone who won't, um..." Again June has to search for the right word, this time going back nearly a decade to that other lifetime. "Communicate."

Now he goes still. The arm around her stiffening, like he's thinking of pulling away. "June, you ain't told me two things about you I could rub together into any kind of story, and you expect me to tell you all my stuff?"

She flinches. Mason's right. June knows she's not exactly the world's best communicator. Not even close. And she's lucky to have found someone who's okay with that. She should let it go. Just let it go…

Instead she says, "My life was perfect."

"What?" The sudden topic change seems to throw Mason for a loop.

"My life…before Razo. It was perfect. That's why I speak this way. Because I grew up in Bluebriar—a small suburb outside Little Rock. I had a mom and a dad. They were both teachers, him by choice—her because her art career didn't really work out. Mom "failed out of New York City"—that's what she used to say. But it worked out for her in the end because she met my dad when she moved back to Arkansas."

It hurts to talk about this, to talk about the fairytale before the nightmare. June is nearly struck dumb by the sadness and regret that pierces her heart as she talks about her parents for the first time in nearly ten years, but she continues. Determined to share her story, so Mason will open up with her.

"My mom used to joke that she only got with my corny dad because he had his own apartment and it was way better than living with her mom. Don't get me wrong, though. She loved him, and he really loved her, and then they had me. I know both of them wished I talked more, but other than that, we were the perfect family. No abuse. No nothing. I don't remember either of them even ever yelling at me. But then Dad died in a car accident. I was fifteen. He was only thirty-nine. Maybe he thought he had time to deal with stuff like life insurance. But the point is, he didn't have any. And the accident was his fault. So there was nothing for him to leave us. Maybe it wouldn't have been so bad, but the thing is…my mom…"

Here it comes. The bad part. June has to take a deep breath, but keeps going. "See, my mom didn't just fail out of New York City. She told me the whole story once when she was high on something that makes people talk a lot. Maybe cocaine? I don't know...anyway, she told me how she'd gone to New York and fell in with the wrong crowd. My grandma came all the way from Arkansas to get her. She put Mom on a bus with her and dragged her home. Scraped together enough money to put her in rehab. Mom was six months sober when she met my dad. She said it was perfect timing, because she'd been plotting her escape back to New York City when they met. Been thinking dangerous thoughts, like if she was going to go out, she might as well go out high. Serendipity...that word was one of my dad's favorites...but then he died. And by then, Grandma was gone, too. That's when I realized my mom wasn't the person I thought she was..."

June laughs bitterly. "I'm still trying to figure out who was the lie. The mother I had for fifteen years, or the woman who died in that abandoned house next to Jordan's mother? Either way, over the next two years I realized I was living with a ticking time bomb. A drug addict who only pretended to be my mother. But she was all I had until I met Jordan. So when my mom and Jordan's mom died, I turned to Razo because I had nowhere else to go, no one else to turn to. And, well, you know how that turned out. Almost seven years of my life, lost. I spent the two years before that following my drug addict mother around from score to score. And the fifteen years before that? Perfect."

She lets out a long breath. "You think Razo's the worst thing that ever happened to me. But I promise you, he's not. Those fifteen years before everything went to shit are the worst thing, and that's why I never, ever talk about the time before. Do you understand?"

"Yeah, I do," Mason says quietly, wrapping both his arms around her. "I ain't never had nothing good to miss. Can't imagine having it, then losing it like you did. I'm sorry that happened to you."

"Me, too," she admits for the first time since her mother's

death. She'd spent so long denying those fifteen years, so long trying to act like they never happened, that this is quite literally the first time in a long while June realizes how much she misses her childhood. Misses her parents. Misses the life she used to have.

They say nothing for a while. June's steeped in her sad memories, and it feels like Mason is giving her and her memories the quiet respect they deserve.

But eventually she asks, "*Now* will you tell me why you feel like opening windows? Did something happen that you haven't told me about?"

"Yeah, but you ain't going to like it, June. I'm not sure how to tell you."

Alarm bells sound inside her head. She thinks about his past. About all the gangs still out there now, spouting the same hateful ideals he once did.

"Thing is, I been falling in love with you for a while now, but that dinner you made for me and Jordan...well it sealed the deal. I didn't realize it 'til just now, but the falling part is over, sweetness. I'm fuckin' flat on my back in love with you. And that shit scares me worse than anything I ever faced before."

June shakes her head. Processes his words. Only to have her mind stutter to a complete halt. "*What*?"

"You heard me."

Yeah, she did hear him. But June still has no idea where this is coming from. "Just because I didn't make tofurkey?" she asks.

And he chuckles, like she's made a joke, even though she's dead serious.

"Yeah, just because of that, sweetness. And just because you put wings with a drive chain on my back. And just because you loved and protected and brought up as right you could, a kid that could have been me. But mostly because I was better from the day I met you. You make me better. You make me wanna be a better man. Also, you're hot as fuck, and you make my dick harder than steel. But other than that, no, there ain't no reason for me to be this fucking in love with you."

"Mason, no...no..."

Strangely, this—not her recounting of what happened before they met—is what breaks her, makes tears pool in her eyes.

"Oh fuck, June. Are you crying cuz I love you?"

Mason switches on the bedside lamp, then curses some more when he sees her crumpled face. "Sweetness, don't cry, oh fuck, please don't cry."

She shakes her head...because... "How can you feel this way about me? I'm so...I'm so..." she can barely choke the word out, "unclean."

He looks down at her, head cocked to the side. "You are confusing the shit out of me right now. You think you're the one who doesn't deserve my love? That you're the dirty one in this relationship? June, I *bought* you while I was wearing White Pride patches on my back. I got so much blood on my hands, I'm surprised they ain't stained red. No, don't shake your head. Look at me. *Look* at me."

It's not like she has much of a choice. He chases her eyes until she gives in. Same ol' Mason. Same ol' June. But now everything is completely different.

"It's okay," he tells her. "Me loving you—it's okay."

But it's not. "You think you're in love with me, and that makes you want to open all the windows and doors. So you can what? Leave? Leave us, even after..."

She stops, finding out the hard way that she's not nearly as brave as she thought. She can't bring herself to say "I" and instead says, "After *Jordan's* gotten so used to you."

Mason shakes his head. "Like I said, this shit is scary for me, too. Makes it hard to breathe. Makes me feel a little—I don't know. Like I got to get out of here, before you hurt me worse than my father ever could. But that's just a feeling, June. It's not truth. I ain't opening no windows, and I ain't going nowhere you ain't. I need you to trust me on this. No matter how bad the feeling gets, I ain't leaving either of you. In fact, you want out this hillbilly love, you gotta leave me. Which you can't, on account of you belonging to me. So that's settled."

Now it's her turn to shake her head. Because she doesn't understand how this could have happened. Why it happened. She doesn't have a clue how to respond.

"I love you," he says in answer to all her unspoken questions, his voice little more than a ragged whisper. "But June, that don't mean you got to love me back. You asked what was bothering me. I told you. That's it. You know what? I don't even want you to love me back. Not until I earn it. So for now..."

He dips his head, bringing his forehead to rest on top of hers. "Let me love you. Can you do that, June? Just let me love you...?"

To sum it up, Mason is a former white supremacist biker— let's call him "retired." And June—well, she's a black woman he bought off a Hispanic drug dealer. There is no reason in the world they should be having this conversation. No reason, save ownership, they'd ever breathe the same air, much less share the same bed.

Yet June closes the distance between her mouth and his, greedily devouring Mason's lips as she pulls his big body over hers. She wants him again. Is crazed with the need to feel him between her legs. To know he's real. That she's not on the verge of starving to death in the Cul while her mind hallucinates some weird, twisted, pre-death fantasy.

But it's not a dream.

She knows this when he raises above her and pushes all the

way in, his thick cock stretching her beyond comprehension. But there's no pain. No pain at all.

"Mason..." she gasps.

He starts moving. Gives her what she needs, what she wants...first in slow and steady strokes, then faster, sloppier, all while grunting, "Fucking come, June. Fucking come before I spill this load in your sweet pussy."

His crass words galvanize her body, and she cries out when the orgasm rips through her. True to his threat, Mason comes soon after with a sharp groan, his body going rigid on top of hers as he spills his load right where he said he would.

They don't talk about it anymore after that. The fucking is too good. It takes away all their words. Mason flicks off the light again, and they settle on separate sides of the bed in silent but mutual agreement. He won't open any doors or windows tonight, and she won't try to talk him out of the crazy thing—the many crazy things—he just told her.

But still, June has to wonder if he's asking himself in the dark what she's asking herself in the dark.

Where do we go from here?

25

JUNE

*T*he answer to that question comes in December, a little over a week later. On a bright but cold Friday morning.

"Where's Mason?" Jordan asks when June walks into the kitchen.

He's already up and eating a bowl of cereal at the table, while finishing the homework that's not due until the following Monday. This is a common sight these days, since Mason won't let him work on the bike after school until all his homework is done. Better to get it done and out of the way so he can do what he wants when he gets home.

"I don't know," she answers, padding over to the coffee machine. "He was already gone when I woke up."

Jordan eyes her jeans and sweater combo. "You don't have work today?"

"Nope," she answers. "Figured I'd bike into town."

"To do some Christmas shopping?" Jordan turns all the way around in his seat and fixes his eyes on her. "Maybe for a new video game system?"

"Nope," she answers.

His face falls in such a dramatic fashion that she almost tells him the truth. She and Mason already picked out a gaming system for him earlier that week. It's wrapped and waiting for him on the top shelf of their closet.

But that would spoil the surprise, so in order not to give into temptation, she says, "Jordan, hurry and finish your cereal. If Mason's not here soon, you and I will need to walk to the—."

The rest of her sentence is drowned out by the sound of a loud motorcycle roaring outside the house.

"Mason!" Jordan yells, jumping up from the table. He dashes from the kitchen before she can nag him to please finish his breakfast first.

June understands why as soon as she steps out onto the front porch. Mason is in the driveway, his denim clad legs on either side of a now gleaming bike that only bears a passing resemblance to the rusted mess he and Jordan brought home a couple of months ago.

"It works!" Jordan yells, running up to him.

"Course it does," Mason answers, pulling his half helmet off. "What'd you think we were doing? Fixing it up for shits and giggles? Purrs like kitten got into the heroin stash now. Seller I found online is gonna be happy when I deliver this baby."

Jordan's face falls. "You...you already sold it?"

"Yeah, kid," he answers. A bit callously, June thinks, until he adds, "Barn's only so big. And we got to make way for another fixer upper. I got a Harley FXRT I'm pickin' up in Bella Vista tomorrow. Real POS. It's going take at least four months to turn that pig into a purse."

Jordan's face lights right back up. "I can't wait!" he says excitedly.

"Me either," Mason replies. "But in the meantime..."

He produces a much smaller helmet from out of nowhere. "Want a ride to school?"

"Uh, yeah!! Hold on, lemme go get my jacket and shit."

"Jordan...!" June says, though she knows she shouldn't be surprised considering how much time he's been spending with Mason.

"Sorry!" he calls out as he darts back in the house.

She looks at Mason, her lips pressed in a thin line. Mason responds with an innocent look that might go a lot further if he weren't also smirking.

"You alright?" he asks. "Sleep okay?"

He knows the answer to both questions, since he's the one who sexed her so good last night, she fell asleep immediately afterwards, like a milk-drunk baby.

"I slept fine," she answers, fighting hard to keep a smile from breaking through.

"You going somewhere?" he asks, eyeing her jeans and carefully chosen graphic tee. On non-workdays, she usually hangs out in her pajamas until after Jordan leaves for school. Today, however, she's wearing regular clothes before nine am.

"I was thinking of biking into town," she replies. "See if that tattoo place might want to take me on as an apprentice."

He grins. "Good idea, but maybe hold off on leaving for a little bit. Got something I need to talk to you about."

Frowning, she nods, wondering what it can possibly be.

WHEN MASON RETURNS, he finds her in the living room pretending to watch the *Today Show* when really, she's desperate to know what he wants to talk about.

"Ah...yeah, we should probably do this in the kitchen."

June turns off the TV and follows him. Watches nervously while he fills a cup of coffee.

"You want some?"

"No, I've already had two." Wow, an answer *and* a reason why.

She wonders if she'll ever get used to how easy it is to talk to him.

Of course right now, her newfound chattiness is definitely in jeopardy because her ravens are spinning with a nervous energy that makes her want to throw up.

Mason walks over to the table. Hesitates. Hesitates some more. Then sits down with his coffee. "So…"

He runs a hand over the back of his neck. More awkward than she's ever seen him. This really isn't helping calm the ravens.

Finally he asks, "You given any more thought to your Christmas plans?"

June shakes her head no, not really understanding what that has to do with his odd behavior. "Uh, no, not really. Well, I have been thinking I need to start looking up recipes for Christmas dinner."

"Thing is…D's been riding me hard to come visit him for Christmas. I don't think I can put him off much longer. But… well, if you want—" he stops, clears his throat, continues. "If you want, you can come with me to Seattle. You and Jordan. I thought it might be nice for you to meet my family. And, you know, have them meet you."

He's not saying the words. Hasn't said them since Thanksgiving night. But they hang between them right now.

"Me and Jordan," she repeats. Then with a tilt of her head she asks, "Is this the same cousin that killed your gang?"

"Our board. But yeah. Same one," Mason admits with a wince. "But I swear he's not like that anymore, June. He's living with a doctor. And they got a baby on the way. When he called to harass me yesterday, he told me he's starting med school come January. So, you know, he's had one hell of a makeover. Also, they got other folks coming. His old lady's family, her best friend, and her husband. He's Russian, huge as fuck, but basically good people if he's not mafia, which I'm still not 100% sure he ain't."

Mason grimaces again. "Okay...now that I'm saying all this out loud, I can totally understand if you and the kid don't want to go. Plus it's colder than a witch's titties up there this time of year."

"Do you want us to go?" she asks, honestly confused.

"Well, yeah."

"Then we'll go," June replies, wondering why this is even a discussion.

Mason smiles, but then it dies on his face.

"What's wrong?" she asks.

He looks away, jaw working back and forth, before he looks back at her and asks, "You saying you'll go because you want to, or because you belong to me?"

For the second time today, June can only give him a look of true confusion. "Does it matter?"

He looks back at her for a long, sad time before rapping his knuckles on the table. "Guess not," he concedes, rising to a stand.

But then he stops. Sits back down. "You do belong to me."

"Yes, I know," she answers. "And I said we'll go to Seattle with you."

"Yeah. But thing is, I want you to want to go places with me. I'm sick of always wondering in the back of my mind if all this," he gestures between the two of them, "if all this is because I bought you, or if you're here because you want to be."

"Mason, I want to be here," she says. "This house is nice. Nicer even than the one I grew up in when I was a kid."

When I was a kid. So many firsts. Not only is she referencing her childhood, she's also not referring to it as "that other lifetime." Like it was a thing that happened in another space-time dimension.

She's saying it now so Mason really understands where she's coming from. Understands how much she loves having a roof over her head, and that she'd never do anything to jeopardize that.

"Me, too, but..." He gives his head a rough shake. "I can't do this anymore. We can't go on living like this."

"You—you want to move out?" June asks, her heart sinking. "But Jordan..."

"Fuck Jordan," Mason bites out. But then stops himself. "I'm sorry, sweetness, that didn't come out the way I wanted it to. I'm real close to that kid, and I know he looks up to me like a big brother or something. I don't understand why, but he does."

He shifts, his leather jacket creaking as he leans forward, places his large forearms on the table. "But every time I try to talk to you about all of this, about how you feel, you make it about Jordan. What I'm asking you...what I really want to know is would you be here if Jordan wasn't a factor? If it was just you and me?"

June looks at him, not sure how to answer, since she wouldn't be here at all if he hadn't bought her off of Razo in the first place.

But for Mason, her silence is answer enough.

"Yeah, that's what I thought," he says. He doesn't cuss this time, but somehow it still sounds like he is.

"Okay, okay..." he says. "I gotta do this. C'mon, Mason. You got to have some faith in something. Gotta have some trust."

He's talking to himself, she realizes, which alarms her big time, because that's the one crazy thing she hasn't seen him do yet.

"Mason...?" she starts to ask.

But then he blurts out, "You're free! Okay. There you go. June, you are free. You don't belong to me no more. I'm done forcing you to be where I want you to be."

Everything inside her, including the ravens, freeze.

Because freedom…it's not something she's ever had before. For her entire adult life (and most of her adolescence) June has been chained to someone or other, whether it be to her mother by guilt, to Razo by force, or to Mason by purchase…

Mason folds his huge hands on the table and stares down at them as he mumbles, "I told you I'd prove myself worthy of your love, but I can't ever do that if ownership is involved. Hell, you ain't a slave, June. That asshole Razo had no business handing you over to me like livestock in the first damn place. I had no business buying you either. So…there you go. You're free. And you know what? You can take my truck."

Say what? "Wait, no! I can't do that!"

"I'm telling you, you can." Mason fishes around in his inner jacket pocket, then drops a heavy key on the table between them. "Automatics are for panties anyway. I'm going to get myself a real truck, so that one's yours if you want it."

"No, Mason, I can't," she insists.

"You can, June. I'm telling you, I don't want it. It's all paid for since I don't like owing anyone shit. So, uh, Merry Christmas."

"No, Mason, I seriously can't—"

He slams his large hand on the table so hard, June is afraid he might break it. "Goddammit, June! Will you just let me do this for you?"

His question reverberates through the kitchen, echoing in her mind, long after the sound disappears.

Which makes it that much harder for her to explain, "Mason, I can't because I don't know how to drive."

Mason blinks, his face suddenly releasing its intense frown. "Oh. Oh! Well, that ain't a problem. I'll teach you."

AND HE DOES.

The back country roads are perfect for driving lessons. Paved and straight with plenty of room to make mistakes, and hardly any traffic around. June is pretty sure Mason must've seen some things in his day, because he barely flinches the few times she slams hard on the brakes, or the one time she nearly runs them off the road and into a tree.

"Just a few more lessons, and you're going to be more than ready to take your driving test," he tells her when they roll to a stop in front of the house a few hours later.

June nods, looking away.

Mason sighs. "June, there's quiet, and there's not saying anything on purpose. Guess which one I think you're doing right now?"

"It's just...well, you've already done so much for us...for me..."

"Yes, and I'm willing to do a lot more, so out with it."

"Well, this car is a beast. Huge and crazy powerful. Like you. I mean, it's probably perfect for a guy like you, but for someone like me..."

Understanding dawns on his face. "Oh...I see. It's too big for you."

She nods with a grimace. "I think I'd always be worried about running over something, or someone. And I'm pretty sure I'm supposed to be able to see over the dash more than just a little."

Mason chuckles. "Relax, June. We can trade this in. Get one of them Minis or Fiats. Something cute and chubby. Like you."

June chuckles, guessing she deserves that. But... "If I stay, will you stop calling me chubby?"

He thinks about it, then answers, "Nope."

She has to laugh, even as she points out, "But I don't like it!"

He shrugs. "I do." He looks over at her with a new intensity in his blue eyes. "And don't tease me about what we were discussing earlier, June. I'm going to go trade this truck in, give you time to think things over, and when I get back, I expect an answer."

The ravens beat inside her stomach, sending her brain messages she has no idea how to interpret let alone relay back to Mason.

"Just think on it," he says, holding her eyes with his. "And try to have an answer for me when I get back. If it's "fuck you, Mason. Go away," I get it. I do. But if it's something else, then yeah, the three of us are going to Seattle for Christmas. And we're going to make each other some promises, promises a lot more binding than the kind that come from a motorcycle and gun exchange. Us Fairgoods ain't made to stay boyfriends for long—"

Mason must sense the ravens are going crazy in June's stomach, choking her. Her inability to respond must be written clearly across her face, because he stops himself right there.

Looks away, directs his blue gaze towards his knees, and says, "I know I'm a fuckin' mess, June. I ain't nobody's prize. But I got some money stashed away and ain't never trying to hurt you like he did. I fucking love you with all my heart, and if you'll have me...if you'll have me, I swear I won't ever give you a reason to regret it."

He himself there, clears his throat. "Now, the kid's going to be here any minute. Get out my truck so I can trade it in for something cute and chubby. Them dealerships take forever."

With a soft smile, June does as he asks. And with her heart hovering right above her ravens, she watches Mason switch over to the driver's seat. Then drive away.

June already knows her answer, the one she's going to give Mason when he returns. She's only surprised he doesn't know it, too.

26

MASON

*H*e loves June. He must, because it takes forever and a fucking eternity to trade in the truck. He has to wonder how folks who actually have to apply for financing get through this shit without punching every last car salesmen in their big-toothed faces.

He ends up with a red Mini Countryman. Cute and chubby, with room for something cute and chubby in the back. He can't say why he's even thinking those thoughts. He knows about June's situation. Knows what the doctor told her.

But still...Mason can't keep himself from wanting to start something with her. Wanting to take what they've found, make it official, and expand it more. Even though six months ago he was convinced bringing her into his life was the stupidest decision he'd ever made.

He thinks back to the drive he took up the left coast with his cousin's old lady, what he said to her, *"You grow up all your life being told you can't have a thing, it's going to make you wonder."*

Back then, he'd been confused. About the black girl he'd bought and left behind. But now things are crystal clear. He feels surer than he's ever been about anything in his entire life.

He loves June in a way that goes way past skin color. And he wants to spend the rest of his life with her and a couple more babies—adopting them if that's what they need to do.

Mason doesn't care how he was brought up. His father and damn near the entire board are dead, so he doesn't have to listen to them whispering in his ear, confusing him with a life view that doesn't make any goddamn sense anyway.

No, he hasn't felt this at peace in long time. Hadn't even known such a thing was possible—

Mason skids to a stop, right there in the middle of the road. It's the house.

It's dark as a grave. There isn't a single light on, inside or out. He has a bad feeling.

No...fuck, no...please...

Mason prays to a God he isn't sure he believes in as he jumps out of the little car, leaving it idling right there in the middle of the road. Not giving a fuck what June said, he leaves the door wide open behind him when he enters the house, flipping on switches in every room, searching, searching...

The living room. Nothing. The kid's bedroom. Nobody. Their bedroom—his mind chokes on "their"—is empty, too.

Maybe they're not home yet. June mentioned going into town to look into that tattoo apprenticeship. But he'd distracted her with all that love and Seattle talk, and then there were the driving lessons. As he makes his way into the kitchen, he constructs a hopeful story in his mind. Pictures June and Jordan walking down the streets of town after checking in at the tattoo shop. Looking for a present for Mason, maybe, and deciding on a whim to eat dinner at a nearby restaurant instead of at home. Of course, that's never happened before. Like ever. June, for all he loves her, is cheap as fuck, and typically refuses to buy a meal she can prepare at home. But there's always a first time...right?

Why didn't she call you, or text, or fucking let you know where she is?

Mason ignores the voice. Has to ignore it as he flips on the light in the kitchen.

No June. No Jordan.

And then...then all hope dies when he sees a piece of June's sketch paper on the table, and what's written on it: *I'm sorry. I can't be yours and you can't be mine. It wasn't in the stars for us.*

June is gone.

He curses at himself. For giving June her freedom when he wanted to keep her with him forever. For pushing her to commit, when he knew how scared she might be.

Mason really thought they reached a new level. That after what they told each other, done for each other...they were strong enough to handle the real shit. Like love. And babies. And a future together.

He was wrong. Instead of staying, she's run, taking the kid he'd been making plans to adopt right along with her.

Mason refused to settle for nothing less than everything with June. And now...

His breath catches as a heart-attack level eruption of pain, regret, and sorrow bursts inside his chest.

Now he's lost it all.

27

JUNE

*J*une is in hell. Enslaved again. Only this time, she's literally in chains. From the rank smell of them, they're the same ones Razo used on his dog. The dog he shot a few months back for daring to bite him.

"June," a small voice whispers in the dark room.

It's Jordan. *No. Don't be here.*

She opens her mouth to say exactly that. But all she manages is a croak. She hasn't had anything to eat or drink since the morning Mason asked her to come to Seattle, and her voice is rusty. Too rusty to talk, or protest when a cup of water is lifted to her mouth.

Tap water. She can taste the minerals after having spent the last several months using a Brita. But it's cold and wet, and that's all that matters right now. It feels good against her swollen lips, busted open by Razo's fist when he brought her through the door of their old house. A few more punches and kicks followed. But he didn't let himself get too carried away this time.

"Nah, *puta*, I got something way better planned for you," he said, before chaining her to the chair.

The first beating did its job well enough. Even the act of swallowing is painful. And June's bruised ribs only let her get in a few sips before she has to stop.

"Drink more," Jordan whispers to her in the dark. "You have to hold on until Mason gets here."

June doesn't have the heart to tell him Mason's not coming.

She thinks of the last time she saw their home. The beautiful home they'd made for the three of them. She was seated at the kitchen table, with Razo and his gun hovering menacingly.

See Razo, not Jordan, was waiting for her when she got to the bus stop. Without a word, he'd jerked his head at her to follow him.

And she had, because June already knew the leverage he had over her. Even before they reached the Suburban, parked on the side of the road, just past screaming distance of the bus stop. She saw two Hijos in the back seat, their guns trained on Jordan.

Razo opened the front passenger door, and without a word, June climbed in. She was surprised when they stopped in front of the house. Then scared when Razo ordered her to follow him inside. She thought for sure he was setting up an ambush for Mason.

But then he grabbed her sketch pad off the kitchen counter, and threw it down on the table. "Write him a note. Say you leaving. I don't want to have to deal with that fucker again after this."

When she hesitated, he raised his phone in one hand and said, "Don't make me send this text. I don't care if that weak-ass bitch is my blood, I will not hesitate to have him offed if you don't cooperate."

She knew he wasn't bluffing.

The Hijos in the back seat with Jordan were not the same who'd been there with Razo at Cal-Mart. June felt certain those men were dead. Likely the recipients of surprise bullets before they even made it back to the Cul. After all, dead men can tell no tales about Razo getting dissed by the white supremacist biker he sold June to.

And the only interest Razo ever had in Jordan, after he proved to be a less than ideal runner, was as a tool he could use to get to June.

June picked up her Sharpie. Kept the note short. Hoping it might hurt Mason less that way. But knowing it wouldn't.

And now she was here. Chained to a chair in a cold room, awaiting Razo's next move, and hating that Jordan was risking his life to get her some water.

June knows she has to talk. For Jordan.

"Jordan," she croaks. "Don't worry about me. Get out of here...escape. Find Mason. He'll take care of you."

"He'll take care of *us*. I'm not leaving you, June. And he's going to come get us. I promise."

"Jordan, please..." she tries again.

But the time for talking is over. Lights blaze on overhead, blinding her after spending so long in the dark. She hears words spoken in angry Spanish. Then there's a slosh of water down the front of her shirt.

Jordan's speaking in Spanish now, too. Begging on her behalf.

"No, Jordan. Don't!" she croaks.

But it's too late. Her eyes adjust enough for her to see Razo backhand the little boy to the ground. He stands over Jordan's crumpled body, spitting more angry Spanish at him.

"Fuck you, Razo!" she yells. Not out of any real sense of rebellion, but because she needs to draw his attention away from Jordan before Razo really hurts him.

Razo whips his head around, eyes flashing with an angry, crazed light. "Fuck me?" he repeats in mocking English. "Don't think so, *puta*. You about to find out who's going to be fucked. Really find out. Do it!"

That's all the warning she gets before her chair is lifted by the two Hijos who'd held Jordan in the backseat of the Suburban. Waves of pain radiate over her body as she's carried down a hallway, through the empty living room, and outside to the cul-de-sac.

It's complete mayhem.

There's a huge bonfire burning in the middle of the main circle, making it way warmer outside than it should be. The massive pile of wood and flames are circled by a mass of trucks, motorcycles, and cars, all blasting the same Reggaeton station at top volume.

Fueling the fire are things June immediately recognizes. The small amount of cheap furniture from the house she shared with Jordan. She sees a few girls, dressed in Hijo colors, throw the clothes she left behind into the flames. The cheap polyester fabric sparking the fire blue in some places.

June peers around, trying hard to orient herself despite the pain, heat, and loud music.

The entire gang is literally here. At least thirty Hijos stand around, watching her arrival with sick fascination. A few are even massaging their dicks through their beige work pants.

She knows what this is. Even before Razo steps up onto the bed of one of the trucks to give his speech, she knows. He's speaking in Spanish, but lucky for her, there's a helpful translation in the form of two Hijos dropping a mattress into the middle of the street. There's no way June can pretend not to know what's about to happen.

After all, she's seen this go down before. Only once, but it's not the kind of thing you forget, even if you run and hide in a house with the boy you've sworn to raise and protect before it all goes down.

It's a ritual of sorts. Usually reserved for women who either turn snitch or dump their Hijo boyfriends for someone outside the gang. See, Hijos never get exed or snitched out to the police. Instead they hand their girls over and let all their boys have a turn. Then throw the body on the fire when they're finished with it.

On the other side of the bonfire, June sees Jordan. Watching, listening, fear and horror carved into his little face. Strangely, all she can think about in these moments is him. How this moment might be the very distraction he needs to escape.

"Run!" she mouths over the cheering, jeering crowd. *"Go now, Jordan!"* she silently begs, because she's almost certain he won't get another chance.

Jordan only stands there, rooted to the spot. He doesn't run, and as far as she can tell, he might not be breathing either.

June starts to cry.

Not because she's afraid for herself, but because she's afraid for the boy. She wants him to grow up safe and happy. To start a family. Live a normal life away from all this horror.

June knows if Jordan stays to watch, even if he miraculously escapes, he will never really leave. Seeing this go down will break him, break his spirit. No matter where he ends up physically, he will forever be trapped here in the Cul in his mind.

But that's not the only reason she's crying.

She never told Mason how she really feels about him. That she loves him. Instead, she wasted all her time and his judging him, holding him accountable for his past, refusing to trust him, trust in them, even when he handed her his heart on a truck-sized platter. And now he will never know.

"I love you. I love you, Mason Fairgood," June whispers into the fire. Hoping he can somehow hear her. "I love you, and I'm sorry I didn't tell you that before."

She chants the words over and over again, drowning out the

mayhem in the background, the pain, the fear, as hands—so many groping hands—reach out to unchain her. But only so they can use her and throw her away like so much trash.

MASON

*M*ason is in hell.

Funny, how he used to think he was already there when he lived under his old man's roof. Under the constant tyranny of his father's fists. Now he knows that was nothing compared to this. Seeing the love of his life taken out of a house, chained to a chair, head flopping listlessly as if she's barely conscious. Listening to Razo make his big announcement about his plans for her. Watching her weep quietly in the firelight.

Mason will never, ever forgive himself. Never forgive himself for thinking, even for a second, that the note on the kitchen table was anything other than total and complete bullshit.

Luckily, he'd found out soon after reading her message that he was full of fucking shit. He'd granted June her freedom, but no way in hell was he prepared to let her go.

After the note, Mason immediately turned on the tracking app, the one he'd added to her phone and hidden in a folder without her permission. He'd feel bad about this later. But for now...

When Mason saw the red dot pop up at a location roughly

30 miles away, he immediately knew where he'd find her. In the Cul. And he was beside himself with fury and fear. See, Mason grew up with a woman who, time and time again, chose to stay with the man who beat her. She did this because his father was familiar, and sometimes the devil you know might seem to be the best option available. But she also stayed because no matter how bad his father hurt her, he always had the drugs Mason's mom needed to make it better. June, however, was most definitely not cut from the same cloth as his mother. He knew she hadn't gone back to the Cul of her own accord.

She'd been taken.

Less than thirty seconds later, he was on the phone with the Russian who'd cleaned up the mess in Los Angeles and made sure it stayed that way.

Funny how Mason always thought his biggest threat would be from other white supremacists who'd want to make an example of him. That's why he'd been hiding here in Arkansas. Staying under the radar, where no one who knew him would ever think to look.

But in the end, it wasn't nationalists or Neo-Nazis who were his biggest threat, but June's cocksucking ex. The one he'd wanted to put down like a rabid dog from the get-go.

And now here he is, hiding beneath a parked truck, watching that fucktard spout off in Spanish about mythical shit that isn't ever going to happen on the other side of the bonfire.

The kid's getting antsy.

Jordan spotted Mason tucked under the truck almost immediately, after stumbling out of the old house he'd once shared with June. Almost as if he'd been looking for him. But to Mason's relief, Jordan was careful not to give away Mason's position. He simply came to stand right in front of Mason's position, as if he were trying to get as far as possible from the sight on the other side of the giant flames, and hide Mason from view at the same time.

This shit is hard to watch, he knows. And Jordan is only a kid. Mason gets more worried as the boy starts bouncing from foot to foot, clearly fixing to do something—anything—that will most likely result in him getting hurt or killed.

He catches the kid around one thin ankle and gives it a squeeze. "Don't do it, kid," he growls from his hiding place beneath the truck, though given all noise and chaos, he's sure Jordan can't hear him.

It works though. Jordan stops bouncing. But Mason still feels him vibrating with the need to act.

Mason looks across the way, past the raging fire, to where June sits. He thinks she might be praying. No, not praying. Even above the music and on the other side of a fire, he can still hear her thoughts, as if she's whispering the words directly into his ear. "*I love you, I love you, Mason Fairgood.*"

"I love you, too, sweetness," he whispers back, so quiet only her subconscious mind will hear him.

Mason's watch dings, and a message appears on the wrist of the hand laced around Jordan's ankle. "***Just landed. ETA 30 min.***" It's from the Russian, the one who has arranged for several of his cousin's personal guards to fly in from Texas.

But June doesn't have thirty minutes.

The Hijos are already at her chair, removing the chains. One rips open her shirt, grabs a breast, and twists hard, making her cry out.

Fuck this. Fuck this all the way to hell.

Mason will be goddamned if he lets another one of those fuckers touch his woman. He releases Jordan's ankle, and scrambles out from under the truck. Bends close to Jordan's ear and shouts, "As soon as I go in, you take June and run like hell!"

He waits a nanosecond to be sure Jordan has heard him. At

the kid's nod, Mason runs like a bat out of hell toward those motherfuckers who dared touch June. He doesn't give two shits if it's thirty versus him. If his life ends up being the price he pays to buy enough time to save June and Jordan, so be it. Because if he didn't realize it before, he definitely knows it now.

His life ain't worth shit if those two ain't in it.

29

JUNE

One moment, hands grope June, twisting her breast, making her cry out in pain. The next...

June hears the sound of boots pounding against pavement. Air displaces as a powerful force comes down on top of one of the men who unchained her. As for the one who'd grabbed her breast...his hand suddenly lands in her lap. Minus the rest of him. Behind her, the man screams and screams, pulling back a stump that still spurts blood from where it used to be joined with his groping hand.

As if closely following some elaborate choreography made for an action movie, the handless Hijo turns just in time to get knifed in the gut, right before Mason—yes, Mason!—puts a gun to his temple and pulls the trigger without so much as blinking. In the next instant, he puts his knife away and turns his gun on the other Hijo, the one who helped carry her out here. June only has a split second to take note of the fact that the man is frantically trying to pull out his gun before he falls back with a bullet-sized hole in his chest.

Mason grabs him before he goes all the way down, and uses

the corpse as a full-body shield as he picks off Hijos, one by one, from behind it.

June's seen a lot go down. But she's never seen anything like this before in her life. At least, not outside a movie theater. She never suspected a guy as big as Mason could move that fast.

Her moment of shock and awe is interrupted by a high-pitched voice yelling, "C'mon, June! We gotta get clear! Mason said!"

The next thing she knows, Jordan is at her side, pulling her out of the chair. "C'mon!" he shouts. "Mason said run!"

So she does. Ignoring the sharp jabs of pain as she follows the boy to the house that used to be their prison, but may now be their sanctuary. Even so, June has a bad feeling about leaving Mason behind. She knows he's outnumbered by the Hijos. And she doesn't see Razo in the melee of people shooting and trying to take cover from Mason's eerily accurate gun. This means he's still out there, somewhere in the fray, unaccounted for.

Where is he?

Sooner than she wants, June has her answer.

"Hey, hey, now...where you going in such a hurry?"

She's suddenly yanked backwards, a wiry but strong arm wrapping around her neck.

"June!" Jordan screams.

"Stay back!" she shouts at him in reply.

There's the soft snick of metal followed by a cold sensation on her neck. Jordan freezes in place.

Not because of her command, she realizes, but because of the knife Razo holds against her throat.

"You didn't do a very good a job with your note, June," he hisses in her ear. "Now I have to kill this fucker. And guess what..."

He squeezes her neck so tight, she can't reply even if she wants to. "You going to help me do it."

30

MASON

*F*or a while, all Mason sees is red. Blood and rage as he takes out Hijo after Hijo.

There's screaming. And the darting shadows of people running to take cover. But Mason barely registers any of this. Can't fully process what he's doing. Can only aim and shoot, aim and shoot. His mission clear: kill as many of these mother-fuckers as possible while he waits for back up.

But then...

"Hey, *pendejo*! Over here, *mamon*! Why don't you come over here and *mamame la verga*!"

The red tint falls away instantly and the world returns in sharp focus when he sees them.

Razo stands about a meter or so in front of Mason. He's holding a knife to June's neck, all while grinning triumphantly. The asshole raises a hand to let the Hijos cowering behind trucks know to hold their fire.

Jesus H. Christ. If Mason wasn't in the middle of a very bad situation, he'd roll his eyes so hard, it'd put a teenage girl to shame.

Because even before the little asshole opens his mouth,

Mason knows for a fact it's not going to be nearly enough for Razo to get him to surrender. No, Razo the Tiny will most definitely want to grandstand the fuck out of this moment, too.

"Looks like you ain't tired of fucking this *puta* yet!" the little man calls out from behind June.

Snickers all around. Yeah, he's a real comedian alright.

"And it looks like you're okay cowering behind a woman like a little bitch," Mason answers back.

That doesn't get any laughs. But it does have the desired effect: a direct hit on Razo's fragile ego. Mason hopes it'll make him do something stupid. Give Mason an opportunity.

"I ain't cowering behind her, *culo*. I'm *using* her. I ain't the one out here on a suicide mission, looking to get killed over some black *puta*."

Mason dead eyes him as Razo's crew laughs. If he could have one wish right about now, it would be to end this motherfucker. He fights the urge to look at his watch, to figure out how far away the Russians are so he knows how much longer he has to put up with this shit.

"Okay, time to drop your gun," Razo says, pulling Mason out of his thoughts.

Well, shit. Looks like Razo finally remembered this is a killing contest, not a battle of egos.

"Drop your gun!" he says again more forcefully. "Now. Or I'm slicing this *puta* up."

Mason drops his gun. Lets it clatter to the ground.

And Razo grins. "Alright, now we're talking business. You want this *puta* back, huh? How much you willing to pay me this time? You best think hard before you answer, because I'm also going to need compensation for the lives you took, for the, let's call it inconvenience, of losing my men."

More snickering, proving to Mason that the majority of this gang is dumb as fuck. They're laughing when they really should be side-eyeing the hell out of a leader who makes jokes after ten of their brothers have been taken out by one guy.

That's what he's thinking, but out loud Mason says, "Anything. I'd pay anything to get her back."

"How bout that bike you used to drop Jordan off at school this morning? And now that I think about it, I heard rumors you didn't turn all the SFK stash over to the feds like you was supposed to. Hear you're still sitting on a lot of cash, even though you got this one working at Cal-Mart."

Razo turns his gaze, full of faux sympathy, to June. "Sorry bout that, baby. Should have warned you about white people. They're cheap as fuck. Always saving. Never wanting to break some off for their dime piece...or to support their friendly local gang."

Mason really wants to tell Razo not to speak to her. Not to look at her. To put down the knife so he can get to the business of ripping the spine Razo obviously never uses out of his back. But he can't risk anything happening to June. So instead, he answers, "Like I said, I'll pay anything. Name your price."

"Fifty K. How's that for a price?"

Mason gives it less than a second of thought. "All right."

"You got that?" Razo says, obviously surprised.

"Yeah," he answers. Taking a note from June's book and leaving it at that.

But Razo's got the scent of money in his nostrils now. "How about *five hundred* K then?"

This time Mason considers it. But only to buy more time, and so Razo won't come back at him with another number. He's not lying about being willing to pay anything, and the truth is, he and D didn't split the SFK war chest. D wanted nothing to do with money, saying it was dirty. He thought it would only hold him back. So he gave every last cent to Mason. Right now, all that SFK money is sitting in a safe in June's barn, waiting for a Russian laundry.

But if needed, Mason would happily give Razo the whole damn safe if it meant getting June out of harm's way.

"Okay, half a million. If that's what it takes," he tells Razo.

"Wow, you hear that?" Razo says into June's ear. Like she's still belongs to him. "You got this white *cono*'s dick so up, he's saying he'll pay a half mill for you. This right here is true love!" he calls out to his boys.

More snickers. It's beginning to feel to Mason like he's surrounded by a pack of hyenas.

"All right, here you go..." Razo shoves June forward. "He so in love with you, *mija*. I'd go to him if I was you."

To Mason's surprise, June hesitates. It's as if she doesn't want to come to him.

Then Razo says, voice dipping lower, "You heard me, *puta*. He want you back. You go to him."

She hesitates again. But then takes a step forward, her eyes wide with fear.

But it's not fear. Mason discovers that a few seconds later when she reaches him.

"I'm sorry," she whispers, wrapping her arms around his wide torso.

"It's okay," he whispers back. "I've got you now, sweetness. Everything will be alri—"

He stops when he feels her hand fist inside his jacket. A moment of confusion followed by a flash of metal when she steps back.

His knife. She's grabbed his knife, and now she's turning back around with it. *No!*

But before he can think to reach for her, stop her, she's running back toward Razo, some kind of ancient, crazed battle call issuing from her throat.

And now it's Razo eyes that have gone wide with fear. June is coming at him too fast, to go for his gun, and almost reflexively he brings his knife down to deliver a stabbing blow. His knife hits its mark, plunging into June's middle with a sickening swick that will haunt Mason's nightmares until his dying day.

But in this case, getting in the first stab doesn't change Razo's fate even one percent. Because nothing, not even a stab to the gut stops June.

Her arm plunges forward, pushing her body even deeper into Razo's knife. And the next thing Mason sees is Razo staggering backwards, Mason's serrated blade now embedded in his throat.

He falls to his knees, unable to scream and dying faster than his mind can process it.

And June...

"NOOOOOOO!!!!" Mason yells, lunging forward.

But it's too late.

June...his sweetness...his one true love...his beautiful avenging angel...she collapses with Razo's knife still planted in her belly.

And then everything explodes.

JUNE

*P*ain. Triumph. The sound of men yelling, "Razo's down! Razo's dead! She killed him!" in English and Spanish. Pain.

Falling. Falling. Hard ground.

Explosion.

Fire and smoke.

The sound of gun shots. Not sharp like before, but deep and staccato. And fast.

Several men drop next to her, their chests lit up with bullet holes, eyes empty and staring.

The ground is cold, slick. She's in a pool of blood. Her blood, choking her, making it hard to breathe.

Sharp pops that are soon drowned out by another round of staccato shots.

More bodies join her on the ground. Then there are voices. New voices. Speaking in another language. Something guttural, fluid. Russian, she thinks.

Mason shouts, "Get the kid, make sure he's safe! My old lady's been hit. She needs help!"

His face is suddenly beside hers. Like they're in bed together, having a talk before they fall asleep. Except he looks really angry and afraid. "Fuck, sweetness! Why did you do that?" he demands.

"I love you," she chokes out past the blood.

He grabs her hand, kisses it. "I know you do. I love you, too."

His head bows over the hand he holds, shoulders shaking.

"Don't cry," she murmurs. "I thought Fairgoods didn't cry."

Mason shakes his head, denying the tears in his red eyes. "I ain't crying, June. Ain't nothing to cry about. Because we're going to be together—fuck!" he yells, then shakes his head at her. "Why, sweetness? Why'd you go and do that when you were almost free?"

"Couldn't let him sell me again. Couldn't let him live on the same earth as Jordan." June coughs up more blood. "I thought it was only way."

Mason rains down more kisses on her face, her hands. "Fuck that, sweetness. There ain't no such thing as an "only way" that involves you getting hurt for any reason. You got that?"

"Okay, yes," she says. Everything goes blurry. She's crying, too.

The conversation hurts on many levels. June feels herself becoming weaken. Not much longer now. She's sure of it. "Please, can I see Jordan?"

"No, you cannot see Jordan," he answers fiercely. "Because you're going to see him later. When you wake up in the hospital. That dead motherfucker didn't give you nothing but a scratch."

"Okay," she says, realizing as much as she wants to say good-bye to Jordan, she also doesn't want him to see her die.

Her eyes flutter. The need to rest, to leave all this drama behind, pulls her under.

"I think you owe me an apology."

Oh, sweet man. He's trying to keep her awake. He thinks she actually has a chance of surviving this.

"Okay," she agrees, though it's taking phenomenal amounts of effort to get the words out.

But June plays along. Stays awake for as long as she can. Because she doesn't want Mason to remember her as the weak thing he found in the Cul. She's strong now. She killed Razo. She's a fighter now. Like him. Because of him.

"Okay, I'm sorry," she breathes out, past the pain. "I love you..."

It's too much. June coughs. Painful and bloody.

"Okay, okay, I believe you," he says, letting her off the hook with tears in his eyes. "Help is on the way."

Help is on the way...

That's the last thing she hears, and Mason's mournful face is the last thing she sees, before she falls into darkness.

EPILOGUE

After she was fully naked, she just stood there awaiting further instruction, which came about a minute or two later.

Bair stopped punching and settled into a nearby leather chair. The piece of hotel furniture was standing so close to the punching bag, it had obviously been placed there for this specific reason. Just like in the other six hotel rooms. Bair scanned her naked form for a second. His eyes cold as black frost.

"Come," he snarled.

She started forward again.

Only to stop short when he said, "You know better than this. Pets walk. Bitches crawl."

KABLOOM!!!!

Theodora is ripped out of the story she's writing by the sound of a soccer ball crashing into her garage office's door. Again.

Freaking neighbors! All the kid across the way seems to want to do in his spare time is hit her garage with soccer balls. His timing is extra bad today because she was finally on a roll with that hot sex scene, but these concentration bombs had been happening ever since the new neighbors moved in a week before the school year began.

She'd actually gone over to confront the junior high schooler, but then decided against it when the man she assumed was his father, or guardian maybe, answered the front door.

He had tats running up and down both arms. Ravens and skulls on one. What looked like nails and gravel on the other. His thick, dark hair was cut into heavy side chops and a handle bar mustache. Seriously, they couldn't have cast this guy better if they'd put out an ad for a vintage biker dude on Casting Choices.

He looked nothing at all like the short tween she'd seen walking to school on her morning run. Probably adopted. So despite his scary looks, maybe he's a nice guy. He might even be an actor. A nice actor living with his adopted maniac soccer fiend son...

Yeah, no. Theodora knows she has an overactive imagination, but there was something sinister about this guy. Something off, she sensed.

And in any case, she'd never been that great at confrontation, so... instead of complaining about his kid, Theodora opted for, "Hi, I'm Theodora! Your neighbor on the other side of your back fence. Just wanted to welcome you to the neighborhood..."

"Thanks," he'd grunted.

And that was all he said.

After a few more awkward minutes during which she told him to let her know if he and his son had any questions about the neighborhood, she gave him a slight wave and hightailed it out of there as fast as she could.

I'll go over after I finish this book, once the kids are back in school, she'd promised herself. Hell, she even put it on her list of resolutions: "Be brave with the neighbor."

But the first few months of the new school year came and went. And now it's Christmas Break, and the kid's soccer practice isn't just limited to evenings and weekends anymore. Her backyard now looks like a black-and-white minefield, littered as it is with soccer balls. At the risk of sounding like a cranky old lady, she's lately starting to identify way more with Mr. Wilson than with that little shit Dennis the Menace.

Theodora sighs, and goes back to work...

Yes, she's been demoted. She'd been told this more than once in the other Benton suites.

Yet she could never just bring herself to do it. To get down on her knees and crawl to him until he commanded it. Trying to ignore the Radiohead song chewing up her chest, she dropped to her knees and crawled to him naked.

However, her quiet acquiescence wasn't enough this time.

KNOCK! KNOCK! KNOCK!

What now?!

With a weary sigh, she flings open the front door. Only to stop short when she finds a pretty black woman on the front steps. The woman's about the same height as Theodora, so short, but with thick hips and softly rounded...everything. Dream curves, she might call them if she were to describe the woman in a book. Except unlike most of her heroines who start off in various states of unhappy distress, this woman is smiling, has a diamond on her left hand, and an extra curve at her front. She's pregnant.

"Hi..." Theodora says carefully. She seems vaguely familiar to Theodora and she wonders if she's a Jehovah's Witness. For some reason, those folks regularly frequent her neighborhood, and often don't see or choose to ignore the huge "No Solicitors!" sign on her door.

"Hi," the pretty woman answers. "I'm so sorry, but my son

has run out of soccer balls, and he wants to know if he can go into your backyard to collect them. But I didn't want to inflict him on you. Trust me, if I send him over to get the balls himself, you'll never get rid of him."

Theodora relaxes with a laugh. "Likes to talk, does he? Sounds like my oldest daughter."

"Oh! I think I met her the other day with your husband," the woman says. "Told me and Jordan all about the guinea pig she's getting for Christmas because she kept her beta fish alive for a whole year. She's very cute."

"Yes," Theodora agrees. "But way too friendly. I keep telling her we're a family of introverts and she needs to start acting like one!"

The woman laughs again and before she knows it, Theodora is walking the new neighbor through her house, and into the backyard.

After all, what kind of person makes a pregnant woman collect a bunch of soccer balls by herself?

Oh, who is she kidding. As much of a hermit as Theodora is, this might well and truly be her only chance to get up in the neighbor's business.

"So...you and motorcycle dude are married?" she asks as they throw several balls over the fence connecting their yards.

The woman nods. "Three years now."

"I honestly thought he was a single dad. I, well, it's just that we never see you around."

"We have weird schedules, that's for sure. I guess you could say we're a showbiz family now. I'm on that tattoo show...*Lost Angels Ink*, and he's on *Bike Kings*, the show about motorcycle restoration."

"I don't watch much reality TV," Theodora admits with a grimace. "And I don't have any tattoos, but..." she squints at the woman, subtracts a few pounds. "My sister loves *Lost Angels Ink*, and I'm pretty sure I saw you in an episode last time I visited her. Are you the one who never talks?"

The woman laughs. "Yeah, but truth is, I've had a lot more to say lately. Weird side effect of being pregnant, I guess."

"Weird pregnancy side effects are totally unpredictable. I ate a ton of salad with my first, even though I *hate* salad, and I wanted to spend all my time swimming in the pool with my second. Hey, sorry I didn't recognize you."

"That's okay," she replies with a wave of her hand. "We're kind of over being recognized. And we try to stick to opposite film schedules, so at least of one of us is here on the regular for Jordan."

On the regular. She reminds Theodora of her St. Louis relatives. Or maybe she's from one of the Missouri border states, like Tennessee or Arkansas?

She opens her mouth to ask, but is interrupted by a deep voice calling, "June! June, where you at, sweetness?"

Theodora looks toward her gate to see the head of the hulky biker she figured for a single father. He's peering over the gate, obviously wanting to be let in. She walks over and unlatches it to let him in. The big guy crosses her yard in a few long strides, his wedding ring glinting in the sun as he reaches out and cups June's stomach with a large, protective hand.

"Hey, Mason. Aren't you supposed to be at work?" June asks.

"We're on lunch, so I came home."

"Did you eat anything yet?"

"Nope. I'll grab something from craft services when I get back to the set. How you doing in this heat? I thought it was supposed to be fucking Christmas but it feels like July!"

"I'm fine," she assures him.

"Maybe you should get inside, though."

"I will, just as soon as we're done picking up all these balls."

"Kid should be doing that. I'll talk to him when I get home tonight."

But June shakes her head. "He volunteered, but I didn't want our neighbor to be mad at him for kicking all these balls into her yard *and* talking her ear off."

Mason gives up with a laugh that's more of a grunt than a chuckle. Then he bends down and starts scooping and throwing the rest of the soccer balls over the wall. Giving his wife a "don't even think about it" when she tries to help.

"Sorry about this," June says to Theodora in a lowered voice. "It took a while and, like, two rounds of IVF to get pregnant," she confesses. "So he's a little over protective these days."

"Totally okay," Theodora answers. "I think it's cute."

Which is strange, because cute would have been the last word she'd use to describe her scary biker neighbor or anything associated with him before his wife showed up.

"Well, alright. I better get back," Mason says when he's finished.

"You know, you didn't have to come here in the first place," June says, but her words are offset by her quiet tone and sweet smile.

He responds to her chastisement with a deep kiss. All but sending June into a full swoon in Theodora's backyard.

But just when Theodora starts thinking about inching back into her house to give them some privacy, he breaks it off.

"Sorry about the soccer balls," he grunts at her before letting himself out through the gate.

"No problem!" she calls after him.

Right then, as if it had been waiting for Mason to leave, a new ball sails over the fence and into the yard.

"Jordan!" June yells out, not sounding as much like a sweet magnolia as she did a few minutes ago.

"Sorry, June," a young voice calls back.

"I better go talk to him," she says, waddling purposefully towards the gate.

"Okay, it was nice meeting you," Theodora says, striding ahead of June to open the gate for her and latch it after she leave.

But she stops, throwing June a curious look. As much as Theodora hates interruptions when she's in writing mode, something about this situation reminds her of that one time in Colorado, when that couple showed up at her hotel room with an off-the-wall story about time-traveling werewolves. Ever since, she's learned not to ignore her hunches.

"Hey, would you like to come in for a cup of tea?" she asks June. "You seem like someone with a good story."

Heyo!

Can I tell you how much I hate to let this couple go? Obviously, they're very close to my heart, and I'm near tears as I write this letter. I began this story purely for June, but was shocked by how much Mason grew on me over the course of it. We can't swap out our parents or change the past, but we can choose what kind of adults we're going to be and we always have a choice about how we'll live our lives going forward. I am so grateful to Mason and June for reminding me of these lessons with their story.

I hope you super enjoyed reading this! If so, please grant me the further favor of leaving a review, so others might find this crazy, sweet couple.

*And if you're wondering about Holt Calson and his mystery woman, keep reading for a very special preview of, **HOLT: Her Ruthless Billionaire!***

So much love,
Theodora Taylor

Make sure to read the complete Fairgood series!

His for Keeps
His Forbidden Bride
His to Own

Forbidden Love... *Holt Calson was born with an 11-figure spoon in his mouth to one of the wealthiest families in the world. The night they met, Sylvie Pinnock only had 11 dollars in her purse, and it was all the money she had in the world.*

They were never supposed to meet, much less be together. But Holt didn't care. He just wanted Sylvie. And what Calsons want, Calsons get.

For one blazing summer, they had it all...until everything fell apart with a terrible betrayal.

Twelve Years Later... *Sylvie is happy and thriving in a solid relationship with a good guy. Until Holt shows up at the hotel where she* *works. She's moved on, but he definitely hasn't. And if Sylvie thinks all is forgiven, she's about to find out...*

Revenge is best served...BOSS

$\sim$

"MR. CALSON?"

I look up from the text I'm sending to Zahir who's in town tonight. Della, the PR consultant we hired when I was named acting CEO of Cal-Mart, stands in front of my office's drop-down screen looking back at me expectantly.

"Do you have any initial thoughts?" she asks. Then she steps back so I have an unobstructed view of the screen which displays the headshots of nine beautiful women, tiled in a three-by-three square.

Della has done a good job, I decide, even though I hadn't listened to a word of her presentation. Looking like a hopeful new crop of *Bachelor* contestants, the women on the screen offer fetching smiles. They're all beautiful and just a few years north of twenty-five. Babymakers who Della believes will provide me with a second heir and merge well into my carefully crafted brand: Holt Calson, Trustworthy Billionaire of the People.

"I'd like to narrow the number of candidates down to six, then we can reach out to the top three for in-person meet and greets."

So, all I need to do is eliminate six in total. Should be easy enough, but turns out it's not. I study the square that makes up the final slide in Della's Power Point deck. There are five blondes, three brunettes, and one redhead. But they're so interchangeable that they remind me of one of those fashion avatar apps that lets users change everything but the underlying body. I feel the same about their bios. Nine women from good families who became doctors, lawyers, professional dancers, and nonprofit associates just like Mommy and Daddy wanted. Not a single disappointment in the bunch—I know this for certain because Della made sure each woman underwent a discreet background check— which means the chances of any of them smashing through a guardrail while loaded up with valium and alcohol is pretty damn slim. Unlike what happened with my first wife two years ago.

Each of Della's candidates is a perfect specimen of womanhood. And I know every last one of them would be thrilled at the opportunity of marrying a guy like me after the prequisite year or two of dating in the spotlight is over. I should feel relief and the faint stirrings of anticipation. Instead, I want to yawn.

My phone buzzes, loudly vibrating on the glass table in front of me. I pull my eyes from the giant square of female perfection and see the green bubble of an incoming text. It's Zahir, replying to the text I sent earlier.

Me: *"Luca says you're in town? Meet up?"*
Zahir: *"Yes. Drinks at Luca's club tonight?"*

It's been a while since I saw either of my former Beaumont suitemates. And though none of us swing that way, I'm a hell of a lot more excited about spending time with Zahir and Luca than I am about taking any of Della's candidates out on a date.

"Holt?" Della asks again.

I force my gaze away from my phone screen and try hard to refocus on the task at hand. But, shit...these women look like younger versions of my late wife, Tish. The same late wife who'd been celebrating our upcoming divorce proceedings when she made a wrong turn on a winding mountain road. And I had only married Tish because she was the complete opposite of...

I clamp down on my memories before I can finish the

thought. Ten years have passed. By now, I should be past wanting to compare women to her. She doesn't matter, and hasn't mattered for a very long time.

"You know what? I trust your judgement," I tell Della. "Go ahead and narrow down the candidates and then work with Allie to get them on my calendar."

"Got it!" Della says with a huge smile that signals she already has a list in mind—and no doubt it's better than any I would have come up with.

I'm not exaggerating when I say I trust Della completely. When I was named acting CEO of a then flagging Cal-Mart, she came up with my current "JFK CEO" branding. She also helped me craft a message and set up interviews and stories about my dedication to serving honest, hardworking Americans, right along with making sure I was in the right media spot at the right time. Because of Della, I was named "Sexiest CEO Alive" by a popular magazine at the exact same time I rolled out a well-received worker's benefit program. Because of Della, America was easily distracted from the series of articles the *New York Herald* wrote up about how, under his father's leadership, Holt Calson cut worker pay and hours until many of Cal-Mart's employees were forced to apply for food stamps to get by. As of now, I enjoy a higher approval rating than JFK himself.

So yeah, if Della is as good a matchmaker as she is a brand consultant, I know her latest strategy will work. Dating the a young, talented, and attractive heiress a respectful two years after my first wife's death will definitely send my Q score into a stratosphere the board wouldn't be able to contend with—even if many of our shareholders, including my father, don't love my plans to start taking on full-time employees and increase worker compensation.

"I won't let you down," Della promises as she gathers up her things.

"I know you won't," I answer, flashing her a perfunctory smile as I grab my phone to text Zahir back.

But before I've typed two words, Allie rushes in with her phone in both hands. "Holt, there's something you need to see."

"I'll get out of your way," Della says, starting toward the door.

But Allie stops her with a, "No, you should probably stay..." Then she bends down to my eye level and presses play on what turns out to be a recently posted YouTube video.

"DO YOU KNOW WHO I AM?!??!!" a familiar voice screams.

He is so loud that both Allie and Della wince. However, I keep my expression impassive as I watch my eight-year-old son kick over a table filled with art supplies, ignoring the gasps and cries of the other children as he shouts, "I will kill you! My father will buy all of you and kill your parents!"

The rant continues with a sobbing Wes throwing paint bottles and other craft supplies at anyone who tries to approach him, including a kind-faced man in a manager's button-down shirt who attempts to talk to Wes in his faintly accented English. He gets a bottle of red paint straight to the chest for his efforts. After a tick of shocked disbelief, the man calls out in Spanish, "*Alguien llame a Vee! ¡Ahora mismo!!*"

Then noticing the camera for the first time, he says, "No, no, Señor. You must put that away..."

The picture tilts and then the screen goes dark as YouTube offers a repeat showing of "Richie Rich Cal-Mart Heir Loses His Sh*t."

So, yeah...I can see why Allie told Della to stay.

With only three months to go until the Cal-Mart board decides whether or not to make my position permanent, my son's epic meltdown ending up on YouTube a mere eight weeks after he was kicked out of his latest private school is not good.

I am *definitely* going to need some solid damage control after this.

THAT MORNING instead of my alarm, I'm awoken by the happy trilling of birds. Sun shines through my bedroom's gauzy employee-issue curtains. It's not often that the sun is up to greet me. It's usually dark out when I leave my bungalow for my job as the director of the three different Kinder Clubs at our vacation village.

At first, I panic. Did I sleep through the alarm? What time is it? Where should I be?

But no, that's not it. I spot the readout on my Samsung. It's Sunday, my one day off every week. And unlike when I worked off-property in Jamaica, there aren't any relatives at my front door wondering if I will be going to church with them. Taking the place of my mother who left me in Jamaica after Lydia's funeral... and never came back.

But despite having worked at the Tourmaline Ixtapa for over a year now, I still haven't become used to being my own woman on Sunday mornings. I wonder if I ever will...

Why am I sitting here thinking about my mother and the life I left behind in Jamaica? It's my day off! I sit up and press play on my Jill Scott Spotify playlist—the perfect music for a chill Sunday morning. Unfortunately, the very first song that comes up is "Jahraymecofasola," the one that never fails to remind me of that summer ten years ago in New Haven...

Nope. Not today, demons. My boyfriend, Arturo, and I are going off-property for brunch after he puts Wes and his V.I.P father back on a private plane. I hit the skip button until I find the perfect tune. And before you know it...

...I am in the bungalow's small bathroom, showering and humming along to a happy Jill Scott song about taking my freedom and living my life like it's golden. Then I sway to the rhythm of another upbeat tune while I take my hair out of crown braids in front of my bedroom's vanity mirror.

When my hair is completely down, I pause and consider the sparse amount of hair products on my dresser. This includes the very last of the Shea Moisture I brought from Jamaica. I bought it in bulk, but my supply is almost down to nothing after a year in Ixtapa. Meanwhile, my hair has continued to grow to where my unbraided curls now reach past my bra strap. The local coconut oil works fine, but there is no way I will be able to wear my hair down anymore if I don't get my hands on a good leave-in conditioner and hair crème. But since today is my date day with Arturo, I decide to break out the Curl and Style Milk and Curl Enhancing Smoothie and spread it liberally into my hair.

After getting dressed, I leave Jill playing in my room and dance out to the living room, so truly excited to be off today.

I truly love my job, I do. But this week has tested me more than any S.A.T. I missed my full day off last week thanks to Wes Hader's giant meltdown during art time at our center for 7-12 year olds. I ended up spending all day with him, and then much of the following week thanks to Wes forming an unexpectedly strong vacation friendship with my usually other-child-unfriendly son, Barron. As a result, it has been two whole weeks since my last full off day.

Barron sullenly informed me last night that he plans to spend the morning with the hotel's local iguana population since, "I will no longer have a friend." Of course, I am sad for Barron, but his absence means I can start my season two binge of *Insecure*. I bet I can get at least three episodes in before brunch with Arturo—

I stop cold and the Jill Scott song I'm humming dies mid-note.

Barron is at the little table in our front room where we take our meals. This isn't the first time I have found him up before me, working on some advanced project or other at the table with a look of such concentration on his face, it isn't a mystery why some of our relatives wonder if he isn't the reincarnated spirit of my super smart sister, Lydia.

However, this morning there is no project taking up valuable table space. Instead, a very familiar tow-haired boy sits across from Barron. It's Wes Hader, the American boy Barron has been hanging out with all week. The very same boy who should be in the lobby with his nanny, Melissa, and his American father after receiving a VIP tour from Arturo. And though I look around the room for the plain clothes bodyguard who was hired to accompany Wes everywhere he goes on resort property, I don't see him.

"Don't be mad, Mama," Barron says at the same time Wes says, "Wassup, Vee." Casual, as if I should have been expecting him at my table this Sunday morning.

"Good morning, Wes," I answer, looking between him and my son. "May I ask why you are here?"

"I got into the Connecticut Institute of Technology, Mama!" Barron says as if he is answering my question about Wes's presence at our table.

"What is this you say?" I ask, turning my eyes back to Barron.

"He got into CIT," Wes repeats as if I did not hear my son inform me he's been accepted into one of the world's most prestigious research universities.

"I heard what he said," I assure Wes. "But I do not understand how this happened."

"I have my GED. That's all you need to apply to a college," Barron points out as if I'm the slow one for not reaching the same conclusion.

"Yes, but..." I blink at the effort of using more of my brain than I am used to before my daily cup of Folgers Tostado Clásico. "You are only ten! How is this possible?"

"I applied online and sent the head of the Computational

Biology department the specs and patent for my bioHelmet," Barron answers. "I didn't think I would hear from him so soon. But he wrote back faster than you would believe and said he'd push my application through for this fall. Yeah, mon!"

Barron stands to high five Wes who, despite being a full two years younger than my son, seems to grasp what is going on much better than I do.

"Hold on...you have a *patent* for that helmet of yours?" I ask, struggling to keep up.

"Yes! I told you about it three months ago, Mama," Barron answers, throwing me a hurt look.

Okay, it's true. I have a bad habit of tuning Barron out when he gets to talking about his bioHelmet project over breakfast, the only time we have for shared conversation since I am usually with the Kinder Club kids for lunches and dinners. But when you consider his helmet project is the only thing he ever talks about aside from video games, maybe you will understand why I am not 100% focused 100% of the time. The truth is, I barely understand the basic design concepts of the wearable helmet other than he hopes it will be able to receive thought commands and allow kids to play videogames against one another using only the device.

But I can tell from the look on his face that he definitely must have told me all about his plans to take out a patent on his invention. More than once.

"Sorry, yes of course," I say, then quickly go to my next question. "But how did you get the money to apply to CIT?"

"Me," Wes says with one of his American boy shrugs. "I paid for it with the credit card my dad gave me."

"Yeah, mon, applying to CIT was Wes's idea," Barron explains.

"We were trying to think of ways to get Barron and you back to Connecticut," Wes explains in a tone I might call helpful if this entire conversation didn't feel like a huge case of overstep.

"I told him how Grandma and Aunt Judith still live there, and how you used to live there, too," Barron adds.

Then Wes jumps in with, "And I was, like, 'then you should move back to Connecticut!' So Ender applied to CIT and now you can come back with us!"

"That's right! That's what's up, mon!" Barron says, and this time the boys exchange fist bumps.

For a moment, I can only stare. Barron must not have told Wes he has never exchanged a single word with his "grandma" in Connecticut because she distanced herself from him after his birth. And I am also overwhelmed by how much effort Barron's new friend has put into lobbying for him. Now, I love Barron to the end of the universe and back again. The moment he was born, I gave up my dreams of going to college and instead, dedicated my life to him, no questions asked. This despite the difficult circumstances surrounding his birth. But the truth is, Barron is not an easy kid to befriend. He is too quirky and too smart for most kids his age to easily connect with.

Which is why this whole friendship thing with Wes so strange. My son has *never* had a friend who wanted to spend more than an hour or two with him, much less one who would conspire with him to move back to the States.

As for Wes, it is hard to believe the determined young man standing here in front of me is the very same boy I sacrificed my last day off to help defuse. As director of the Tourmaline's Kinder Club Program, I have seen my fair share of fast friendships between the kids we supervise while their parents—or, in Wes's case, his poor nanny— get some much-needed R and R. But I have *never* seen a friendship take this quickly or firmly.

I am torn between disbelief and respect for all the plotting they must have done behind my back. However...

"We can't just fly back to Connecticut with you," I say to Wes.

"Why not?" Wes asks, his voice taking on a snide tone as if I am an idiot for not going along with his plan. "Ender got into CIT! And he says he already talked to you about college."

Barron knows better than to speak to me in such a tone, but he turns pitiful eyes to me as if to punctuate his friend's point.

"Yes, but...Wes, my friend. I do not have enough money saved up to send Barron to such a place," I explain. "On top of paying back the fees you charged to your father's card on Barron's behalf."

"You don't have to pay him back," Wes insists.

"They are giving me a full scholarship," Barron points out.

"Wow, that *is* impressive!" I say because it is, and I'm so, so proud of him. But, "A full scholarship does not cover everything you will need for school—especially if I am also going to take classes as we discussed. There are textbooks to be purchased, and other necessities as well. I will have to save up more money before we can make this dream of ours happen."

Barron shakes his head at me, his expression a gut-wrenching mixture of heartbreak and disappointment. "So, I will never go to college?"

"No! That is not what I am saying at all. I will do my best to save up for your college dream—for *our* college dream—by this time next year. And if Arturo gets that transfer to the Tourma-line Florida that he asked for, we can look for a good university for you to attend there."

"Arturo?" Wes asks Barron. "Isn't that the guy who's always asking me, like, a million times if I need anything else or if I'm having a good time? What does he have to do with this?"

"He's the hotel manager *and* her boyfriend," Barron explains, not bothering to hide the eye roll in his voice even if it doesn't show up on his face. His father might not be in the picture, but

Barron has made it more than clear he has no desire to replace him with another man.

"Oh ...you can get a new boyfriend in Connecticut," Wes informs me. As if getting a new boyfriend is as easy as going to the store to pick up milk.

"And it's C.I.T., Mama! *C.I.T!*" Barron points out. "They have TWO clean rooms at their tech facility *and* animals other than iguanas to experiment on. I will be able to develop my bioHelmet there. And after that, we'll be rich and will never have to worry about money again!"

"Barron, come on now..." I say, squatting down to talk to him. "You know money is not a thing we should be worrying about. We have everything we need right here." I will admit there is some pain in my voice as I try to convince him of this. After Lydia's death, I worked hard to provide for him and be the best mother I could. The thought that I might be failing him in the same way I failed my sister sits uneasily on my heart.

And as for what his young American friend is arguing... "Wes," I say, turning a stern gaze upon him. "Boyfriends are *not* as replaceable as toilet paper."

"Yeah, they are," he answers with the certainty only an eight-year-old can achieve. "My dad gets a new girlfriend, like, every other month."

"Okay, well, I am not here to argue with you about this grown folk business," I answer, trying not to laugh at Wes's all-knowing tone. "My point is, we cannot just hop a plane to Connecticut. Barron must stay with me, and right now, my job is here."

"But it doesn't have to be," Wes says. "We live, like, fifteen minutes from C.I.T. You could live with us. I'll make Dad fire Melissa and hire you instead!"

"Hold on, child. You are trying to fire your nanny now?" I ask, shaking my head at the boy.

"*You're* the one who calmed me down last week, not her," Wes points out. "I haven't had a meltdown all week because you don't make me mad when you tell me what to do. You're a way better nanny than Melissa will ever be."

"Wes has that right, Mama," Barron agrees with a solemn nod. "I mean, you've been doing the nanny's job all week, isn't that right? Wes and his father will be lucky to have you."

"Plus, you can have as much money as you want. My dad will pay for Barron to go to C.I.T., too. I'm serious! He'll do anything I ask if I promise to behave at public school until he can find another private school willing to take me. All he cares about is me not embarrassing him anymore."

And that is how I know I have definitely not turned into my mother, because I can only imagine how she would respond to two boys trying to manipulate the affairs of grown-ups.

But that doesn't mean I am not feeling the sharp pricks of impatience. Which is why my ability to continue speaking in a calm, civil tone feels like a small miracle as I respond, "Okay, Wes. I can see you would like very much to see Barron again. I will make sure he Skypes with you after he talks with his Aunt Judith next week. But you will not be talking to me anymore about blackmailing your father. Because you are a child and you are not in charge of me or of your father, do you understand?"

Wes rolls his eyes.

"Wes, I am not here for you to be rolling your eyes at. I asked you if *you understand*?" My voice has taken on a hard, no-nonsense tone I was not even aware I possessed until the first time Barron tried to talk back to me when he was a toddler.

Wes doesn't respond. But as I did the day he threatened to kill everyone if he did not get his way, I do not let him off the hook. I stand quietly making eye contact with him until he finally huffs and says, "I understand. But it wouldn't be blackmail—"

"Okay, Wes. Now I must text Melissa," I say, cutting him off. "She is most likely worried out her head about you."

I go to my bedroom to fetch my phone. The return trip doesn't take long. While the two-bedroom "family suite" I share with Barron is generous by onsite employee standards (as Arturo is always quick to point out), it is little more than a small living room with two even smaller box bedrooms attached. Barron's bedroom is so tiny, I am a little surprised he didn't decide to nickname himself Harry, after the boy wizard who lived in the cupboard under the stairs, as opposed to Ender, the boy who was smart beyond his years. Though now that he's gotten into CIT at such a young age, I have to admit the nickname he insists everyone call him makes more sense.

"Barron belongs at CIT!" Wes shouts from the living room as if he is thinking the same thing. "We've got a lot of space at my house. A whole guest house out back. You and Barron can have it."

I sigh and pick up the phone. Sure enough, I am greeted by a screen filled with messages from Arturo. The pile starts with a calm *"tienes Wes?"* at the bottom. Then a few Missed Call notifications on top of that. Followed by several *"Llamame!!!!"* and finally, in English, a *"Please tell me Wes is with you"* as if Arturo is afraid I might have forgotten how to read Spanish since his first text.

"si, he's conmigo," I type as I walk back to the living room, using the staff Spanglish that only a bunch of Spanish-as-a-second-language speakers who work with native Spanish speakers in a resort, catering to mostly English-speaking guests could understand.

"Just name your price," Wes says when I return to the front room, as if we never paused the conversation. "Whatever it is, Dad will pay it."

The phone explodes in my hand and instead of answering Wes, I say, "Morning, baby," to Arturo. "Wah gwan?"

"Thank you for your message, Vee," Arturo replies, his usually warm tone so crisp and professional that I know Wes's father must be standing right there with him. "Are you at home?"

"Yes, I am, and I'm bringing Wes to you now..." I reply as I head to the door. "Come, Wes. You can bring Barron with you if you like, but we are going now," I tell him over my shoulder.

And I don't wait for Wes to agree before I open the door and head out. Over the past week, I have found it is better to give him a choice and leave him to decide how he will respond than trying to have a discussion with him.

"I don't want to go home!" Wes shouts. But as I suspected, he also follows me right out the door while he is making his point. As my mother used to say, "Hard heads be hard the world over."

"Are you in the lobby?" I ask Arturo.

"Actually, I am heading over to your place right now," Arturo answers.

"No! Stay in the lobby. We will meet you th—"

I never finish my sentence because of who I see coming toward me on the narrow back road path that leads to the staff quarters.

Not just Arturo, but a very tall man. A tremendously handsome man who reminds me of someone I used to know long, long ago. And without warning, the starting melody from "Jahraymecofasola" unfurls inside my head, even though it can't possibly be...

But I stop dead in my tracks, because the tall man has the same sharp, preppy good looks I remember from the graduation photo they ran with the story about the ten-year anniversary of Holt's mother's death. He also has the same square jaw and "I own everything, including you" aura that even drugs and alcohol couldn't completely suppress back in the day. But...*it cannot be...*

I refuse to believe it. Even as Wes rushes past me yelling, "Dad! Dad! Tell Vee she has to come home with us and be my new nanny!"

Oh, c'mon, you can't stop there.
Finish the first bestselling standalone
in the RUTHLESS TYCOONS series.

ALSO BY THEODORA TAYLOR

THE VERY BAD FAIRGOODS
His for Keeps

His Forbidden Bride

His to Own

RUTHLESS TYCOONS
HOLT: Her Ruthless Billionaire

ZAHIR: Her Ruthless Sheikh

LUCA: Her Ruthless Don

RUTHLESS BOSSES
His Pretend Baby

His Revenge Baby

His Enduring Love

His Everlasting Love

RUTHLESS BUSINESS
Her Ruthless Tycoon

Her Ruthless Cowboy

Her Ruthless Possessor

Her Ruthless Bully

BROKEN AND RUTHLESS
KEANE: Her Ruthless Ex

STONE: Her Ruthless Enforcer

RASHID: Her Ruthless Boss

RUTHLESS RUSSIANS

Her Russian Billionaire

Her Russian Surrender

Her Russian Beast

Her Russian Brute

HOT AUDIOBOOKS WITH HEART

The Owner of His Heart

Her Russian Billionaire

His Pretend Baby

His Everlasting Love

Her Viking Wolf

HOT HARLEQUINS WITH HEART

Vegas Baby

Love's Gamble

ALPHA KINGS

Her Viking Wolf

Wolf and Punishment

Wolf and Prejudice

Wolf and Soul

Her Viking Wolves

ALPHA FUTURE

Her Dragon Everlasting

NAGO: Her Forever Wolf

KNUD: Her Big Bad Wolf

RAFES: Her Fated Wolf

Her Dragon King

THE SCOTTISH WOLVES

Her Scottish Wolf

Her Scottish King

Her Scottish Warrior

HOT SUPERNATURAL WITH HEART

His Everlasting Love

12 Days of Krista

(only available during the holidays)

12 Months of Kristal

(newsletter exclusive)

ABOUT THE AUTHOR

Theodora Taylor writes hot books with heart. When not reading, writing, or reviewing, she enjoys spending time with her
amazing family, going on date nights with her wonderful
husband, and attending parties thrown by others. She now lives
in Los Angles, California, and she LOVES to hear from readers.
So....

Friend Theodora on Facebook
https://www.facebook.com/theodorawrites

Follow Me on Instagram
https://www.instagram.com/taylor.theodora/

Sign for up for Theodora's Newsletter
http://theodorataylor.com/sign-up/